THE WALKING MAN

THE WALKING MAN

Be light!
Be smooth!
Be open.

Paul Dore

a novel by
Paul Dore

IGUANA

Published by Iguana Books
720 Bathurst Street, Suite 303
Toronto, Ontario, Canada
M5V 2R4

Publisher: Greg Ioannou
Editor: Kate Unrau
Front cover design: Ellen Yu
Book layout design: Kate Unrau

Library and Archives Canada Cataloguing in Publication

Dore, Paul, 1978-, author
    The walking man / Paul Dore.

Issued in print and electronic formats.
ISBN 978-1-77180-077-8 (pbk.).--ISBN 978-1-77180-079-2 (epub).--ISBN 978-1-77180-080-8 (kindle).--ISBN 978-1-77180-081-5 (pdf)

    I. Title.

PS8607.O734W34 2014   C813'.6   C2014-906494-2
                                               C2014-906495-0

This is an original print edition of *The Walking Man*.

This novel is dedicated to Carol and David.

Part I

Summer: Fear and Loathing in Jordan

Lemme just get this out of the goddamn way: I'm nervous as all hell. Nervous because you may or may not relate to the mess that follows. Of course, I hope that you do because it would confirm to me that the time late at night, before we fall asleep, when our bodies sink into mattresses while our minds remove the armour — during that moment when all our deep fears appear ready to jump into our dreams, at some base level, what we all have in common is the ability to admit that we don't know what we're doing.

Maybe it's just me. Maybe you don't relate. You're well-adjusted and have no idea what I'm talking about. If you're content and simply slip into soundless sleep, dreaming of nothing but skiing on cotton-candy snow wearing skis made of french fries, if you wake up refreshed, ready to tackle the challenges of the day, if you refer to them as "challenges of the day" and you're looking forward to said challenges, this might not be for you.

Or maybe you're like me: you wake up late — always — and your back hurts. Feels like someone punched you directly on the brain. You're hungover but didn't drink a drop the previous night. You wear sunglasses even on cloudy days to hide the bags under your eyes that reveal the terrifying yet forgotten dream state buried deep in your subconscious — the dream state that left you restless. You can't imagine talking to someone until the clock turns to afternoon, and then still, still, you cannot perform the simple societal exchanges that represent the hallmark of being a functioning person participating in this world. You want to just walk into a café to get a coffee because you need it desperately to wash away the blanked-out nightmares, but this simple excursion involves true existential dread — yes, dread — in order to even attempt a reply to the barista's quizzical "for here or to go?" If you're still following me, if you're still here—

You are my people and I've been looking for you my entire life.

Because forever—

I've been mad as hell. So goddamn tired.

Mad and tired without knowing it. Unable to admit that perhaps I wasn't as self-aware as I'd thought, successfully pushing these two elements so far into the depths that my everyday disposition failed to register any anger, any fatigue. Just sailing along with no feelings at all. I thought I'd had those feelings, but my sensitivity hid the fact that I wasn't feeling much at all. I realize that many people, including myself, would like to just say, "Stop whining and get on with things." To those people, including myself, I say (or want to say, wish I could say, but am too cowardly to say) shut the fuck up. 'Cause the thing is, it's not so easy.

Besides, aren't you tired sometimes? Mad?

For too long, I've hidden behind stories and inside the minds of characters. I thought this was the best scenario, that who I really was and what I had to say should be expressed through fiction. That way if anyone asked, if anyone found fault with what I said, I could place responsibility on a fictional character. After awhile, these fictional characters became facets of my personality. Replaced me. I've realized this was both cowardly and dishonest.

Last year, I took a creative-writing class focused on memoir. Wow, a writer writing about being a writer. Brilliant.

Stay with me. Please.

This has to work.

The class was undertaken in an effort to develop some kind of authentic voice. The idea made me uncomfortable from the outset because I'd convinced myself long ago that my life simply wasn't interesting enough to document. Why would anyone want to read about me? I couldn't think of anyone who would. As the weeks went on, I felt I was producing some of the worst writing I'd done since trying to compose poetry in my twenties, those sparkling and rhyming renditions expressing how alone I felt surrounded by so many people. The pieces I read out in the memoir class were not much better — so stoically earnest, so Antarctic cold, so utterly humourless.

Just hold on. Keep holding on. Stay with me.

The whole thing fell apart for me when I wrote a piece about going into depressions — an enormous mistake, not in the content but in the execution. Writing about depression should help take you out of it, not push you further into the fog. The subject was important to me, something I have fought with and continue to fight with, yet I couldn't articulate what was happening internally in any tangible form. Embarrassed, I did what I do best — I shut down, tuned out, turned off my emotions. A dial on a radio.

I've quit many things in my life. I feel no shame in quitting; it's highly underrated and I think more people should try it. I feel shame in admitting that I can go down for days into a depression. Sure, I can function and people generally don't notice, but I just don't feel the need to generate pity by dragging my life into the lives of others.

Justified by my enormous failure in the writing class, I spiralled down into thinking that perhaps I should finally give up writing. Very dramatic, but I'm prone to making everything into a high-stakes situation. Unfortunately, I tend to lose these games, setting myself up for failure from the outset. This is how it goes with me. I don't just think, *Not a good class today, we'll get 'em next time.* Instead, if there's one thing I'm good at, it's beating myself up. I should bite off my own ear and get a tattoo on my face. I really have no idea how to get out of my own way. Could someone please tell me how to get out of my own way?

In my head, this all led to one scary thought: if I couldn't write about myself in an honest way, then what did I actually have to say? Like really have to say? The only answer I came up with was nothing. Stewed in this for a few days, which was both stupid and unhealthy. Maybe the whole thing was a bad idea. Maybe I should focus on other things like finding a partner, having dependants, you know, growing up. As I said earlier, I have no shame in quitting. The thing is, writing is the single part of my life that has remained consistent. I've been through a few jobs, a few careers, schools, relationships, friendships, all kinds of ships. The one thing that's made it with me through everything is writing.

How could I quit?

This is my last chance.

And then my computer got stolen. I want to say that I had everything backed up, including the novel I was writing. Some of it was backed up. Anger and rage and madness and desperation were focused on the thief. I wanted to find him, beg him to give me thirty last minutes with my computer so I could get my files, and then he could have the damn machine. Just give me the work back. Give me my life back. Years of stuff, gone. Then I thought perhaps this was a good thing. Sometimes it's hard to change, to let go, unless your hand is forced. Sure, I still had old printed drafts of the book and could piece a manuscript back together, but what did all this work really mean to me?

On an exceptionally warm summer evening, when the wind blew across the urban landscape, disrupting discarded debris and releasing cement dust into the air and into my lungs, and the sirens of rushing ambulances filled the soundscape, I built a fire using some of the manuscript pages as kindling. I had never built a fire before this night, a potential problem I had failed to consider, but nonetheless, that fire shot up like a goddamn phoenix, quickly — a bit too quickly — like an explosion that could be seen for miles. Perhaps it was the ink on the pages or the poor choice of words that formed the poorly constructed paragraphs. I tossed in each page of the book I'd filled one at a time, and with each page the fire grew and grew, and after throwing in the last page, I danced around that fire and raised my arms to the heavens. If you had been watching me from afar, I must have looked like an insane shaman intending to resurrect spirits from the other side. To raise people from the dead.

Really, I had no choice.

That book — burning away, the pages crackling in the fire — was very different than this one, but I just couldn't write it anymore. I scratched it, decided to write as if I were sending you a letter — whoever you are out there, wherever you are out there. I needed to picture someone. I needed to build on some form of connection, no matter how superficial, no matter how constructed. A person who loves my work, loves to hear about the potentially uncomfortable stories that follow. Loves it, and I love them. The problem was processing, where the awareness of just how mad as hell and how goddamn tired I actually had become over the course of thirty-odd years could no longer be denied. I pushed it all down, too far down and for too long. The anger was bound to surface. These two dispositions — the love and the exhausted anger — cancelled each other out, resulting in not much feeling at all. Cracks were forming.

No more screwing around.

I don't want to think about who you are, except for that one person I'm writing this letter to. It's a long letter, but one I hope reaches from me to you. I'm focusing on you because I've gotten lost in there somewhere. And what do I have to say if I'm not the one saying it? And if I want your trust, if I want you to go along with me on this, I need to trust myself. And, and, and.

The problem I saw with my work and its failure to really connect came from my precious attitude toward it and, by extension, toward my life. By "precious," I mean playing it safe. But writing isn't precious and life shouldn't be safe. One piece I wrote for my class was about a work experience from a few years ago. After it was finished, I thought, *Who cares?* I was writing about people who didn't matter. So write about something that does matter. Some people can write about tragic pasts with a clarity that astounds me. I can't do that, plus, what tragedy? What do I write about? My stories are generally nice and polite and precious and safe.

Boring.

Burn it with me.

And that's the point of all this. I think that anyone wanting to express something through writing or other artistic means is curious about the world and interested in becoming a better person. I'm not curious about plunging into my past — a lack of interest I understand to be a form of denial — but how can I write about it in a sincere way if I'm not interested? I'm just going to write about what matters to me. Whether it's about something serious or about the old guy that farts while he's on the treadmill at the gym. 'Cause inside of that smelly, shitty fart could exist The Answer.

When I found myself in uncomfortable situations, my immediate thought was to disappear. I figured it would be best for all involved if I became invisible and let's all pretend this didn't happen. How does one become visible? My desire to fit in, to please, constrained my writing. When I came to something important and it made me uncomfortable, I moved away from it and missed the mark. And therein lies the connection for me, the thought that brings the whole thing together in a flash of lightning. Above, I just said, "My desire to please constrained my writing." I could easily have said this about my life in general. My mad-as-hell anger and my tiredness stemmed from how I perceived others were perceiving me. This was no way to live because, in the end, after I removed all the layers of who I thought I was, when I got to the core of myself, when I stopped pretending, stopped fooling myself, I was faced with the reality of the situation. Man, does it suck when you get a glimpse of your own core and you are not impressed.

Burn it.

Excuse me for this long diatribe, reeking of self-indulgence and presented in a way that makes me, and potentially you, uncomfortable. I'm tired of the shame, tired of the need to please, tired of wanting everyone to like me. The truth is, I'm just going to sit here, I'm going to write whatever I'm going to write and say whatever I'm going to say, and I'm going to do it in what I think is the right way. It might get messy, and it might not be pleasant all the time, but screw it.

Stay with me, you have to stay with me.

So this story, this new story, covers about a year. There's heartbreak, love, loss, long walks, fear, anger, and a talking dildo. Can't forget the dildo. And burning. The metaphorical burning began in the deserts of Jordan, very soon after the computer was stolen and I danced around that fire. There was nowhere to hide in Jordan. Trust me, I tried to hide. Carried around a straw in case I decided to bury myself in the sand. In the end, I decided against it. I feared the near silence, where the only sound would be my laboured breathing through a straw, the straw my only connection to living.

Jordan was the idea of my girlfriend, Hannah. We had wanted to travel together, but she got a job in one of those big towers downtown and couldn't get away. She told me to go visit one of my best friends in Jordan, even though I'd miss her birthday. She didn't seem to have a problem with this. Hannah's not my girlfriend anymore. More on her later, in the part of the story that displays my desperate attempt at love and my belief that I understood it — love, that is. But really and completely and truly, I had no idea.

So that's how I found myself on a plane to Greece. When the wheels of the plane hit the tarmac, all the passengers erupted with cheering and applause. I almost expected plates to be passed out and smashed on the ground — there's a poor joke made poorer due to stereotyping. Were they clapping because we had made it across the Atlantic alive? Were they just really happy to be in Greece? I wasn't in Greece long enough to determine if I should be happy about it. Happiness is relative, and I had no gauge for happiness.

Transferred to a much smaller plane heading to Cairo. The guy beside me was of Incredible Hulk size, his elbow stabbing me rib range for the duration. On arrival, we circled Cairo and the Sphinx and the pyramids; these cultural icons always seem so much smaller in real life. I once questioned someone on religion and the existence of god, and he replied by asking me if I'd ever seen the pyramids in person. When I said no, he questioned my firm belief in something I had only heard about or seen in pictures. He was arrogant and felt this was proof of the existence of god. Clever, but only in an immediate kind of way because, when I thought about it for five minutes, I came up with several rebuttals, all of which went unheard. I'm good at this: coming up with responses when no one's listening. I suck in the moment. I can safely say the pyramids do exist, but don't take my word for it. I don't know what that says about the existence of god.

As soon as we got off the plane, a couple kneeled in the corner, started praying. Notable differences of dress in Cairo — no shorts, no short sleeves, no skin showing whatsoever. I was trapped in the airport for a ten-hour layover. Walked up and down those limiting hallways so many times. Emailed with Hannah for a bit, she seemed disinterested that I was in Cairo. I found it very interesting. Maybe she was just disinterested in me.

Landing in Amman, ready this time, I clapped when we hit the ground, cheered and everything. My solitary clap echoed throughout the cabin. Perhaps because it was late at night? Maybe these passengers were not so happy to be arriving in Amman. Maybe the clapping was just a Greek thing? Whatever the case, everyone regarded me with mild confusion.

Inside the terminal, the thought occurred to me: what if my friend Andrew doesn't show up? It was about 2:00 a.m., and I didn't see him anywhere. Maybe we got the times mixed up? I'd been so focused on just getting there, making all the transfers, waiting, walking, and cheering, that I hadn't considered the possibility. My loitering caused the taxi drivers to keep offering me rides. Probably projection, but the looks on their faces held questions as to why I was there. I wondered why I was there. Finally, Andrew burst through the doors, threw his arms up, and yelled, "Welcome to Amman!" Lifted me off the ground in a bear hug. A slave to these societal rules we cling to that hold no meaning, I used to find it uncomfortable to hug men. Andrew taught me to hug other men, that I might even enjoy it.

We rushed out to the waiting taxi and into the Amman night. The driver was very enthusiastic to have us in his cab. The car actually got significant air whenever it hit one of the many speed bumps, and the driver was undeterred in his speed. I was glad my introduction to driving in Amman happened in the middle of the night, with few cars on the road. Driving in the city was like nowhere else. All roundabouts and rocky roads. All the cars were pockmarked from nudging into each other. As the saying goes, "Jordanians are an accommodating people until they get into their cars." Roundabouts ruled intersections, and drivers were well schooled in the art of shielding themselves with surrounding cars in order to arrive alive. As in many places with crazy drivers, it was organized chaos, but everyone managed to get where they had to be.

We ended up in a quiet part of the city. The apartment next to Andrew's was empty and his landlord allowed us to use it. We had been roommates many years ago in Toronto, and we'd be roommates again in Amman. We couldn't sleep, didn't sleep — loudspeakers informed us it was time to pray. The announcement was made five times per day, instructions arriving through a series of outdoor loudspeakers that could be heard everywhere in the city. The call was somehow comforting, even though I knew not what was being said, nor did I feel inspired to pray myself. It was the collectiveness of it that moved me. The people around us formed a community where everyone was, if not participating, at least aware of the time when prayer occurred. I was struck by the intensity of the sun as it rose, and lights flicked on, illuminating rooms in the apartment buildings surrounding us. Andrew told me his story about moving to Amman — that's his story to tell. Still unable to sleep, we walked the streets past the ubiquitous grey garbage bins and the feral cats looking for scraps. Walked up a steep hill, overlooked the valley, and watched nomads emerging from corrugated-roofed shacks and tending to herds of goats. We passed soldiers strolling casually with machine guns. Finally, I crashed in my own bed in Amman.

Woke up.

Where am I?

Halfway across the world from home.

But what is home?

Checked to see if Hannah had replied to my last email — nope. I was caring a little less each time I didn't hear from her. Besides, Andrew and I had an early-morning bus to catch.

The Captain gave new meaning to the term "handlebar moustache." Wore a dark jean vest over a white shirt with military-style patches, and a brown corduroy fedora tilted to the side. Only the Captain could wear this outfit and make it not only respectable but also damn cool. I didn't know if he was really a captain of anything, but that's what he told us to call him. He drove the bus coolly, while drinking from an open cup of steaming tea, smoking out the window, playing DJ for the rest of us, and clapping to his music. The music seemed unravelled from the fabric of everyday life here, all beats, foreign tongues, and unidentifiable instruments. There was a No Smoking sign at the front of the bus, but who was going to tell the Captain he couldn't fire up his Marlboro Lights? Not me, no goddamn way. As we left the city of Amman early that morning, the Captain cranked the volume and yelled into the microphone at his passengers, "Why aren't you dancing?"

Our destination was the desert. The Captain would be the one to bring us there.

The city quickly disappeared, the box-like buildings fading, growing smaller in the rear-view mirrors. The brown land on both sides was flat, the horizon visible. Signs for Wadi Rum led us away from the rolling trucks, and rocks became visible then grew larger, developing into hills, mutating into cliffs and mountains. After having driven deep into the valley and being surrounded by mountains, we turned off the road and headed into the desert. We were off-roading in a large coach bus. I had faith in the Captain. Sand kicked up from the wheels, the dust clouding in our wake. Coming around a steep rock face, we rolled to a stop.

Wadi is the Arabic term for valley. Wadi Rum is sometimes referred to as the Valley of the Moon and is located in southern Jordan, some sixty kilometres east of Aqaba (a place I only knew from a slight obsession in my youth with the movie *Lawrence of Arabia*). The highest elevation of Mount Um Dami measures 1840 metres, and from the top, it is possible to see Saudi Arabia and the Red Sea.

It was mid-afternoon by then, and although the sun was hot, the temperature was tolerable. We grabbed our bags and walked into the Bedouin camp. Sadly, my reference point for Bedouins also came from *Lawrence of Arabia*. The camp had a large square in the centre for the entertainment, and the square was flanked by rows of tents.

Time to eat and time to dance. Though there was no formal entertainment, the Bedouins had a full sound system and blasted music loudly enough that it probably echoed in every corner of the desert. Some visitors got up and danced while others sat around the perimeter of the stage, eating and smoking hookah. The Captain sat and chain-smoked his Marlboro Lights, a pot of tea resting next to his cracked toenails. I wanted to talk with him, have a sit down, but no goddamn way.

The sun went down and it was time for us to hit the desert.

Walking up a hill covered in sand is much more difficult than you may think. My feet sank into the sand up to my ankles and little headway was gained with each step. I knew I'd be rewarded at the top and Andrew and I kept going higher, following along the rocks, giant steps leading up to the sky. Not exactly rock climbing — easier — but once I reached the top of the rock cliff, I realized this was not a place to get lost.

A group of people emerged from the camp and we headed back down the hill to join them, walking deep into the desert. My concern over getting lost diminished — the others seemed to know where they were going. There was very little conversation — we just walked. Andrew and I walked at a distance from the group, but soon a young boy broke off and insisted we join them. There's strength in numbers. I can't tell you how long we walked. Didn't matter to us how long.

Sometimes you have to walk around aimlessly. Sometimes you do it alone, sometimes with others.

Andrew was up near the middle of the pack. I lingered, fell to the back. I got lost in our nomadic pursuit, in my footsteps disappearing behind me, in the repetitiveness of the foreign chatter ahead of me. The camp was well behind us, the lights getting lost, flittering farther away with every step. I stopped mid-step. I wasn't tired, nor was it a conscious decision or thought telling me to stop — my feet just came to a standstill. On the desert horizon, illuminated by the moonlight, a cloaked figure moved in the distance, on a trajectory perpendicular to the walking group and the camp. I thought maybe this person was lost, or perhaps afraid of us. In the same manner I had stopped, I took a new step with no conscious thought — a step toward this person who had just disappeared over the sand dune. I figured I'd just make it to the top of the dune, and if the person didn't want to join us, then I'd return to the group. The problem with this plan was that when I reached the top of the dune, the cloaked figure seemed even farther away. Stopping, I looked back at the walking group, small figures in the distance by then. I turned toward the cloaked figure — dammit — with every step I took, it seemed like he took five.

Kept after the cloaked figure. Maybe he was lost. Maybe he needed help. Just up and over one more sand dune, I thought. One more and I'll go back. I couldn't keep after this guy forever; I didn't want to get lost myself. One more. Up and ... He was gone. I turned and ran back up the last sand dune, couldn't see anyone from the walking group. I didn't even know which way the camp was. Nothing but sand and the moon. Nothing.

Shit.

There was only one thing I could do: walk.

Sometimes you have to walk around purposefully. Sometimes you do it with others, sometimes alone.

Intentional Emergencies and the First Walk

I was born to walk. Crawling was never fast enough — there were too many places to see. Through tough trials and considerable errors, I got my feet moving as quickly as possible. My curiosity could not be contained, but my physical body soon had something else to say about it all.

If you can believe it, I failed to receive the vaccination for polio as a baby. You wouldn't think this a problem, but this oversight of the family doctor combined with a family trip to Spain during a small outbreak resulted in my contracting the disease before my age hit the double digits. We got the entire thing under control, but not before the muscles in my left leg were attacked and annihilated, and not without my being trapped in the house for a year at the age of nine. A bed was moved, and for a while my world consisted of the first floor of our house.

I was no longer allowed out except for emergencies.

The first emergency was unintentional. I inhaled a small Lego piece. I don't feel it necessary to describe in detail how the plastic block got up my nose. The front door opened, and the sun blasted, blinding me until my eyes grew accustomed. The smell of dirt and exhaust filled my unplugged nostril. The air lighter. The light brighter. In the back seat of the car, pulling away from the walk-in clinic, holding a bloody tissue to my newly Lego-free nose, my mind plotted.

The emergencies that followed were completely intentional. Swallowing objects or shoving small pieces of toys up my nose necessitated a clinic visit. Depending on the item swallowed or shoved, the hospital was also a viable and very realistic option.

Miniature flatbed trucks. Arms and legs of assorted action figures. All swallowed. Every trip was a revelation. With each outing I noticed more details: multicoloured houses, well-groomed lawns, soccer-playing kids. Traffic! Emergencies were planned in conjunction with rush hour. More time on the road meant more time out in the world. A freakishly bloody kid with forehead pressed against the window, I waved at confused passersby.

Boldness breeds carelessness. I finally got caught with Optimus Prime in my mouth up to his legs. Optimus Prime was large — try swallowing your fist. I was slapped hard on the back, and he flew across the room, slammed into the wall, magically transforming into his tractor-trailer alter ego. My mom and I stared at the truck, eyebrows raised. Something other than Optimus Prime had to transform.

We started hanging out in the backyard for an hour each day. At the time, I failed to recognize that this set-up resembled a prisoner's mandatory one hour of exercise out in the yard. No one expressed any significance to this new routine, and I was just content to get outside consistently. The middle of the lawn used to be a swimming pool but had been filled in with cement after we acquired the house. I limped laps on the artificial turf that outlined the kidney-shaped ghost of the pool. An old oak tree quietly sat in the corner and raspberry bushes lined the wooden-plank fence. On my hands and knees, behind the raspberry bushes where I couldn't be seen, I pressed my face against the fence, peeked through the cracks, desperately wanting to see what lay beyond.

A part of me wishes I had never left that backyard. A part of me wonders, had I been confronted with knowledge of the future, would I have been so curious, so desperate to rush out and experience the outside world?

The discovery of the old dog door marked another revelation. We didn't have a dog, but the previous owners had. Must have been a big one. A well-concealed wooden plank had been nailed to the lower third of the backyard door. One day while I sat enjoying a peanut-butter-and-jelly sandwich at the kitchen table, a rainstorm raged outside. I heard a banging noise and, with some investigation, came to understand that the top-right nail of the wooden plank covering the dog door was loose. I wiggled the plank. Lightning crashed and I froze. Listened. Wiggled. A loose flap of rubber slapped against the wooden plank as the wind blew. With each slap, the cool, misty air shot forcefully into my face. I listened again. Wiggled the bottom-right nail free. Turned my shoulders at an angle, planted my feet on the floor, and pushed my head and torso through the dog door.

One of the single most important discoveries of my life.

I returned inside and covered my tracks. Patience was one of my virtues before I knew what it meant. I replaced the wooden plank, but left it loose.

The silence of night barely concealed my excitement. At 1:37 a.m., I slipped out of bed, pulled my hidden backpack from under the bed. Contents: flashlight (clicked on to double-check other supplies), light jacket, shoes, hammer, loaf of bread. All will be explained.

I padded in sock feet down the stairs. At the door, the two right nails unhinged easily, and the hammer came in handy for the left side. I removed the wooden plank and set it quietly against the kitchen counter that ran perpendicular to the door. The bag was pushed through the rubber flaps and gently placed on the porch floor. Feet planted, headfirst. My waist caused a bit of a problem. I shifted weight, switched position, pressed with my toes, jammed through with a suction noise, and landed on the porch with a thud.

Crumpled on my side, I listened for movement. Satisfied, I pulled on my shoes. Kept the flashlight handy but off. The sky was clear, the rain gone, the stars shining, the moon a night light. Behind the raspberry bushes, next to the old oak, I knelt down in front of the wooden fence. The hammer had been a good consideration. The claws poked between two planks and wrestled the ends free. Enough room for me to lift the planks up and scoot underneath.

The outside world beyond my backyard.

Next: bread crumbs. Ripped a few pieces of the white bread with my right hand and held the crumbs with an upturned left hand until the slight wind carried them to the ground.

And I walked, trailing bread crumbs behind me to find my way back home. Home was getting farther behind me with every step. A trail led to a school soccer field. I limped across the field to a tiny pond. The wind sailed over top, the still water untouched. My reflection looked back at me. I looked up, saw a silhouette at the entrance of the trail. Pretended not to see anyone. When I moved, the silhouette moved. I walked over to the playground, slowly climbed the play structure, sat down. Waited for the silhouette. Looked in the windows of houses, listened for signs of life pouring out of open windows. Nothing. Just me and the silhouette. A stray car or truck could be heard every few minutes. The silhouette sat down across the field next to a tree. The stars started to fade, the black sky grew lighter by the minute. It was time to return home.

The wind picked up in the early morning. After making my way off the play structure, I realized the bread crumbs had been picked up by the wind, scattered in every direction. An intermittent snowfall, the flakes fallen in random places. According to my brilliant plan, the bread crumbs were supposed to have led me home. According to the bread crumbs, home was every direction on a compass. The silhouette stood, motioned for me to follow it. So I did. The silhouette moved slowly enough that I could follow but still maintain a safe distance.

At the school, the bread crumbs had not scattered but disappeared. The culprits revealed themselves: two squirrels had hit pay dirt, scurried to collect as many as possible. Robbers at a heist. The silhouette stopped at the entrance of the path that weaved its way back to my house. The early-morning sun rose, revealing the face of the long-haired girl who lived next door to us. A purple birthmark formed a crescent around her left eye. She pulled a plank up from the fence surrounding her house, crawled into her yard, and quietly put the board back in place, disappearing before a word could be exchanged between us.

Found the wooden planks I'd used to exit, but they took some help opening and a while longer than expected, long enough for a missing persons report, and the sun. At least I wouldn't have gone hungry, with most of my loaf of bread left over. My bread crumbs may not have worked as intended, but that venture beyond my house and my backyard and the hospital revealed a deep desire to explore. Back home, my parents had even called in my grandmother Margaret. She waited for me on the back porch, smoking a cigarette. While my parents were frantic, Margaret just stood there calmly, didn't say a word while I made my way back into the yard, her eyes darting over the fence, over the walkway that separated our house from next door, watching the neighbour girl sneak into her house.

This walk also introduced me to the single most important person in my life — I just didn't know it then. For the rest of the time I was sequestered in my house, I couldn't get that girl out of my mind. Her purple birthmark was tattooed on the inside of my skull. Chloe.

The Mary Manifest

After returning from Jordan, I created a podcast with a friend of mine. I'd started a blog a few years earlier, after just about everyone else on the planet. Ever since I joined the podcast revolution as an avid listener, I had a secret desire to start a podcast myself. Behind the trends again. Something intrigued me about podcasts. Here were people finding their voices and their audiences, and doing it on their own, producing content they wanted with no interference. The most democratic form of expression we've come up with yet.

Another secret desire was to work in some capacity as a journalist. Not necessarily as a newspaper journalist, more along the lines of a Jon Ronson type. Someone who would follow his curiosity and seek out stories that were personal to him. Also, one of my favourite things is to talk to interesting people and engage with their experiences and stories.

Before starting the podcast, I made some recordings — recordings that no one will ever hear. Terrible. I know that everyone hates hearing his own voice, but mine sounded especially grating, monotonous, and boring. Shelved the idea.

I talked to a friend so often about this stuff that she finally said, "Why don't we do a podcast together?" Something clicked for me. It would be easier if I were speaking to someone else, and there was no one else I'd rather do this with. We decided on an interview format with some banter between us at the start and end of each episode.

We got some microphones and the learning curve commenced — I came from a television background, with no radio experience. My friend was proactive and quickly had two interviews in the can. Time for a little banter from the hosts. We got together and set up the microphones. When she threw it to me, I could barely speak. We tried a few more times, but it didn't work. My respect for my friend and other people who talked on microphones so freely and openly went through the roof. It wasn't easy.

Here's where it gets weird.

You see, I have this bitch of a personal assistant living within the confines of my mind. She's there with me every step of the way. She was wrinkly, old, and crinkly-voiced, and she smelled like someone poked a hole in a catheter. I named her Mary.

Most personal assistants are helpful, they bring you coffee, and file shit, and organize things. Mary had files all right — she had a gigantic cabinet of files. These files encompassed all of my failings and low points, and the reasons I was a terrible person. She actually had two cabinets, a small one beside the big one. This smaller one contained the positive things I'd done with my life, but it was the size of a shoebox.

Oh, how Mary loved to go through the big cabinet. She would remind me of my deficiencies at every opportunity. For example, whenever I stepped up to the plate, like trying to speak on the mic and getting my voice heard, Mary was right there waving a goddamn file in my face. "You gotta see this," she'd say. "You have nothing important to say and no one wants to hear from you." I generally replied to statements like this by telling her to fuck off. The problem was that she wasn't fucking off, no matter how many times I asked her to.

One aspect of her physical appearance that I had concocted was that she was missing one of her arms. I made up an elaborate backstory that she'd lost it as a little girl. She grew up on a farm, and her father always told her to not play around the large machines and equipment. One day, her hand got stuck in a machine and pulled her in right up to her shoulder. At least by removing her arm, I had established a weakness in her. I'd never exploited that weakness, but some day that arm — or lack thereof — might come in handy in an effort to finally cast her off.

After a few days of thinking, of listening to Mary, of studying the files she showed me, I realized I was overthinking. Sometimes I can fight Mary off. Sometimes. I'm not a broadcaster. But dammit, I had shit to say and wanted to give this an honest try. Had to do it my way, trust my friend, and just go with it. And so we hit record and started talking and it went well. I tripped up a few times, but I had to give myself permission to screw up before I gave up.

Things got better and I contacted an old friend of my grandmother for an interview. Curiously, her name was also Mary — Mary Hammerstein. She was over ninety years old and sharper than most people a third her age (most obviously including myself). Originally from Germany, Mary was a retired ballet dancer and choreographer, and had survived the concentration camps during World War II.

I went to the Lighthouse Retirement Home to talk to Mary and record her experiences. It was like walking into a dream. We had arranged a time early in the morning. The sun popping up over the hazy horizon created a desert-like feeling of mirage and an unfiltered fuzziness that made my eyes unfocused. A ring of light emanated from the Lighthouse, a rainbow in one shade. The golden colour played at the fringes of my periphery, melted the sidewalks under my feet, played with the opacity of the outlines of the building. The streetlights heaved at the weight of their being, everything tilted to the side like I was walking into a funhouse.

The catheter smell hit me as soon as I entered the place. This smell triggered a spell as I wound my way through the hallways and found her room. I knocked and something went thud against the door. The thud will be explained later. I knocked again and heard some vague swearing and mumbling. My bitch of a personal assistant sounded like she had a megaphone inside my brain: *You are a failure! You won't be able to engage with this person in a way that would be interesting to others!* Finally, the door opened and…

Here's where it gets even weirder.

Mary — my bitch of a personal assistant Mary — was quite firmly established in my mind. I could pick her out of a police lineup of old ladies. When Mary — my grandmother's friend Mary Hammerstein — opened her door, she was wrinkly and old, her voice even more crinkly than the Mary-voice inside my head. This Mary also was missing an arm. This bears repeating: inside my head I have a personal assistant whom I consider to be a bitch, and around whom I have created an elaborate backstory involving her missing arm. Standing in front of me was a real genuine person who seemed to embody these parameters exactly.

I shrugged off the thought, because what else was I supposed to do? Stepped inside and set up. We drank gin and tonics and ate cookies, and we sat for over five hours. For the first while, Mary talked about her childhood and coming of age when the bombs started dropping. I'm including excerpts from the interview here. What remains unspoken is her story to tell.

MARY: You want to know about the war, yes?

ME: [unintelligible] ...mmmhmm...

MARY: You can't imagine. You have no idea. You have
no frame of reference. My father failed to recognize the
seriousness of the situation. He was a businessman. He
decided that they would not come for us. We had
curfews. Then they wouldn't sell us food at the store.
People started disappearing on the trains. Still my father
was blind. But I knew the severity of the situation. They
took the old people first, my grandparents. The next week
they took my parents. There was nothing to do but wait
for them to take me. When we went to the camp, you
filled out on a piece of paper your name, age, and
occupation. I wrote down that I was a ballet dancer,
which I was, as you know. It so happened that the soldier
in charge of the camp was a fan of the ballet. Can you
believe this? He pulled me out of the factory work, my
job became to clean the houses of the soldiers. Much
safer than the factories.

ME: Wait, because you put down "ballet dancer," this
basically saved your life?

MARY: Many small things saved my life. But yes, this
was the big one. Two days a week I worked in the
factory. All day they would call people's names and they
were brought to the trains. At the end of the day, I would
be the only one left. The soldier in charge gave me a
special pass that said I was not to go on the trains.

ME: What happened to your parents?

MARY: My father, fooling himself to the end. I worked
in the factory and my name was called. Afraid because I
thought they would disregard my pass. No, my parents
were being put on the trains and they allowed ten minutes
for me to say goodbye. The last time I saw them, they

waved from a packed train car, my mother's arm sticking out of a barred window waving. Then I was brought back to the factory.

ME: Do you think that some people are wired for survival?

MARY: You want to live, but this didn't make any sense. None of it. All day, you are surrounded by death, people starving. Madness. I wanted to live, and I would do anything to survive. One night, the soldiers had a party and they asked me to perform. I had not practiced for a long time. I was sure they would see me as a fraud and take me immediately to the train. This is the danger, always there, over your shoulder, watching you. A man following you in a black suit. I danced and they didn't notice how bad I was because they were all drunk.

ME: How did you get out of the camp?

MARY: The Russians. You could feel them coming, not only in the sky and the air, but in the faces and actions of the soldiers. They started leaving, one by one, until the Russians finally appeared and no German soldiers were left. They told us to go home.

ME: They just left you there?

MARY: There was still much to do for them, the war was almost over, but not yet. No support for us. For a few days, I rode on top of a Russian tank, on the outside of it. This is where I met your grandmother.

[Mary got up, walked across the room, took a framed photograph off the wall, handed it to me.]

MARY: She was there as a journalist from America. This was one of the famous photographs she took, and it was of me. That's me riding on the tank. The tank ride finished, I needed to go in a different direction. Margaret and me started talking. We walked together until we reached my village.

ME: So you just walked home?

MARY: How else? Have you not ever done something out of pure necessity? Been in a life or death situation? Because you had no choice? Margaret and I walked for days. We found food in the forests that weren't burned. One day we were foraging when we heard a click of a machine gun. A Russian soldier there asking us who we were. Two women: one Canadian and one German. Not a good mix. He told us to give him anything of value. He pulled back his sleeve, at least ten gold watches fastened to his forearm. He wanted Margaret's camera. We were liberated just to be pillaged again. But Margaret, she refused, she grabbed my arm and turned our backs and told me to walk away, told me he would not shoot two women in the back. I protested, but she said to trust her. The Russian shouted, clicked his gun, shot at the ground at our retreating feet. Margaret told me to keep walking. He didn't shoot us and didn't follow us. We walked and walked. She asked me to tell her all that I've told you — about the camps, about growing up. When we reached my village, our feet and legs about to fall off, we knew everything about each other. I found my house and there was another family living there, a family that was given the house. I was alive but my life was taken from me. Margaret helped me get out of Germany and out of Europe and finally to America.

ME: You know, I've been thinking about Margaret a lot lately.

MARY: You visit where she's buried?

ME: Not since I was very young.

MARY: Why? Me? If I didn't live in this damn place, I'd visit her all the time.

ME: It's just a gravestone.

MARY: It's a symbol. Come on, get your ass over there. When you go, I'll go with you. Get me outta this place for a couple of hours. I got something to show you. It's time for a cigarette anyway.

As she lit up, a bang on the door disrupted the recording. Mary retaliated by grabbing a glass ashtray on the side table and whipping it across the room at the door, shattering it into pieces. Every morning at six and every evening at six, the Walking Seniors gathered their members and did laps of the building. The group was organized by Mary's purple-haired arch-nemesis, Edith, who insisted on signalling to every resident — Walking Senior or not — by banging on doors with canes and walkers. The banging, which had initially started for the many members who were unable to hear, had become a tradition. In the morning, Edith and her crew woke everyone up — Walking Senior or not. Mary joined them one morning for the first and last time: "They're too slow. I kept getting too far ahead and had to wait. They pashawed when I lit up, so I blew smoke in their faces. Bunch of frickin' little kids. I've had cancer seven times and they're complaining about inflamed hemorrhoids? 'Oh my hip! Oh my swollen lymph nodes!' Yeesh. Deal with it." Edith led the walks every morning with her right-hand woman, Leena, a mysterious Estonian woman. Edith was focused. She had seven different walking outfits — each in a different shade of purple.

I went to the door and out into the hallway. You should have seen those old fogies as they shuffled down the hallway in all their glory with their canes, walkers, limps, fake hips, false teeth, and thick glasses. Once the members had all been collected, they went down to the main foyer to make a starting line. They waited for Edith to give the signal. Nervousness swelled around them. Mary told me about the time she saw the running of the bulls in Spain. The men had all glanced nervously at the angry bulls behind them. Gunshot! And they were off running for their lives. The old fogies also ran for their lives, albeit slowly and for different reasons. Imagine the running of the bulls with four-pronged canes.

When the group was gone, I returned to the living room where Mary sat, eyes closed. Her head leaned to the left side as usual. Cigarette burning in the ashtray. This position would be uncomfortable for most, but it was the only way she could stave off her pain. The left sleeve of her blouse hung flat against her body, the missing limb a remembrance of the past.

Her mouth was open. No drool.

"Mary?"

I crossed the living room and bent over for a closer look. Cupped my hand over her mouth, checked for breathing.

"Mary?" I asked, louder.

Her eyes opened and she yelped. The force shot me back a few steps.

"Ah, hell. What's the deal?" She squinted at me. "Trying to scare me to death?"

"I didn't see any drool."

"I'm over ninety. I don't have any drool left." Mary adjusted her empty sleeve. Her left arm had been amputated when she was fifty-four, during her third bout of cancer. Mary managed to do more with one arm than most people accomplished with two. She had problems with her back that caused her neck to fall to one side. The constant head-tilt made her look like she was sizing you up, judging you. She was.

Mary reached for her chrome four-pronged cane. Placing her weight on the cane, she rose to her full height of 4'7" and looked past me into the kitchen. "Where's Marathon Margaret? Thought that's who was at the door."

"Margaret's dead," I said. "Remember?"

She blinked three times. Recognition.

Mary motioned for me to follow her. We walked through the hallway and into the bedroom. Inside the bedroom, a giant cabinet went all the way from the floor to the ceiling. I was trying to figure out how the hell she got it in here when another trigger shot through my brain, similar to when I first entered the Lighthouse and smelled the catheter. *A cabinet?* Mary rested her cane beside the cabinet. The hinges squealed as she opened the doors.

Okay, now this was one of those moments that I can't really express the truth of because whatever I might say, you will most likely not believe it. So, I will just tell it the way I remember and allow you room to interpret as you will.

"Your grandmother gave all this to me to keep for you," Mary said.

Inside the cabinet were row after row of very neat files. The files were organized by year. I went to grab one of the files—

"No, no, no!" Mary yelled, slapping my hand away. "Only me. I know where everything is."

In addition to being tall, the cabinet was also very deep. Half of Mary's body disappeared as she went through a few piles.

"Yes," she said, moving to sit on the edge of the bed. "Here it is. Whenever you got around to visiting me, before I showed you anything else, Margaret wanted me to show you this."

Mary took out a framed photograph, handed it to me.

"And she told me to call you an idiot."

The photograph was one I hadn't seen in years. A close-up of the two of us. Me and Chloe. She was looking into the camera, squinting, squirming, and laughing because I had turned right before the camera clicked, kissed her on the birthmark around her left eye. It's quite a spectacular picture — the light sparkles in from the top left-hand corner, creating a blue-tinted effect, capturing all our best features. I can't quite articulate it, but when you see two people in a picture during a certain part of the day, in a specific moment when their guards are down, that photograph can capture something, a moment in time when you can almost read the thoughts of the people in the photograph, you can see them like thought bubbles. You can see the emotions going back and forth, you can actually feel what each person is feeling toward the other, there's an electrical force bouncing back and forth. Well, my grandmother Margaret was a photographer, after all. I remember exactly when this happened: it was one of the times we visited Margaret. She was pissed off because we had moved her out of her apartment and into a retirement home, similar to the Lighthouse. If there's one thing that Margaret valued over anything else, it was her independence. She was also resistant to understanding her limitations. Mary let me stare at the photograph. As though she were waiting for something, when a significant amount of time had gone by, she slapped her hands on her lap and stood up slowly.

"Okay," she said. "We have a lot of ground to cover in how much of an idiot you've been. But first we must smoke."

She led me out to the balcony. She lit a cigarette and told me about the residents of the retirement home. She knew that her neighbour had broken her dentures in a very embarrassing fashion when she'd gotten drunk with old Mrs. Wilson. Mary had discovered the five-day-old corpse of Benny Balduchi after trying to figure out where a most peculiar smell had originated. Although the autopsy revealed Benny had died of natural causes, his rumoured ties to organized crime were whispered about in the hallways for months. She knew that the widow Ballantine upstairs had the Big C and urged her to see a doctor. She knew whose grandchildren visited and whose didn't. Who was angry, who was bitter.

If gossiping were an Olympic sport, Mary would've been reigning champ. It took training, discipline, commitment, determination. She didn't say what Edith had done to earn her arch-nemesis status. All I knew was this: she was going down. It was only a matter of time before Mary discovered the vital piece of dirt that would bounce Edith from her throne.

31

With speed beyond her years, Mary dropped her cane, grabbed a water gun that was leaning against the wall, and shot at some pigeons.

At ninety-three, she was attentive to many details. The folders were impeccably kept — my grandmother's life's work that contained details and reminders of my experiences, a collaboration between these two women. A conspiracy, if you will.

"You missed quite the match last night. Stainless Steele used his blowtorch. It kills me every time." Mary moved on to her favourite subject: professional wrestling. Mary was *the* number one fan of the International Federation of Professional Wrestlers (IFPW). If you referred to wrestling as "entertainment," you'd surely get a swipe of her cane to your head. Yes, she used the cane for walking, but it was really more of a weapon. A knight's sword. Mary often gave people nicknames that resembled those of the steroid-induced megamen from the IFPW. She called her best friend (and my grandmother) Marathon Margaret. When Mary and Margaret lived next door to each other, they often held court at the local sports bar down the street. Marathon Margaret and Mary "The Hammer" Hammerstein commandeered the corner table whenever wrestling was on television. They sat in front of the big-screen television, drank high balls, smoked like hell, and argued for hours about who was the better wrestler: Stainless Steele or Margaret's favourite, Smackdown. The Hammer broke her hip after she jumped off a table trying to demonstrate Smackdown's signature move, the "Flying Elbow."

They made a great team and they knew how to have fun, but when that first folder was pulled out of the cabinet, it opened a door to a completely different side of them that I'd had no idea about. Truly, I was an idiot — for a variety of reasons.

We went back inside. Every room of her small apartment was a different country, decorated with collected souvenirs from Mary's career as a travel writer. I collected the glasses and plates and brought them into the kitchen, China. Her plates, bowls, and tea sets were from Beijing. A didgeridoo from Sydney sat in the corner of the living room — she was quite the player, even with her smoking. Her bathroom cabinet was full of Tibetan herbs, such as saffron, aweto, and snow lotus. And there were photographs, all taken by Margaret: Mary riding a camel in Morocco, sky diving in New Zealand, and atop Mount Tai in China. I could travel the world without stepping outside.

Mary walked with me down the hallway. She pushed open an emergency door that triggered an alarm. As we walked toward the lobby, the hallway filled with the other residents of the Lighthouse.

Edith was also the Treasury Secretary of the Board of Directors. If an alarm went off, it was her responsibility to check that emergency procedures went according to plan. She appeared, purple-haired and holding a clipboard, rushing around to check the quality of the fire drill execution. When she saw the far door open by the south entrance, Edith wasn't happy about it. The crevasses on her forehead deepened her already pronounced scowl. Edith shook her head at the blinking emergency light, making a cluck-cluck-clucking noise with her tongue. She saw the director of the retirement home and ran after him, tap-tap-tapping her pencil against the clipboard.

"Keeps her on her toes," Mary said, watching them all scurry. "That dunce, she'll get hers."

I shot her a quizzical look.

"Hey, don't look at me. If that purple-haired freak gets taken away in cuffs, I had nothing to do with it." There was a knowing glint in her eyes.

The emergency exit was where we started our walks. We headed out to the wooded area behind the Lighthouse, followed a path cut through the trees. Mary started with that first file, the one that included nothing but the photograph of Chloe and me.

"Margaret, your grandmother, she's kept track of everything you've done," Mary explained. "You didn't think she was paying attention, did you? Everything."

That night, long ago, when Margaret waited on the back porch for me to return from my first walk, she was really with me all along.

"Besides the fact that she was your grandmother," Mary continued, "she felt a certain connection to you. Besides the fact that you're an idiot and didn't visit her enough, didn't spend enough time with her, she had a very strong sense that you needed help to make the right decisions."

"What, like a guardian angel?" I asked.

"No, not like a goddamn *guardian angel*," she said, smacking me over the head with the file folder. "You mustn't be so stupid. This is serious. You need to change things."

Mary went on and on like this for our entire walk. We eventually circled back around to the entrance of the Lighthouse.

"Go visit your grandmother's grave. Idiot," she said, and we parted.

As I walked away, I turned back to wave at Mary, who looked like a large garden gnome, resting on her cane in the foyer.

I walked to the subway, clinked through the turnstile, felt the train coming before headlights were visible. Strewn papers swirled. Voices were drowned out. The tunnel held its breath until the train erupted from the darkness. I wanted to touch the subway as it sped past and came to a stop.

The doors opened, the chime sounded, and we were off. Subways are indifferent to people and do not discriminate. Two years earlier, the Transit Commission had installed automated stop announcements. The announcements had already broken down, the usually pleasant female voice constricted to that of an alien scratching her chords between two sheets of sandpaper.

I sat in the front seat of the lead train. Checked the orange cushions for signs of used gum or spilled drink, neither of which I wanted to take with me. The door to the driver's compartment swung open. A lot was packed into that tiny booth: blinking lights, odometers, flips, radios, switches. The driver nodded at me. A guitar case leaned against his chair — he would not be defined by his job. He wanted to talk. "You notice the difference between trains?" he asked.

I shuffled uncomfortably in my seat. "Difference?" Was he talking to *me*?

"Yeah. This is an old train." He shifted gears as we approached the next station. "They're difficult to drive though. New drivers aren't allowed to take them on. Nope. Only experienced ones."

"Like you?"

He looked at me funny. I always said something wrong.

"What's so hard about driving them?" I asked.

"Difficult to handle. Yep. And can be a stubborn bitch to stop."

"How fast does it go?" My courage blossomed.

"You want to see?"

I nodded.

"Okay, wait until we've cleared this stop."

He stuck his head out the suitably tiny window. All clear: doors chimed, slammed shut. He smiled at me and spun the throttle all the way into the highest gear.

You could feel a change in velocity but no other passengers seemed to notice. The tunnel lights blinked as we passed. And still we went faster. It might have been my imagination, but I thought I could hear the screech of the tracks as we pressured them to work harder than usual. Through the side window, I saw sparks shoot from the wheels. And still we went faster. A great beast awakened. We challenged it and it took on the challenge. But the driver was in complete control. Focused. And still we went faster. Not fast enough. I wanted us to keep going, forget about the station stops, forget about responsibility, just keep driving, accumulate kilometre after kilometre of distance. We would get to the end of the prescribed route, but it would not be the end. Our speed would allow us to jump the tracks, burst through the walls, emerge unhurt. Unhinged. And there would be a metal-sounding sigh as we drifted into the sky, carried off by the clouds, through the atmosphere until we reached our final destination: the moon. And there we'd float for the rest of our days. Not even gravity could keep us down.

Fall

I was out there somewhere in the deserts of Jordan, the wind incredible. Climbed to the top of a small rocky area in an attempt to see what I could see. If I could see signs of life. The wind could take you over. If you leaned into it and let go, it supported your weight. I stood, watched the moon move incrementally, and sat down — just sat, not feeling anything or forcing a moment. There was no forcing of moments, no need. The weight of the desert overcame any thoughts, instead forced you to focus, not on anything specific, but on the vast emptiness before your eyes.

Just sat. A scorpion scuttled past me. At least, I think it was a scorpion. The Captain told us green scorpions were poisonous and we'd probably be dead before we could get any help. The black ones were okay. Wait, or were the black ones poisonous and the green ones okay? I saw a black one and it didn't bite me.

I'm still here, so I'm fine for now.

From there, the world seemed visible in its entirety. Have you ever been camping? Or far out away from where any city lights take away the power of a clear night sky? The sky, full of stars, pressed down, immediately above, like you could reach out and touch them. I lay down. I felt as though I was lying on the edge of the world, clinging helplessly to the earth. Everything went away. It's at times like these when people say they feel small. But with the wind supporting me and the vastness of the desert, I felt like I was a part of something larger. You're not small, you're a piece. A required piece.

I'll wait for the sun to rise.

The sun will show me the way home.

I listened to the wind.

Chloe, Then Hannah, Back to Chloe

Before I left for Jordan, my girlfriend Hannah and I were not doing well, but I had no idea. I never wanted to be in a relationship where the other person harboured resentments, buried them deep down, waited for them to surface in explosive ways. She had gotten a job in her chosen field — sort of. I say "sort of" because what she wanted was to work creatively, but due to parental pressures, she started working at a large firm downtown in the financial district. She seemed pretty miserable from the start, and perhaps I wasn't as supportive as I should've been. I was trying to be whatever she needed. Or so I thought. It's a problem — I tend to lose my sense of myself in a relationship, trying to give that person all they need when all they really want is me. So I told her that she should take the job and still pursue her creative endeavours. She didn't feel the same way, felt overwhelmed and frustrated by work.

These feelings of frustration, of course, bled into our relationship. I was older than she and had more perspective. Felt that a relationship ebbed and flowed, had peaks and valleys, and all that crap. I do admit that the passion of our two years together felt different once I returned from Jordan, but I attributed it to the many changes going on in our lives. This was a good thing, right? We were evolving and changing with each other. She didn't feel the same way.

Our sex life was pretty healthy, or so I thought. Claiming she wanted to practice more on her own for both our benefits, she mused about buying a dildo. Maybe this was a sign that things weren't so good, but I took it at face value. I might be older, but you can be naive at any age. After all, this was something we could do together, kind of like a team-building exercise, so we shopped online for the right one. Shopping for dildos was definitely a new experience for me. There were wooden ones that made me think of splinters, one called the Silver Bullet that made me think of werewolves. We finally settled on a traditional model. Since she lived with her parents, we had it delivered to my house.

The dildo arrived a week later and I removed it from the postal packaging. It looked larger than the picture. I kept it in the box, wanted her to handle it. I placed it in the corner of my office on the floor. It was strange having a dildo in my office, made me feel insecure. Made me think about why I felt insecure.

I'm not really that interested in marriage. Sure, the thought crossed my mind when I was with Hannah — the first time I'd really had this thought about anyone — but more than anything, I felt like I was actually in love with her. It was a somewhat scary feeling for me — I'd felt it before, but I must admit that, with Hannah, it was the strongest it had ever come on. I wouldn't have even said we were having problems; we just were growing apart, and I believe she was pulling away, knowing that she didn't want to be with me anymore, whereas I thought we were just going through a rough stage.

A rough stage, that's a good way to put it. I was fooling myself, and the stress surrounding the volatile ground my relationship stood on started playing with my mind. How can I explain this without sounding totally batshit crazy?

While I was sitting at my desk alone in my home office, someone started talking to me. I live alone and my space is relatively small, so I'd know if someone came in.

"You love her, that's your problem," the voice said.

I looked around, saw no one.

"This situation with her work," the voice continued, "it's bullshit. You're scared, you're afraid. And when you're afraid, you make excuses. You look for ways to remove yourself from potentially hurtful experiences. How very childish and immature."

The voice seemed to be coming from the dildo sitting in the corner of the room. Now, I understand how this sounds, but sometimes the unexplainable combined with a poor mental state can make anything plausible. The voice was gravelly, spoke as though it were down in a well or, in this case, inside a box.

"You get close to things, but not too close. No, not you, you wouldn't want to live happily ever after. Or even try. You won't know anything, can't figure anything out unless you at least try. There are some things called vulnerability and sensitivity, the ability to let someone in. These things are all part of growing up into a full adult, something maybe you missed along the way? You're even intimidated by me, an inanimate object. That amuses me greatly."

The dildo laughed. There was darkness in that laugh.

"Wait—" I started but was cut off.

"I ain't finished yet. This inability to let someone in, to actually be intimate in a completely authentic way has crippled you. A hardening of the heart, a closing of valves. I'm not here 'cause of a lack of sexual desire, I'm here because she's at a loss with you, just like all the others. She tried, she really did, but being with you is like being with an empty shell. The more you continue like this, everyday will be one more day that the veins are closing and without knowing it, you'll get an aneurysm, drop dead without even feeling it."

The dildo had a point.

I'll never forget when Hannah called me and wanted to talk. We rarely spoke on the phone, either saw each other in person or wrote or texted each other. After a twenty-minute conversation, she dumped my ass. I got no real explanation, no real anything. I can honestly say it was the first time that I really had a physical reaction to getting dumped. I actually felt it in my chest, like someone had sucker-punched me. And like the weak person I sometimes consider myself, I simply accepted what she said. I mean, where was the fight? If I felt so strongly about this person, where was the desire to get to the real truth of the situation and maybe save what I thought was a good thing? No, I had no moral authority over my gut. I had a bottle of champagne sitting in my pantry for a special occasion, and during those twenty minutes, I popped it open and toasted myself. Cheered to the long road ahead, a road of loneliness and of being alone. Opening the champagne made me think of the dildo and how much of what it had said rang true. Also made me think that I'd never buy a dildo for a girlfriend again. I drank down that goddamn bottle of champagne and went for a long walk. Maybe more of a stumbling.

I'd like to think I'm a good boyfriend. I try to make the other person happy. Honestly, I didn't think it was fair to break things off in this way. I understand that people's feelings change, but still, I'm human and deserve to be dumped in person with an explanation. Maybe after a few weeks of going out, a phone call would suffice, but after a couple of years?

Here's the thing: since I had no real explanation, I could basically make up whatever I wanted, so I just blamed her.

I had to catch a flight to Dallas the next morning for meetings with some people down there. It was one of the biggest opportunities of my professional life — and she knew that. The good part was that I went to Dallas pretty numb and everything went fine on that end.

But is this the entire story? Truthfully?

The hotel in Dallas was attached to a shopping centre. The shopping centre was an oval shape, five levels high, and when I had half a day off, I walked for hours in circles past stores full of advertisements for beautiful people and happy couples made happier by sunglasses, new clothes, and the latest technological devices. When I walk like this, I get deeper and deeper into my psyche. I started at the top floor of the shopping centre and moved downward, level by level, further into the depths. Somewhere around level three, certain things came to the surface that maybe I can discuss here in order to shed some goddamn light. But I'll warn you: these aren't pleasant things to talk about, especially when I'm admitting my own incompetence and inability to partake in a proper relationship.

It seems that I am good for one thing. In a completely unscientific study of past relationships, it looks like I am the guy women go out with right before finding the person who goes on to be their lifelong partner. I'm the guy women make mistakes with and learn from, and then they go off and apply all the lessons to the next person. Not every relationship, but most. I'm playing a numbers game and I'm losing.

I'm thinking of starting a new business called the Intermediary. You can hire me to be in a relationship for a limited amount of time — one to two years seems to be enough — and I'll help you work through certain problems that keep you from finding the perfect mate. Commitment phobic? Not after being with the Intermediary. Intimacy problems? Let me help you explore, but not too much, leaving room to apply all the positive lessons to your next relationship. Call it a "pay it forward" system.

The Intermediary offers no emotional attachments. Not for you, that is. You can break things off with me whenever it suits you. You'll learn many things about yourself. Soon you'll be ready to meet someone special — someone willing to provide not only the superficial elements to a relationship, but also what the Intermediary cannot. You know, those emotional requirements that are supposed to go with the deal. When that time comes, you can cut me loose and I'll be sad, but I'll find someone else in a transitional place to spend time with for a while.

But is this the truth?

I can't really blame the other people from my relationship history. I used to like to, because who wants to take responsibility when a relationship falls apart? In the end, it's my fault. Always has been and, unless I figure my shit out, always will be.

One specific incident always pops into my head. It was Chloe — the girl who followed me on that first walk, the girl with the birthmark on her left temple, the subject of Mary's first file. I didn't listen to what she was really trying to tell me.

It was toward the end of our relationship, and I remember sitting beside her on the old blue couch in my old apartment. She was asking me why I would not fully let her in. I pretended I didn't know what she was talking about, and I tried to remove myself from the situation. She reached out to touch me on the arm, and I stood up and started to walk out of the room. I remember her pointing at me and saying, "This is exactly what I'm talking about." And that was it. We were done shortly after that moment. Because where do you go from there?

This scene has played over in my head after each successive partnership deterioration. I am superficially very good to the people in my life. We do interesting things, and I support them and encourage them. I give everything to them. I give everything except the only thing that is important — letting them in to the real me. By shifting the focus to the other person, there was no focus on me. I thought this was a good thing, that I was treating the other people well, that I was giving them what they wanted. I thought this would make them happy. But I missed the entire point. They were with me because of me. And if I weren't willing to show myself to the other person, what choice did she have but to leave?

I did not intend for this to be a self-pity party, where you regard me as sad and pathetic. At first I tried to formulate this section as a humorous want ad about the Intermediary. But I couldn't — it was stupid and juvenile, and above all else, it sounded like a misdirected untruth, making it look like I was taking the high road and all the blame. I'm not sure if I'll ever figure this relationship stuff out, even after all these years. And it frightens me that I have this impassable gulf between me and the people in my life.

I believe that I have been loved and have loved others. Fallen hard in love. Perhaps the hardest thing I've endured has been when someone — with no fighting or arguing or throwing of things — quietly falls out of love with me. I do not talk of love lightly, and even talking about it in this way makes me feel squeamish and unintentionally lonely. Squeamish because just thinking about the stupid things I did in the name of love makes me embarrassed to admit that it hurts me right in the goddamn chest. Unintentionally lonely because talking about it brings back too many memories, memories where I foolishly thought I was crossing that gulf to another person only to be brought back to reality and to my position as the Intermediary.

Why am I writing about these things? Perhaps I want people to know that the Intermediary is a person as well, and even though people like us are difficult to reach — need a bit more hand holding to draw us out, a little coaxing to get out of our constantly thinking heads — we do get attached the odd time and have potential that is sometimes hard to see. We are not bad people, and under the surface, we have a secure hyper-awareness of self, except for that one blind spot, the fear of revealing too much of ourselves.

This fear is what I really want to talk about. Took me a while to get here, a couple of pages at least, and I wonder if I took so long with all the above crap just to turn people off, hoping that few would get this far, most would skip this part. It's a scary thing to think about being alone. I'm in my mid-thirties, and many people around me are married and have popped out a few kids. My fear isn't about disappointing society by not participating in the acts of lawful partnership and procreation to further the species. My real fear, a fear so deep-seated as to give me actual nightmares, is that everyone just goes away. I enjoy my time on my own, but only if there is the potential to not be alone when I choose it. Just as I have a need to be alone, I also get strong desires to be with other people. Selfish, really, when you think about it — I want people around when it's convenient for me.

I'm not necessarily afraid of being alone. My fear is the feeling I get when it's all done and they're gone. That feeling, even though you throw out any photographs or residue of their existence. Weeks later, you're cleaning, perhaps sweeping the floor. A stray hair floats into view and you stare at it for a few minutes. My fear is that feeling when you get good news and you go to call the first person you would share your good news with, and you have to stop yourself with the reality that she's gone. Or on a nightly basis, you arrive home, hoping that she will be sitting on your stoop, having waited all evening for you with the intention of telling you just how wrong she was. But instead, every night you walk up your vacant stairwell. The only way to avoid these fears is not to attach yourself to anyone.

I'm all over the place here. It feels like I'm having an argument right here on the page. One part of me — arguably a large part — totally agreed with the above statement about avoiding attachment. But another part says this is bullshit, that the risk of losing someone, the threat of those moments of complete loneliness are worth the risk, just like the dildo said. It has to be worth the risk, right? I have to believe that. In a way, I have no choice.

And here we get to the real fear — the thing that, after thinking this through and attempting to organize these thoughts, led to something else popping into my head. *What if I am unlovable?* There you go.

Listen, I'm not sure what all the bumbling around in the dark on this page is all about. I just wish my goddamn heart and my mind would work together a bit better. I'm tired of being an Intermediary, I'm tired of being the middleman, the guy people work out their problems on and then dispose. In order to fully retire from my position as the Intermediary, I need to be more demanding, to reveal myself in a different way. Expose my inner workings and just be who I am instead of pretending. Maybe that's the way out. Maybe it'll take a while. Maybe I'll figure it out in the next relationship before it's too late. Maybe.

Phew.

When I returned from Dallas, I emailed Hannah, by then my ex-girlfriend, and asked to meet. She refused. Desperate, I told her that on the following Sunday, I would go to a coffee shop and wait for two hours. If she decided to show up, we could talk; if not, then I'd be there the following Sunday. If she didn't show up again, I'd drop it. If you can believe it, at almost the same moment I sent that message, Mary called me up and demanded I visit her. She suggested exactly the same time on Sunday that I had told my girlfriend — er ... ex-girlfriend. It seemed that something was telling me to make a choice. I could sit in a coffee shop like an asshole, waiting for a woman who was never going to show up, or I could meet with a person who has a profound connection to my past, someone I continually learn from?

I went with Mary. I didn't know it at the time, but I eventually came to understand that you have to make a choice in these circumstances, and the choices you make can affect you for years. My choices were to harden my heart or to use this experience to really break myself down and start over. I wrote back to Hannah and told her to forget it. I've never spoken to her again.

So, on that Sunday when I might've been sitting pathetically, desperately alone at a coffee shop, I went to the Lighthouse, and Mary and I went walking in the woods behind the place. She brought a file with us, a big one stuffed with many photographs and notes. But she didn't open that file folder. Instead, she wanted me to explain, to relive what it was about Chloe that made her the person I continued to return to in my mind.

I started at the beginning.

Before Hannah, once girlfriend now ex-girlfriend, there was someone else — Chloe, someone from deep in my past but who had been part of almost a third of my life. Chloe had a birthmark on her left temple, a half circle around her eye. Purplish and yellowish, it looked like someone had punched her on the side of the head. She often joked around when people asked her about it, said she got into a lot of fights, but she quickly realized this was not a good answer. The first time I saw her was during my doomed first walk, and because of my failure, I did as I was told and didn't leave my house for the rest of that year. I was able to go only as far as the backyard, and I caught glimpses of her in the spaces between the wooden fence. I didn't dare leave the premises again. I was being watched. The year went by slowly.

When I returned to school, I knew nobody. For a few years, I pretty much walked around the school like a ghost, invisible to most other kids. Walking in the hallway between classes one day, I saw three boys surrounding Chloe at her locker. I knew Chloe, or at least I'd always been aware of her. It wasn't until then, until we were teenagers and becoming interested in things like the opposite sex and parties, that she noticed me. Perhaps I was finally at the right place at the right time. The boys made fun of Chloe's birthmark, saying in loud voices that her father beat her up. Called her derogatory names because of her Chinese background. Pulled on their eyelids to make fun of her eyes.

I'm a lover not a fighter, but I'd had my share of run-ins with these guys. I walked up behind them unsure of what to do. One of the boys made another crack at Chloe's father and she turned, kneed him in the balls. As he fell to his knees, she took a heavy textbook and smacked the second boy in the face, grabbed him, and shoved him into the third. Slammed her locker, pushed past them, and knocked right into me. She paused, looked at me for a moment, grabbed my arm, and pulled me down the hallway with her.

We walked fast out of the school, walked and walked across the field and into the forest area that surrounded the school. Slowing down once we were off the school property, we followed a path that went deep into the forest. The further in we went, the more wild and dense our trail became. Animals could be heard as we walked. Squirrels stopped, regarded us with questions. This time she led and I followed. Tried to match her steps. The distance between us was minimal; the energy between us, palpable. She walked fast. My limping was still evident from the polio — something I could usually hide by taking it slow. No hiding from Chloe.

We came to a clearing and stopped, and Chloe dropped to the ground cross-legged. I was completely oblivious to the fact that we were now skipping school. She cried. I sat across from her. I didn't know what to do. Something strange happened. Maybe it was my new-found interest in the opposite sex, maybe the attention of this beautiful girl. Maybe it was that we were doing something that involved truancy, or maybe it was some unseen, pent-up anger or frustration that I didn't even know was there. Whatever it was, I started crying with her. Tears came down my cheeks, and I couldn't remember the last time this had happened. My tears pulled her out of her own world — she looked at me and laughed. Not at me, but because we were both sitting there crying for very different reasons, but also for many of the same reasons. We laughed through our tears. We didn't say much, didn't have to. She took my hand, and from that moment on, we were seldom apart.

Whenever Chloe's parents were away, she threw huge parties. One weekend I went over, the house was filled with people. I still wasn't the most social guy, even after being in high school with many of these people. I just went to see Chloe. I walked by people drinking out of red plastic cups. Smoking cigarettes. I reached the stairs, and there she stood, as though waiting for me. She cocked her head when she saw me. Hands on hips.

In her room, the only evidence anyone lived there was the books. Her shelves were stacked. Other than that, no pictures on the walls or the bedside table, nothing.

She played down her background. It surfaced later. She couldn't ignore it. The birthmark burned on her temple. Her frame was small, clothes slightly too big. She was unpredictable. One blue eye and one grey eye, dimpled cheeks, small balletic hands that danced around the cup they held. The cup sloshed, threw droplets on her thighs, on the floor. She didn't notice.

We sat down on her bed. Something was different today. She wore a skirt. I talked to her knees, reminded myself to look up every once in a while. I remembered those knees, attached to calves and feet that didn't stop moving. The dancing hands. While she talked, they had minds of their own, and she wasn't afraid to touch in order to make her point. Electricity every time she touched me on the shoulder or the forearm. Her last name was Qi — translated into English it meant *energy flow*.

The party went on without us. Late that night, after everyone else finished dancing or passed out or did whatever kids did back then, we sat in her darkened room, just the two of us, just talking. Chloe tucked hair behind her ear, revealed her birthmark. I imagined that she wanted me to see it, trusted me to see it. There was no exhausting of issues or subject matter. Specifics are fleeting. We were there, we were present, we were aware of what was happening to us, right in front of us, not waiting for our turns to speak, but listening to each other, desperately wanting to hear what the other thought, wanting to tell everything. In some ways, if it were up to me, we never would've left that room.

Neither of us were big drinkers or drug-takers, but that night she pulled out some mushrooms. After a disappointed hour, we felt no different. We took the remaining drugs but still felt nothing. I turned to Chloe at one point, as she attempted to do a headstand on her bed.

She said, "I don't think they're working."

I replied, "I think they are."

Chloe wanted to tell me her story. It had been bottled up for far too long. Perhaps I would listen, not judge her or try to fix her or give answers. Listen. She started and stopped. She made her thinking face: eyes racing around the room, the area between her upper lip and nostrils puffed.

She grabbed a black marker out of her desk and wrote her story all over the blank white walls of her bedroom. Reading over her shoulder, resting my chin beside her neck, I followed her around the room. The tension broke apart with every word she wrote. She would pause, touch fingertips to lips, meet my eyes. She needed to compose herself. The words formed a lattice that contained her life, held it together. When she ran out of room, had filled up all four walls with her life, she pushed the sleeves of my shirt up and wrote on my arms. I rolled my pants up so she could write on my legs. Soon my shirt was off and she finished somewhere around my left shoulder. After that, we lay in bed with our arms around each other and didn't say a word.

"Margaret's right," Mary said. "You're an idiot for screwing this up."

Mary and I walked in silence for a while. When we reached her door, I could say only one thing: "I'm beginning to think the single biggest mistake of my life was ever leaving that room."

Winter

The sun quickly rose in the desert. I slept under a small rock cliff, but the sun found me. Creeping over the rocks, the light caught me faster than I anticipated. Grew hotter in intensity within what seemed only minutes. I watched a scorpion skirt across my eye line. Didn't move in case it was a poisonous one. But another part of me didn't care if it was.

When I closed my eyes and instructed my body to get up, I felt it shift. However, when I opened my eyes, I hadn't moved. Felt like I was in some sort of dream or hallucination. Closed eyes, up and moving and finding my way home. Open eyes, stuck in the same position.

THE WALKING MAN

Eventually, I talked my body into sitting up. Headache, parched lips that parted with much effort. With a groan, stood up.

When your system starts shutting down, the complex operation of running your body becomes streamlined and basic. First, I felt the blood running through my veins being distributed through my entire body. Then the organs, one at a time, feeling what each of them was up to instead of them working collectively to run things smoothly without me noticing. It becomes more complex before it gets simple. Once it simplified, I didn't feel the minutiae of working organs, but the singular desire to do what I needed to do in order to stay alive. The only thing I worried about was being able to stand on my own two feet. Which I did, albeit shakily.

Took off one of my shirts, tied it over my head. The sun rises in the east, right? Or the west? I don't think it mattered at this point. I just took a step right toward the sun, going one direction really wasn't any better than another. Had to start walking, had to start moving.

Cuba

I went to Cuba because of the aforementioned dumping by Hannah. Before I get too far into this, I wanted to say that it was not my intention to write about this situation for the purpose of hurting anyone. However, I will say this: I was also involved in this relationship and feel I have the right to write about my perspective, keeping out details that implicate the other person. I am a damn writer, and we do like to write about pain. And I'll be honest, for some reason this breakup was painful. In the aftermath, I became even more convinced that I was actually in love with this person, and I didn't really have a way to deal with that. Maybe I'd say I was confused about how wrong I'd been at the time. The reason I wanted to write about this stuff was that it all ended very abruptly, and I found myself a little bit in shock — although I shouldn't have been shocked — and I didn't really feel I got to say my piece. Closure was not an option.

For about a month after being dumped, I didn't feel depressed — I felt nothing at all. Numb, I wandered through my everyday world in a stupor, as though I had been prescribed antidepressants, but I took nothing. Flatlined, became a fixture of the background, a ghost people saw right through. I had to do something, couldn't keep going on like this. You see? Isn't it funny how the universe works? As my personal life succumbed to the inevitable, opportunities in my professional life kept popping up. I called up a few friends I had been ignoring, and thankfully they indulged my need to be around people.

And to those out there who might be reading this and thinking I'm publicly attempting to garner sympathy for my perspective, it's sad to me that you think this because it means you know me even less than I thought you did. Maybe you are not my people. This was what happened, and sure, it might not be anyone's business, but hopefully it makes for a good story. I'm in the story business.

Being busy helped, and I had my usual plans to visit my family in Ottawa for Christmas. However, something gnawed away. I didn't go back to work until January 7, and that first week of the new year scared me. Both New Year's and my birthday fell within those seven days, both events which, until a few weeks before Christmas, I had hoped would be spent with my ex-girlfriend, and plans had been made accordingly. All that thrown out the window, I didn't want to be alone that week or I knew I'd drive myself crazy. For days, I tried to find an affordable flight back to Jordan, but alas, it was not meant to be. It was less than a week before Christmas and I was getting desperate. It looked like I would be travelling somewhere alone rather than visiting someone, but I didn't care. I'd rather be somewhere else alone than at home alone.

At the end of my last day of work before the Christmas break, I decided I would walk into a travel agency and not leave until I had booked an all-inclusive trip. Usually I arranged everything myself, but I had run out of time and didn't want to worry about all the little pieces. When I stepped into the travel agency, I ran into my upstairs neighbour. We never talked, and I was slightly intimidated by her — she wore a leather biker jacket most of the time. I didn't know she worked there and we shared an awkward pause until she smiled. She stayed with me for an hour after closing and suffered through my various awkward requests: *yes, I'm going alone; yes, I'm going alone for New Year's; yes, I'm going alone because ... (inaudible); please no kids and minimal couples.* She suggested Cuba because the resorts there don't charge double-occupancy rates.

Done.

My parents are very patient and forgiving people. I spent Christmas moodier than usual. I got back to Toronto as a snowstorm started, but I didn't care how dangerous it might be: that plane to Cuba needed to take off. And it did, barely. It was a small charter plane that rose almost perpendicularly into the air, the hull shaking and making that awful sound metal makes when it's doing something it doesn't want to do.

But we arrived and it was warm. I found the bus to the resort and checked in with no problems. Found the room suitable and beer in the fridge. A balcony. And the ocean.

I woke up late and went for a walk along the beach. The wind was too strong for swimming, and still, people were swimming. The poor lifeguard, the sound of his whistle heard for miles, kept having to kick stupid people out of the water. A local guy approached me asking if I wanted to buy any Cuban cigars. I said no and we talked for a few minutes. He told me about god and then asked if I smoke weed. When I replied that I didn't, he asked if I wanted coke, said I looked like more of a coke kind of guy. Emphatically, I said, "No, thank you," continued walking, and wondered why I looked like a coke kind of guy. Sure, I hadn't been eating properly for the last few weeks — three people had asked if I was okay because it looked like I'd lost weight — but still, skinny doesn't mean I did coke.

Then I imagined, what if I were a guy who did coke? What kind of guy would I be? By the end of my long beach walk, I made a decision. Don't worry — it wasn't the decision to buy coke. I decided that, here in another country, totally on my own, around complete strangers, I could be anyone.

This was largely the point of wanting to go away. To learn how to be alone again. It should have been a warning sign during my relationship: I let myself get too attached to another person. Reluctantly came to realize that attachment was not such a bad thing, but when the relationship is unbalanced — as mine had been — basing the fundamental aspects of said relationship on the unhealthy fear of losing that person means it's probably doomed. Hindsight is a bitch.

Most of the time I'm pretty comfortable spending time on my own. I'm rarely bored except when I'm wired on too much caffeine. My relationship with Hannah had been based on the pretense that we had our time together, but that we were also independent and needed time on our own doing other things. This sounded perfect to me. But what I didn't realize was that when you fall for someone, you want to be around them. Christ, that's such an obvious statement, but apparently not to me. Maybe I should have been better at explaining this to her — that I wanted to be around her more — but I felt things would naturally evolve. They didn't. And as my desire to spend time with her increased, she realized that she wanted to spend less time with me. Again, a warning sign. I thought this was just a transitional phase. I was wrong. And I found myself alone, but I shouldn't have been so surprised.

I'm good at being alone, and I think what shocked me was my desire to be with someone. Attachment was never my forte, so this was unchartered territory for me. When that attachment severed, like I should've known it would, well, let's just say I wasn't very pleasant to be around. Just ask my parents about Christmas.

And so, once again, I needed to develop that sense of security in my aloneness. And I hoped I could hold on to that sense of attachment because, goddamn it, sometimes it did feel good to have a partner in crime. I just needed to find the person who wanted to be attached to me so we could attach to each other. I'm so naive at times (see, there's that person on my shoulder telling me it ain't going to happen already).

My plan was to spend my days getting a tan while reading, getting in shape, and writing, and my nights meeting some people. With every person I'd meet, I'd introduce myself as someone different, each persona here for different reasons.

The first night I went to the bar. A man approached two women and asked if he could sit down. It was that easy? The problem was that I'm not that kind of guy. I'm quiet, shy even, and although I'll talk a wild blue streak to the point of your wanting me to shut up, it's hard for me to get started. I walked over to the pool bar. A drunk man passed me, stumbling around the perimeter of the pool and falling down across a lounge chair. His head hit the ground and his arms sprawled out, spread-eagle like. The pool might not be such a good place to serve alcohol.

I ordered a beer and sat across from two leathery-skinned old people. From their accents, I determined they were German, and when polite conversation came around to who I am and where I'm from, I told them I was there from Dallas, Texas. They inquired about my lack of accent and I explained that I was originally from Canada, but had just been transferred. Since you can't fly from the United States to Cuba, I'd hopped on a plane through Mexico. You see, on that first night, I was a marketing executive, specializing in sport-event promotions. I worked for the Toronto Maple Leafs, but hockey was having its labour problems, and when an opportunity popped up to develop and market hockey in the state of Texas, I'd jumped on it. I explained that hockey was very popular in Texas when the Dallas Stars were winning, but programs had suffered since they turned into just another losing southern expansion team. However, that brief stint had generated a hockey infrastructure, and the people behind these institutions wanted to continue developing Texas into a robust, vibrant, and long-lasting hockey community.

This was all not so far from the truth. I did recently visit Dallas for a business trip. Well, okay, that's about the only truthful element. I don't live there, and I've never worked for the Maple Leafs, but I knew someone who did. We talked a bit more about hockey, something I know very little about, but I guess the average Canadian digests a certain amount of information about the sport, like it or not. The old couple were there from Munich, both retired teachers enjoying their twilight years. We had a pleasant evening and said goodnight having enjoyed each other's company.

New Year's Eve. Never been much of a fan of New Year's Eve. A number of years ago, my roommate and I had a party that everyone came to. It went all night. Before then and since then, New Year's Eve has usually been somewhat of a bust. This time, I'd been dumped a few weeks before, but I've actually been dumped on New Year's itself. Can't say which is worse.

I walked into town — about two hours — and people honked and shouted and waved at me. I was looking for a good time at one of the many clubs. When I arrived, no one was around. I ended up having a beer alone in a Beatles-themed bar watching Eric Clapton on a big screen. Not as much fun as it sounds. Caught a convertible taxi, paid him way too much to take me home. Things were jumping back there. I sidled up to the bar and found myself talking to a group of women from Calgary.

This night I was a writer on assignment. Commissioned by a Canadian travel magazine called *Destination*, I was to write a review about resorts in Cuba. But really, I planned on using this week to edit and start rewriting my novel. Again, not so far from the truth. One of the women, trying to be cool, had heard of the fake magazine, which amused me to no end. Midnight came and all the couples kissed. I felt nothing.

Saw another guy around alone at the pool and at the restaurant. An older guy, with whom I had purposely avoided eye contact, so as not to see something recognizable, or have to talk to him and hear about the similarities between us.

The beach went on forever. Kids made crappy sandcastles; people collected shells. The sound of the waves was hypnotic. I listened, but the waves provided no answers. Back at the room, I turned on the television for the first time. Strangely, found myself watching a Canadian network for a while. Then Wolf Blitzer reported on CNN about falling off the fiscal cliff. See? Politics can still be poetic. They say you shouldn't fall asleep with the television on. I suppose they're either right or wrong depending on how you interpret things. Rarely remember my dreams, but I remembered the one from this night.

My father was escorting me to see the president. We waited in a back alley in front of a back door. My dad warned me that Barack was a hugger. I had gained the insight that my parents had been working as secret agents all these years. Nobody told me, I just knew. A procession of people appeared coming down the alley. Circus freaks, jugglers, animals, little people. Barack's kids came first — Sasha and Malia — and he appeared with his arm around Michelle. He took my hand, leaned in for a half hug. He was smiling that smile. We went inside. I don't remember what the room looked like.

"You're nervous," Barack said. "Don't be. Here's the situation. At the Olympics in Sochi, Putin has challenged me to a skating race. He likes to show off his physicality, you know, with the shirt off and flying with the birds and all that. I want to kick his ass. Thing is, I can't skate. I want you to teach me. Will you do it? You have until all your teeth fall out to make a decision."

My teeth started falling out one by one.

And that's it, that was the dream. I didn't know what it meant, but dammit, I dream so rarely that I tend to place a lot of stock in them. It occurred to me that I had to choose something. Had to make some decisions.

I went for another longer walk along the beach. Still no answers. Maybe I'll swim in the ocean, but not today. I'm always a bit hesitant to swim in the ocean. Sharks. Sure, this is an irrational fear, but look at it this way: although the chances of a shark attack are slim, it's still within the realm of possibility. I had just watched *Cast Away* in Spanish, and the idea of being shipwrecked in the middle of the ocean scared the shit out of me even more than the goddamn sharks. Walking on the beach, I did come up with the new beginning for my novel rewrite. Maybe those waves did have something to say.

I took the night off from my identity crisis. Sitting bare-chested on my balcony, sipping a cappuccino, writing, listening to a salsa band's music pouring out of the bar below. I felt some kind of change occurring, don't ask me to put my finger on it or give it a name. My reasons for being there differed from those of the couples, the groups of Germans, the single people. Don't ask me to describe those reasons either.

Withdrawal. There was no internet at the resort, except for a computer in the lobby with a slower connection than my 1990s computer. I monitored emails every few days but didn't send any. No Twitter. No status updates. I had brought my iPad to write on but forgot a plug adaptor. Stupid. And no one knew what I was talking about when I asked for one. No caffeine, or much less caffeine. I was trying to eat healthy, but there was a serious lack of fruit, no shortage of meat. After my iPad battery went dead on the fourth day, I was left to writing in my notebook and reading under the sun. And after another day, I was okay.

Took a bus to Havana. The resorts were definitely segregated from the real city. Kids tapped my arm in the street, pointing at their bare feet, holding out empty hands. That day my name was Ernie, short for Ernest. Apparently, my parents were obsessed with Ernest Hemingway, who lived in Cuba for a time. Found the hotel he stayed at — the Ambos Mundos — and ordered a mojito at the bar.

The woman next to me asked if I was Canadian. Found myself introduced to Kim and Glen the Giant next to her, a meathead, larger than the Incredible Hulk. Sure, meathead is a derogatory name for those ridiculously large guys pumping iron at the gym. And yes, I'm biased against them. Glen owned a tattoo parlour (of course he did!) and showed off angel wings on one arm (curious) and barbed wire around the other (cliché). A knife ran down one leg, a snake down the other. More hid under his clothes. Kim was a social worker, and I wondered how she'd hooked up with the meathead. Told them I was there to drink where Hemingway drank, I'd already been to the cat house in Florida, and I was saving for a trip to Spain for some bullfights.

Glen had heard of Hemingway: "The book about some old guy fishing, right?" He proved to be an attentive listener and posed many questions. I told them about Hemingway's Fourth Dimension, that there existed an abstract and intangible potential in literature found between the words. Glen grasped something I didn't. Hemingway was on to something with that Fourth Dimension.

On one wall of the bar hung photographs, a tribute to Hemingway. I took Glen through the photographs — one where he was with Castro, another with his wife at the time, don't remember her name. And there he was — the old man that Hemingway fished with. I tend to draw meaning sometimes where there is none. But that was definitely the old man from the book, and there was something about his eyes. Kim, Glen, and I polished off a few more mojitos and clinked glasses to Ernest, to me, to them, to the old man. Maybe I'm wrong about meatheads.

As an early birthday present to myself, I sat outside that night drinking seven-year-old rum and quietly smoking the same kind of cigar as Castro.

Okay, so at dinner I finally talked to the other guy here alone. "You look like a man who has answers." He smiled, introduced himself as Günter — another German. Lots of Germans around here. He asked my name — The Texan? The writer? Ernest? I told him my real name. He said exactly the words I needed to hear: "Let's walk." I have paraphrased his points.

"Have you been off the resort, yes? You notice people always smile at you, especially if they are selling you something. Yes, poor, poor people here, but poor with smiles on their faces. Not all, but many. More than the people where you and I are from, yes? You walk down the street, and where is the smiling? Where is the happiness? So much worry, so many things, everyone needs the latest new things. How can we be happy when there is such worry? Everyone has many worries, but are we worrying about the right things? What are the right things to worry about?"

We got more drinks from the pool bar, moved out to the beach. The beach was different in the darkness. We talked late into the night.

Günter continued: "But what can you do? I mean in general. Yes, Cubans seem to smile a lot, laugh a lot, but theirs is a very difficult life. This is a Communist country, people are very poor, but there is money being made somewhere. But what is right? There are free democratic societies, but still, these contain strict moral rules. Right? Capitalism is good for some, not so good for others. The economic unification of Europe, not so good either. We are running out of options, yes? There are dictatorships that kill their own people. There are monarchies — what relevance does the Queen of England represent? It is the people who suffer. We all suffer in some way. Some more than others. Broken. The kings and queens don't make decisions for the people. We must make our own happiness. Make our own rules. We must be individuals from society, find what makes us happy, and allow it to invade our hearts. Only then can we see there is no right or no wrong. Look at things from a different view."

In the end, the disguises of those few days still didn't conceal the pain. I understand that it's pathetic to keep going on and on about this. The thing I realized was that this wasn't really about Hannah. What I couldn't get by was *why*. In my mind, there were myriad possibilities, and I think she dumped me because of things she couldn't control. This was what I believed, or what I chose to believe. In a way, I admired her for leaving, for having the courage to stop the pretending, or at least for making a decision. I still felt sad that I would never be able to speak to this person again, so that's why I'm writing this. A message in a bottle. Yes, I'm writing this for me, to gain some closure, but really for one reader, most likely someone who will never see it.

Last day. Screw the sharks. Let's do the ocean.

The beach had a yellow flag waving, meaning caution. There were high winds making big waves. Fine with me. Let's throw the flag to the wind.

Marched into the water unsure — sharks, remember? — and the first wave hit my knees. I went further. Waves slammed into my chest and I liked the pain. I went further, the water up to my waist. I jumped over the next wave and turned so it slammed into my side — is that the best you can do? I went further toward where I saw the biggest waves crashing. They started coming one after the other, and I jumped through them, over them, darted from side to side trying to find the biggest ones until finally two waves crashed one after the other. The first one I jumped over, but the second hit like a fist, pulled me with it. Under the surface, my mouth filled with water, the wind was knocked out of me. I was under for good, I was sure. I couldn't breathe, couldn't find the surface. Just as I found the surface, another wave crashed down and I was back under, taking in more water. I opened my eyes, goddamn salt water. Waited for the shark, waiting, WAITING, goddammit, like I always waited and never acted. I burst through the surface, gasping for air. I let a wave bring me along, floated back to the beach, crawled, and lay down on the sand, the tide nipping my feet, tried to stuff air into my lungs.

Don't try to beat nature. Nature always wins.

I sat up, scanned the water for where the biggest waves were crashing, leapt to my feet, sprinted to the water, moved like a shark, moved with the water instead of against it, rolled over small waves, waiting for the big one. It came, and I punched through it with my fist — is that all you got? Dived through another one, jumped through, and I saw it approaching — a double wave. I planted my feet in the sand, jumped the first wave, smashed through it. The second one was bigger. I slammed through it with my shoulder, but I felt no pain, as though the water were passing through me. I let the next wave carry me in a bit then I stood, allowing the waves to crash into me, but I didn't move. I only moved when the waves told me to and then — really, I'm not making this up; there are things I will not lie about — the wind died down, the waves stopped crashing, settled, gracefully touched the palms of my outstretched hands. I loosened my planted feet, and I let the water flow around me, and I let go I let go I let go...

I waited outside the hotel for the bus to the airport, where a cab driver also waited for some customers. He sat down next to me. He was supposed to pick up a family at 7:00 p.m. It was already 7:30. I told him my bus was also supposed to have arrived at 7:00 p.m. Right after he pulled away in an empty taxi, a family of four came looking for him. Then, no joke, the band in the bar started playing "Happy Birthday." It would be my birthday in a few hours, when I was in the air. Right on cue. I pretended it was for me.

Sure, I felt a little weird at times on this trip, and I did what I do best, placing thoughts in the minds of others. For example, that person must be thinking, "Look at that sad and lonely and pathetic guy sitting alone. Who comes to a resort alone?" That might've been the case, but also, and this is a new and strange concept for me, that person might not be thinking about me at all. The whole week I had actually felt my confidence growing, but as usual, something happened to keep me grounded, to remind me just how alone I was and that, sometimes, I should just disappear.

I got on the bus taking us from the hotel to the airport. I stepped up into a sea of couples, most of them ignoring me as I lugged my baggage to the only seat in the back. An important distinction should be made: this seat was on top of the back wheels, so it sat higher than the rest of the seats. Let's call this the Single Seat, overlooking the couples. We stopped at the last hotel and one more couple got on the bus. They were struggling, looking for two seats together because it's against protocol for couples to split up in situations such as this. The tour guide, who had no idea of the impact of his words, walked down the aisle, pointed at me, and said, "You sir, you are alone?" Now, he didn't really ask me directly, but made a loud sort of pronouncement that sounded to me more like, "You sir, YOU are ALONE!" At that moment, every couple on the bus, as though they had melded into one giant *über* couple, turned toward me with one, giant *über* furrowing in their collective brow, as the tour guide continued, "You are by yourself?"

I could barely speak, but uttered a weak, "Yes."

One half of the couple, the woman, said it was okay, she'd take the seat next to mine. So we sat there, her ignoring me, her husband maybe glad he had a break from his wife, me staring into the dark black sky feeling bad and inadequate that I couldn't find someone, feeling that maybe there was a defect in my operating system, that I couldn't seem to hold things together, reveal enough of myself to another person for them to love me enough. What was it I was missing? Was there something I could fix? Something I could do?

Examinations

Cuba worked — for a time. Winter can be difficult on walkers. But what is all this talk of walking? It's how I figure my shit out. The sorting out of accounts, of trying to figure out who the hell I am. 'Cause no matter how well things go, there's down time.

Stepping into a store a few weeks after returning from Cuba, I was feeling crappy already, and the automatic doors didn't open when I approached. Felt like Bart Simpson in the episode when he sold his soul. Felt my powers of invisibility growing stronger again. Ever since my return from Cuba, I had been feeling better. Something did get out of my system. But old habits are like Bruce Willis. Lately I'd been examining my moods with a little bit more self-awareness. I used to think I was just moody, but was beginning to think it was something more.

Mary was right there with me, challenging me, as the cold weather and snow and ice slowed us down. Mary was persistent, demanding that we had much to talk about. On every walk, she brought files with her, files from deep in the cabinet. She knew things I'd never want to admit and things that I hadn't thought about in a while. Everything was there, a collection of my greatest fears and losses and secrets.

"Wow, you're really a constant disappointment to yourself and those around you," Mary said.

"Yeah, thanks," I replied. "You really know how to break things gently to a guy."

"It's not me," she said. "It's the files. Your grandmother kept track of everything. But not just what you were doing, what was going on in your head."

"'Cause she knew that," I said.

"She guessed," Mary said. "But let me ask you this: has she been wrong yet?"

I paused, because what do you say to that?

"Right," Mary said. "Let me continue. You've squandered any talent or potential that you might've had. You've managed to run away from opportunities. It will really be impossible for you to sustain any type of meaningful relationship. And so on."

True, but I wasn't going to let Mary know that. These thoughts I've had aren't reflecting any sense of logic, and I know that and don't worry.

However, if a thought is conceptual, that is, if it appears in our brain due to some strange combination of external forces, our past and present experiences, and whatever else is firing in there, these are a different kind of thought. They just exist, waiting to be taken out of the cabinet. But they are sometimes more real than you can imagine. Truth is elusive, and even though these thoughts are not based necessarily in any truth, there is no questioning them. They just are.

For a span of time, after arriving home from Cuba, I accessed a part of me that I liked. Operating on some other plane, I put aside my polite, always-wanting-to-please self. That annoying person who has no feelings of his own, very little in the way of a belief system, he's a man with no soul, such that even automatic doors in grocery stores do not register enough warmth to open for him. Invisible. I decided to kill this person off. I walked around with the ability to feel and was filled with joy that I could do this.

But as in any good soap opera, the dead side of me returned and I crashed, and here we are back at the beginning. I can't go to Cuba every few months.

And I'm walking around here yelling at Mary, "Well, how do you get back there? How do you change? What the hell do I have to say?" The truth is, I'm tired of fighting this whole thing, and maybe there's value in just allowing myself to feel shitty. Who cares? I'm driving myself mad fighting for the opposite — when I'm down and out, I think I should go the other way, and when I'm up and doing well, the thought *why should I have the privilege of these feelings?* is gnawing away.

Sometimes I just have to let go and realize that if I hold on to this stuff, it won't go away, but will just keep growing and gnawing and building up. It's okay to feel scared, but really — and I know this is lame — we've got our time here and that's it. So I'm going to stop being invisible. At times it seems very easy, and at other times, not so much.

"How very conveniently abstract and vague," Mary said.

"It's just the way it has to be now," I replied.

Worked through things, telling myself the fact that I was talking about this was a good thing. Better than some of the other things I tell myself.

I wanted to get inside this feeling while it was happening. And it was happening. Even in the cold, it felt good to be out there with Mary, to be walking, to need to walk because I was feeling crappy. I'd been inside all day working, hadn't talked to anyone, and as the day progressed, a shadow came over my mind. Yeah, that's the only way to describe it. Happened every once in a while, and I tried to tell myself that I was just stressed, that I had a lot on my mind. For some reason, when I get distracted with the necessities of life — work, bills, money — I have feelings of going nowhere.

Sitting at home and feeling down, feeling blue — oh, goddammit, will I just admit that I was feeling depressed. Finally admit that maybe I have a condition, that I have the tendency to slip into bouts of depression. I used to tell myself that these bouts were for no good reason, feel guilty knowing that others had it much worse, all of which only compounded my feelings of feeling shitty.

In the past, I've tried to write about this, mostly wrote around it without ever truly discussing it head-on. But I've always tried to do it after the fact, and this time I was in it. I could feel it. I was afraid, but I wanted to explore it. Is it weak to say these things? I believe that most people, once they remove daily life distractions, once they get a goddamn chance to just sit and think and let their minds wander, most people have dark thoughts. It's normal. Is that what all these distractions, like television, and worrying about getting more shit we don't need, and status, and other things, keep us from thinking? Look at me, I'm veering away already. I didn't mean to make some general proclamation about the times we live in.

This is about me.

The first place I go is thinking that I'm a failure. The work I'm doing is not good enough. Now, let's look at this. If I were to learn from the past, I'd realize I am pretty good at the work I do. Many more times than not, the feedback from my clients is overwhelmingly positive. At times, I feel shy and embarrassed over the praise they heap on me. So why in the hell, with every job, do I feel like it's only going to end in disaster? Where is the insecurity coming from here? Or, perhaps I should ask, why is there insecurity at all? My excuse is that if I expect doom but then everything goes well, then it was good I expected the worst. But whatever I think the worst might be usually has very little reality attached to it.

So, is this insecurity supposed to compensate for my actual abilities? Maybe I'm not as good as I think, or maybe the results of my work have not been as successful as my clients tell me. Jesus, even as I write this, it feels like a fight. But I have to tell you something: when you slip into feeling bad, your awareness goes out the window. You see, after you — dammit, just say I — after *I* come out of it, I always think that the negative and depressing thoughts I had were ridiculous and that next time they won't affect me so much. But when I'm in it, I just feel the thoughts, and they are real. I can't see outside of them enough to have any awareness of them. Does that make any sense?

I'm a good worker, and I get everything done on time and usually under budget. So what am I afraid of? I'm afraid of people finding out I'm a fraud. Whoa, I just wrote that without even thinking about it. A fraud? Why would I consider myself a fraud? Maybe it's because I've given up on everything I've wanted to do, and by placing other things in front of my desires, I have an excuse when those desires don't happen. I didn't even give myself the opportunity to show how much of a fraud I am. I'm talking about everything I've pursued creatively. My film work? I was just getting somewhere when I stopped myself dead in my tracks. Sure, I've done a lot of things I wanted to do, but when it came time to try moving to the next level, I froze. I couldn't admit that I was maybe just a little scared. Do I have a disposition where I'm afraid to be happy, or even try to be happy? There's another sentence I didn't plan on. What in the hell does that even mean? *Afraid to be happy?* Have I just grown comfortable being frustrated, feeling like I haven't reached my potential, living in the land of stasis?

This is another theme when I get like this: stasis. I feel like there's no room to manoeuvre; the only thing left to do is move. Walk. I close my eyes as I walk to combat the stasis, and I think about the physical feelings. I actually feel like there is a weight over my eyebrows. Not a headache — I rarely get headaches — but a weight. I only feel it when I furrow my brow and try to unknot it. My shoulders are up over my ears, and when I think about them, they drop, and tension releases from my neck at the base of my skull. I believe the mental and the physical are intimately connected, and when I get like this, everything tightens up, like my body is holding its breath, pausing, waiting, and hoping this will pass. It's a form of protection. At the same time, I am emotionally ridiculous. I could watch the wrong kind of movie trailer, and it would make my eyes well up. I could read about someone who has taken the kind of risks I've failed to take, and see that the risks paid off for them, and I'll start thinking about an alternative universe where I also took those risks. I could hear music, like I'm hearing right now in the background of my mind, a piece by my friend, a song full of his violin quietly moving across strings, plucking at them, and it will sound to me like the violin is crying, the strings like a human voice. And I'll keep walking, feeling like an idiot because this song makes me think of someone I knew too long ago, but whom I think about far too often, especially at moments like this.

Veering again. Keeping within the creative work and being a fraud: writing. There's the fact that I don't call myself a writer because I don't believe I am one. I don't know what a writer is. A common description would be "someone who gets paid to write." A professional. Well, I've gotten paid to write, so why don't I consider myself a writer? Maybe it's because I haven't really written something that I consider good, something that turned out the way I wanted or that reached the audience I wanted it to. Something so intertwined with my life, so risky that it penetrated my psyche and blew off my appendages. But looking at the flip side—

"Have you done everything within your power to get to where you want to go?" Mary asked.

I didn't answer.

"Well?" She poked at me.

"Hold on," I said. "I'm thinking about this last question."
"Since there was a pause," she said, "the answer must be no."
Hmmm.
Excuse me, my mind has gone empty.

No, I haven't done everything within my power to get where I want to be. Why not? I'm afraid. Afraid of what? Being a fraud. But I already call myself that. You know, a funny thing just occurred to me: a lot of times I refer to these things — fraud, fear, failure — in very general ways, never really distilling them down to details or essence. Come on, what are the details? What are the specific things that I am afraid of? But as I'm writing this, I don't really know. Sure, there are logistical things to worry about. But as far as actual concrete things keeping me from moving forward, well, it all seems rather ridiculous and silly, doesn't it?

And when I reach a place where I'm building toward a project, something that I believe people will want to consume, when I'm utilizing all my skills and could potentially be creating something meaningful, I lose my fucking mind. And then when I get down, when I feel shitty, those ideas go away, or I talk myself through all the ways they're not possible. Every opportunity that might bring me to the next goddamn level, before it even gets started, I'm the one saying it's not going to work.

So I'm walking and wondering about my ability to self-sabotage. Why am I not going all the way with my work? I am and I'm not. Not going all the way. I think, why am I not doing this now, tomorrow, and the next day? I mean, what's stopping me? And when I walk with this question, the answer is nothing.

And obviously, when down in the depths, I start thinking of my inability to maintain a relationship. But I had this thought today — it was kind of a sad thought, but it was a true thought — I've never woken up beside someone on a regular basis. This is something I've always wanted. Sure, I've woken up next to people and felt good, but these times were fleeting as I never lived with anyone. And I thought about all the people who are married and who maybe don't enjoy waking up next to that same person everyday. What's worse: waking up alone or waking up next to someone you don't love anymore? And see what I did? I'm not even considering that I could find someone I would want to wake up next to. My mind just jumps to the thought that at some point I would be unhappy with that person. How about believing that I could find that person who I would wake up next to, someone who would make me feel like a better person just by looking at her sleeping face? I wonder if this could be possible for me. I wonder. And just the fact that I'm wondering is quite a change, let me tell you. Because when I think about this question, the answer is yes, it has to be yes.

But what am I really trying to get at here? I need to stop whining. I can't get out of this. I'm not afraid to admit there are competing voices in my head. And now, one of these voices, through some form of advanced meat puppetry, has leapt out of my head in the form of a one-armed woman with whom I am spending an exorbitant amount of time. Someone who is calling me out on my shit. One of my writing teachers once said that you have to decipher between the voice of doubt and the voice of the devil. I don't think she meant the devil in any theological sense, just the manifestation of evil a person can conjure in his own head. There is a voice of doubt that questions my actions, a voice I trust and that I think is healthy. But there is also the voice of Mary, a voice that never shuts the hell up, her vocal range fluctuating, always with more files to show me, always wanting to dig through the cabinet. When Mary takes over, she presents a version of me that is weak, useless, and unattractive, and I am able to talk myself out of almost anything. Mary's voice is charming, confident, and convincing. When I fall into this state of mind — my blue mind — this voice, whether inside or outside, becomes the truth. No matter how ridiculous. I can temper that voice, but it is still there, quiet as it waits for a moment when my world turns blue. It says, *Why did you call that person? You will not get that job. You will fail. You will always be alone, lost, angry. There is no way out of this for you.* I can go through a day and believe that everything is conspiring to make me feel worse. From getting splashed by a car speeding through a puddle, to a bad day at work, to getting dumped. When I'm feeling down and I'm in this state, every tiny detail holds meaning, pointing to the fact — the truth — that I am useless. On the flip side, the exact same things could happen on a day when I'm feeling okay, and I won't have even one thought like this. So I understand that the events happening around me are completely interpreted by my state of mind. It should be simple, right? If it's all simply a state of mind, then a state of mind I can change. Right? Um ... right ...?

You see, you have to understand — you, and Mary, and the rest of you, I desperately want you to understand — that although this may be a state of mind, a state I've conjured in my own mind, it's very real to me. When things become too much, it's like I separate or disassociate from myself. Not exactly like watching myself, but similar. And there's no way to talk myself out of it. What I am learning more and more is that it's just a feeling and it will pass. But every time I get into this mood, it feels like it will never lift. I just have to remind myself that the past repeats itself, and I will come out of it.

The weight above my brow is still there but lighter. And the music. I wish you were here in my head as I walk, and as I hear my friend and his violin between my ears, because this one song came on and halfway through he breaks into "Ode to Joy" — he covered Ode to fucking Joy, and it's amazing, and I can feel it and I can feel my body releasing the tension, and I'm kind of dancing while walking. And I'm trying to hide my stupid tears from Mary and other passersby, trying to wipe them off until I decide that it's okay, decide that sometimes it's just a good idea to feel what you're goddamn feeling, knowing that you'll get through it and that there's some semblance of peace on the other end. A quietness that is not a tightness of the heart, but a silence of the mind.

But it returns. You break through only to have those feelings return.

I was lying awake a day after I left Mary, and I couldn't sleep. Thought maybe I was lapsing into some form of lucid dreaming — the only way I can explain it, the only way I can justify the feeling. I've never gone into lucid dreaming, but how do you really know if you're doing it? Anyway, I'm avoiding the issue. It was a Sunday, and I ended up sleeping the entire day, then found myself unable to get to sleep at night. And I knew I had to get up early in the morning and I hate getting up early in the morning. I was sleeping on my mini-couch because if I make myself uncomfortable enough, I won't go too far into REM mode, and I would still be able to wake up to the five alarms I've set. Five alarms and I can still sleep through them.

But I'm avoiding the issue.

The walk must have stirred some things up. We've been talking about rejection and being a fraud, and where to go from here, and what to do, and how to change. I'm talking about a big blob of rejection and how, taken individually, rejection is not so bad, but thinking about all those rejections at once, well, that just sucks. I was lying there, uncomfortably, unable to sleep, maybe lucid dreaming, with all these things — rejection, fraud, change — swirling around in my head, and I started to notice this physical feeling running from my neck to my pelvis. I felt permanent, immovable. What I could only describe as a mini version of the monoliths from the Stanley Kubrick movie *2001: A Space Odyssey*. Void of space but full of density.

Okay, so I was probably dreaming, but the feeling was very real. It didn't feel like the monolith was on top of my torso, pressing down; it felt like it was under my skin, applying pressure both internally and outwardly at the same time. I didn't feel depressed — I know that feeling — but it was like those damn monoliths in the movie, just standing there with no features, begging me to apply my pathetic attempts at interpretation.

Bullshit. I'm telling you, I really know how to talk myself into believing that what I'm feeling is actually a step forward, that the changes I feel I've been making continue no matter what. I can convince myself that there is always forward motion, but I also know how to make things safe, mediocre — my attempt to be insightful in an incredible and annoyingly cute way. I'm trying not to do that anymore. Listen to me: I wonder what all this means. Fuck off. Here's the thing — the monolith thing actually happened. Well, not really exactly, but the physical sensations and thoughts did. Where I veered off course here was in wondering what it all meant. I knew exactly what the monolith was: fear.

You see, I'm trying to change the way I'm thinking. Challenging. It was quite a revelation when I realized that the majority of my anxieties were conjured in my head and that, in a way, I have a choice in how I think about things. Doesn't sound so revelatory, but whatever. It was to me. The fear was about diving headfirst into new and weird territory. I feel I've been hiding, that really the person I am internally bears no resemblance to the person I present to the world. I spend a lot of time apologizing for nothing, hiding what I'm really thinking, not saying what I want to say. Tricky because when I start telling people what I think, they want to keep me in the same box I've been tying myself up in for my entire life. How do I bring together these two parts?

This thought scares me because it's more abstract, and it's crossed my mind that maybe it's one more thing I am conjuring. But that's bullshit too. Ask me what the fear is, and I'm not sure I could tell you. There is definitely some form of blockage going on that I can't see through. Makes no sense, none, when you actually think about it, so I tried to think about it.

When I was lying there, the monolith pressing inwards and outwards, I thought about how alone I was, the fact that this is it. I'm preparing myself for a life of panic in the middle of the night with no one to panic to. And anyway, who would want to be that for me or anyone else? This is a major block that I've always had in my head, at least somewhat, but that has become more prominent lately. When I actually think about it, I can't see myself with another person. I used to think I knew what kind of relationship I wanted, but that has sort of gone out the window.

Yeah, sure, the first step is awareness, and that may be true, but then what do you do? There's the idea that if you imagine what you want, it will manifest itself, that the universe is listening. Sure, there might be something to this, and things happen everyday that I wouldn't even think of trying to explain logically. But at the same time, especially with that damn monolith, I can't help but feel that this is it: I'm completely alone. There is no system, no pattern. The world is absurd and random, and how do you impart change to absurdity and randomness?

And then I think, *Oh, shut the hell up. Just relax.* So what if there's a monolith pressing down from inside and pushing out. It's probably just a figment of my imagination.

On the next walk with Mary, she had a new file with freshly printed sheets of paper.

"You know this internet thing?" she asked.

"Yes, I'm familiar with it," I replied.

"All kinds of stuff on there. I found some questionnaires about something you should really take a look at."

I'd always assumed I was just very organized and neat. My house is generally clean, and I actually dust with a duster every week. My two bookshelves are organized alphabetically according to the author's last name. Seemed like common sense to me, until I was at a friend's place and the books were in random order. The friend said she placed them wherever there was room. Wherever there was room? My god. I fought the urge to rearrange them.

Toiletries are set up along the side of the sink in order of height, tallest closest to the mirror. Standing tube toothpaste, deodorant, cologne. My toothbrush and razor lay side by side, the longer instrument closer to the wall.

Bed is made everyday and adjusted so it matches with the three pictures hanging above the headboard area. My only secret is that I stuff things in places where I can't see them. Closets can be messy, and there is an inordinate number of items bulging out from under the bed. Sure, I have guilt and shame about this, but I can't see these things on a daily basis, so "out of sight, out of mind."

My home office is the most organized room in the house. A cabinet separates my business paperwork into various categories: expenses, bills, research, current projects, production, writing, and miscellaneous. The miscellaneous drawer is the messiest. It's a catch-all, where my wild side comes out. A guy's gotta live a little. The current book I'm reading is placed, along with my Moleskine notebook, on top of the cabinet whenever I return home. These two items generally travel everywhere with me. A corkboard, containing plans for current projects and detailed breakdowns for each plan, hangs above my desk. This is updated on a weekly or biweekly basis. The computer area is clean with no extraneous trinkets or notes. Wires and plugs are messier than I'd like, but you can't win every battle. All notes are made on a pad of paper placed to the right of the computer mouse.

This pad is also used for lists. I love making lists. What's even better than making lists? Crossing things off lists. A weekly list of to-dos usually contains a few easy crossing-outs and gets progressively more difficult. Multi-year lists, yearly lists, monthly lists, weekly lists, and sometimes daily lists. Sometimes more than one daily list. These are just grocery-list type lists. A comprehensive and detailed breakdown of what is required for a particular situation.

78

"Obsessive-compulsive disorder," Mary said.

"This doesn't apply to me," I said.

"You're so sure? Happen to have a test right here."

Mary asked me a series of 20 questions, and I answered them as honestly as possible. The thing is, these were all yes-or-no questions, and because I'm obsessed with explaining myself, I needed to justify my answers.

Instructions: This is a screening measure to help you determine whether you might have an obsessive-compulsive disorder that needs professional attention. This screening measure is not designed to make a diagnosis of such a disorder or to take the place of a professional diagnosis or consultation.

Part One: Have you been bothered by unpleasant thoughts or images that repeatedly enter your mind, such as ...

1. Concerns with contamination (dirt, germs, chemicals, radiation) or acquiring a serious illness such as AIDS?

No. I felt confident right outta the gate because I'm not too concerned about this kind of thing. I like to be clean, but only up to a point.

2. Overly concerned with keeping objects (clothing, groceries, tools) in perfect order or arranged exactly?

Yes. As explained above, I see no problem with having your surrounding area in neat working order. Some people claim to have "organized chaos" and navigate their ways through clutter. I don't know how they do it — scares the crap outta me.

3. Images of death or other horrible events?

Yes. See, this is tricky. I rarely think about death except in the abstract. But horrible events? Sure. From my journal: "My aptitude for failure has reached such a height that the only outcome in all this is that I'll lose my job, my house, my car. Everyone will truly stop talking to me, truly and finally give up on me, and I will inevitably end up on the street where I will die a lonely death under an overpass, sighing a last breath, saying a last word to no one." Well, I guess I just caught myself lying when I said I rarely think about death except in the abstract. This seems pretty concrete.

4.   *Personally unacceptable religious or sexual thoughts?*

No. This one was easy. I never really bought in to the whole religious-sexual-repression thing. Not sure why, it just didn't seem like a good idea.

5.   *Have you worried a lot about terrible things happening, such as fire, burglary, or flooding in the house?*

Yes. Oh, yes. Well, not so much fire or burglary, but flooding in the house? All the time. I have a recurring vision that my toilet will finally explode. These thoughts usually occur when I've been away on a trip for an extended amount of time. I always breathe a sigh of relief when I walk into my place and realize that none of my fears have come true. Not yet, anyway.

6.   *Car accidents. Accidentally hitting a pedestrian or rolling down a hill?*

Yes. Again, tricky. You see, I do have this strange awareness while driving that we are manoeuvring machines that could kill someone. Especially in areas with children, I drive extra slowly, which makes people behind me nuts, but I don't care. Tricky because I've never even thought about it rolling down a hill. Not until now, that is.

7.   Spreading an illness (giving someone AIDS)?

No. Sometimes I can be pragmatic: how can I spread AIDS if I don't have it?

8.   Losing something valuable?

No. This one made me think. I don't think too much about valuable things, maybe because I don't have many. I take care of something like my computer, but I don't worry about it. Strangely, I focus on cheap things, items that have little or no value. When I was a kid, I remember there was a towel hanging outside drying. A huge rainstorm came, and I worried so much that the towel was going to blow away and disappear. Wasn't even my favourite towel. This makes no sense to me now, but here I am writing about it. Must mean something. Towel = Rosebud?

9.   Harm coming to a loved one because you weren't careful enough?

Yes. Tentatively. One of the stranger questions on the list because who doesn't think about something like this? Maybe I am so far down the spiral that I am not aware of my abnormal thoughts. This is perhaps my biggest fear: not being aware. Walking through life with a certain perspective and getting to the end and realizing that I was totally perceived in a different way. I mean, I know I'm wrong about a lot of things, but I hope that I have a healthy personal point of view.

10.   Have you worried about acting on an unwanted and senseless urge or impulse, such as physically harming a loved one, pushing a stranger in front of a bus, steering your car into oncoming traffic, inappropriate sexual contact; or poisoning dinner guests?

No. This one gave me pause as well. Now, I'm going to admit something here and I'll probably sound like a bit of a maniac, but here goes: unequivocally, my answer to this question is no. But say, when I'm standing on the subway platform, I've wondered — wondered — what would happen if someone fell on the tracks. It's more about witnessing something like this: what would it look like? What would I do? How would it unfold? Perhaps this is a senseless urge, but I do not worry about acting on it. And if I invite you over for dinner, do not be afraid I will poison you. My food might taste bad, but it's not poisonous.

11. Have you felt driven to perform certain acts over and over again, such as excessive or ritualized washing, cleaning, or grooming?

No. Okay, admittedly, I said above that I clean my place on a regular basis, which I guess is ritual. However, I think this should be more specific. It's not like I dust my house five times a day. I like things neat, so goddamn sue me.

12. Checking light switches, water faucets, the stove, door locks, or emergency brakes?

No. Really. I often think that I didn't turn my headlights off or lock my front door, but they're passing thoughts. Look, this test is getting quite personal and making me think about things that are a bit uncomfortable. I stick to my "no" answer because I wouldn't say I perform these acts over and over. I am really justifying myself here and even getting a little defensive.

13. Counting, arranging, evening up behaviours (for example, making sure socks are at the same height)?

Yes. Not counting, I've never been good at math. Arranging and evening up? Absolutely. The weird thing is that I don't really care about pictures being evened up. I'll get them so they look aesthetically pleasing, but that's it. And I mentioned my closets. But something like files and work areas? The first thing I have to do is arrange everything the way I want it. As an editor, you have to be organized. You're screwed if you're not organized. Editing is the perfect job for me: all you're really doing is arranging things, placing them in order, and keeping things organized.

14. Collecting useless objects or inspecting the garbage before it is thrown out?

No. I'm actually the complete opposite of this. I have a rule that if something is not used by the next time I move, I throw it out. Nothing ever gets moved twice. The problem is that throughout my twenties, I moved a lot, resulting in very few excess items. But now I'm in a place I'll probably be in for a while. Things are starting to stay.

15. Repeating routine actions (in/out of chair, going through doorway, relighting cigarette) a certain number of times or until it feels just right?

No. This has never been a problem, this counting thing. Again, math is not something I want to think about.

16. Need to touch objects or people?

No. Actually, I'd prefer if people didn't touch me. I'm just getting to a point where I don't flinch when people pat me on the back. My handshake is firm, but I'd rather avoid shaking hands. I'm also just getting used to hugging friends, both women and men. I never used to do this, and you know, there's something about a nice hug. Comforting.

17. Unnecessary rereading or rewriting, reopening envelopes before they are mailed?

Yes. And I answered yes because sometimes when I am reading, my mind wanders away from the page. And rewriting? The thing is, wouldn't most writers be considered obsessives? I've rewritten this goddamn novel almost eight times — not out of compulsion, but out of the realization that my life experience has grown, so what I wrote two months ago, six months ago, last year, bears no resemblance to what I'm thinking now, how I want to express myself, and what I want to say. Yeesh, this is getting a little depressing.

18. Examining your body for signs of illness?

No. This has never been a problem. But like question six, hadn't occurred to me until now.

19. Avoiding colours ("red" means blood), numbers ("13" is unlucky), or names (those that start with "D" signify death) that are associated with dreaded events or unpleasant thoughts?

No. However, this kind of thing fascinates me. From a mythological perspective, I understand that the number 13 is an unlucky number, but I've never really believed in luck all that much. I believe in being unlucky, but that's an entirely different story.

20. Needing to "confess" or repeatedly asking for reassurance that you said or did something correctly?

Yes. What do you think my life is all about?

Part Two

➡

"Wait," I said. "There's a part two?"

"Shut up, we'll finish when we finish," Mary replied.

Part Two

1. On average, what amount of time is occupied by these thoughts or behaviours each day? None, mild, moderate, severe, extreme.

Moderate. To me, much of my worry is ingrained in my behaviour. It's not conscious, but deep down in my psyche. So although I'd say I worry a lot, I don't know how aware I am of it until the thing — whatever it is — happens or doesn't happen, and I am either relieved or just completing a self-fulfilling worry prophecy.

2. How much distress do they cause you? None, mild, moderate, severe, extreme.

Moderate. I'm going right down the middle on these questions. Again, I don't necessarily think about it, but there's always a worry just out of view.

3. How hard is it for you to control them? Complete control, much control, moderate control, little control, no control.

Moderate control. Well, most times I think I keep my worries in check, and in a way, they keep me in check. Keep me from getting too confident. Again, I'll quote from my journal, which speaks for itself: "I wrote an article a few months ago and sent off the finished product to the clients. I didn't hear anything for a few days and during those days, I went from 'They're just busy' to 'Oh, no, what have I done?' to 'They're not answering because they're trying to figure out how to get out of this deal with me.' Sure enough, they got back to me saying the article was great and more than they expected. My mind takes giant leaps to the worst possible outcome, and I am trying to trace these leaps, following where they go so I can dismantle them one at a time in order to realize that the worst I could think of happening is really not going to be the end result. Sometimes this pragmatic approach works. Sometimes."

4. How much do they cause you to avoid doing anything, going any place, or being with anyone? No avoidance, occasional avoidance, moderate avoidance, frequent and extensive avoidance, extreme avoidance.

Occasional avoidance. Okay, I'm talking about in general here. When it comes to relationships, obviously, I avoid certain things. I am working on these things, give me a freakin' break. Sometimes I like being alone. Is that a bad thing? Oh, look at me getting defensive.

5. How much do they interfere with school, work, or your social or family life? None, slight interference, occasional interference with functioning, frequent interference, extreme interference.

None. Always have been and always will be functional when it comes to my outside life. I am good at hiding things, which comes in handy. Sure, I might be moody, but I try my best to repress my feelings. Oh, that's healthy.

"Result: score of 15," Mary read. "Based upon your responses to this screening measure, you are most likely suffering from an obsessive-compulsive disorder. This is not a diagnosis, or a recommendation for treatment. However, it would be advisable and likely beneficial for you to seek a professional diagnosis from a trained mental health professional in your community immediately."

Here's the thing: as Mary and I went further into this questionnaire, I kept thinking, *People will think I'm some kind of maniac.* And then I thought, *Who gives a shit?* And then I thought, *How clever you are in avoiding what's really going on.* It seems that no matter how much I get to a place where I feel comfortable, I immediately slip into old patterns of being clever, of placing the mask back on my face, of not being honest. Rereading this a day or two later, I chastised myself for not allowing the truth of the situation.

Yeah, sure, I admit this test was actually an interesting experiment. I'm not saying I'm taking it as a professional assessment, but the questions did make me think. It made me see just how much of a control freak I can be. Conveniently, I called this "being organized," but if being organized means an inability to let go of certain things, how can I ever move beyond this? Can someone actually change? Is it a constant stream of returning to old patterns, re-breaking them, returning to them? Does this become the new pattern?

I'll tell you this: I'd rather be aware of my faults, embrace them, and pull them apart in painful ways. In the end, what am I supposed to do? How does knowing these things translate to being helpful in any way? From my recent experiences, I believe that a person can get to a breaking point, a point where I will either give in to my inadequacies or really and truly attempt to understand them. Oh, I am interested in that point, in that moment where the buildup of repression and obsession finally becomes too much. And I'm interested in the expression of what it could be: violent creation, musical inspiration, poetic rage, expression through exposing my internal self. Reconnection after all these years with someone while we ignore all the lost time between us. Dislocation or isolation or confusion or wondering what the hell I'm supposed to do, when really, just the fact that I'm so broken that I'm asking that question—

That question is exactly what I fear. I let go of my search for answers, gave in to the realization of how much I don't know, how little of life I've lived. And by falling downwards, by being beat, beat down, bottoming out beneath the pressure of my own mind — is that the place to finally STOP being organized? That's a clever way of justifying my control issues. And the body I've been tightly winding up all these years comes loose, and shoulders lower, and maybe, just one goddamn time, I can hold my head a little higher, stop furrowing my brow, bow to a pretty lady in the street just for fun, and just — could I please just relax?

We returned to Mary's room at the Lighthouse. Stepped over the pieces of a smashed vase that had been aimed at Edith and the Walking Seniors. I have an affinity for older people. Maybe I was looking for the wisdom that life brings through experience. Maybe I was looking for a sense of history. Whatever the case, maybe because I was getting older myself, I'd gotten more interested in my family history and where I came from. Mary knew everything about my grandmother. I imagined that everyone had someone in his life who knows everything: a keeper of the flame, a vessel of history, and a holder of secrets.

Mary and I walked downstairs for lunch. I had set up a podcast interview near Niagara Falls at Caesars Hotel and Casino with a musician for the next day. One of the first things Mary told me was that my family had settled near there on a plot of land on the Canadian side. Now there's a casino on the same land. I told her about my planned trip to Niagara Falls, how it would be my first time there, and that I'd be meeting someone at that casino. Mary smiled at me then narrowed her eyes.

"You should go visit Margaret's grave," she said.

Okay, I didn't know if god was in those details, and I didn't know how any of this worked. But I couldn't deny that there was something in the energy and particles and atoms and vibrations around us. Maybe it was random, and every once in a while this randomness connected, and the electricity pulled people together. The great thing was that I didn't know. I couldn't explain it. Sure, there are scientific reasons or I could logically explain away these coincidences. In the end, I just wanted to keep being amazed by these experiences, accept them, and continue to bumble around in my perceived randomness. The one thing I did believe in was patterns. To me, patterns govern my experience. Maybe this is why I enjoy spending time with older people. Given enough time, you earn the privilege of connecting the dots.

Spent all day with Mary. We ate downstairs in the dining room. We laughed, we paused at certain points, and there was poignancy and truth in those pauses. I was put to work — getting things for other residents (with Mary's approval) from high shelves, for example — and was offered chocolate fudge for my help. Maybe I'm just storing up karma so younger people will talk to me when I'm older, do errands for me. But I think I can say honestly that this was not the case. We walked downstairs to the parking garage, and she showed me her Lincoln Mark VI, now dusty and unused. She paid to keep the vehicle stored here, a red fiery beast of a car with a long hood, round headlights that resembled the wide eyes of a stranger, and bucket seats.

After many hours and another meal with Mary, I was unleashed into the night, my usual guilt in check, and I continued toward

Caesars Casino. Stayed in a crappy motel down the street from Caesars. I've always liked staying in those anonymous motels. For some reason they make me feel more at home than home. I went for a long walk that night, along the Falls, in the very place where my distant relatives had settled. I felt they walked with me. What I didn't do was visit my grandmother's grave, but this would all come in time.

One story Mary had told me popped back into my head. She had been on assignment with Margaret, driving out of town to photograph and interview residents from a small town whose drinking water had become contaminated. Their partnership extended beyond the work. The writing, the journalism, the books were all merely reasons for them to hit the road together. And I saw them in my mind's eye, Margaret sitting in the passenger seat while Mary drove her boat-sized Lincoln Mark VI, stick shift with one arm, cigarette drooping from her lips, tumbler of gin and tonic with a wedge of squeezed lime balanced between her thighs, manoeuvring the steering wheel with her knees, constantly honking at "frickin' jerks" — cars, bikes, pedestrians, and basically anyone else on the roads — to get out of her way. Shifting between puffs and sips, Mary drove fast and was no stranger to riding in bus lanes, bike lanes or, on more than one occasion, the sidewalk.

But what is the reason or pattern of moving my way from the Lighthouse Retirement Home to Niagara Falls? I don't know.

Maybe this can explain it, maybe not. Behind the main foyer at the Lighthouse was a wall-length mural of stained glass. The mural was a colourful representation of the solar system, complete with planets and moons. Quite stunning. For some reason, I thought this was unusual, but as things have been going, I just went with it. I was the one all caught up in the notion of what all this meant. As Mary walked me out of the Lighthouse, she showed me the mural and asked what it meant to me. I said that I didn't know, just that it made me feel small, but that for some reason that was okay. She nodded and we moved on. She shuffled off, leaning on her cane with each step, and I remember feeling — not thinking, but feeling — that this "not knowing" was okay. I learned a great deal on these two days. I learned that the more I figure out, the less I actually know.

Spring

The sun was getting higher. Hotter. The morning turned into noon, turned into the afternoon, turned into my seeing what I thought was real, but which was obviously, in retrospect, not.

I thought that the idea of mirages in the desert were something created in movies. A way to show that the desert was not only a place that was extremely dangerous physically, but also one where you could lose your mind.

I was losing my mind all right. Whatever was left of it.

I just kept walking, my steps disappearing behind me, lips drying out, eyes drying out, the sweat drying down the centre of my back. Things were not going the way I had planned. My life, or what was left of it, could have been better. As my body turned in on itself, collapsed from the weight of my stupidity at getting lost out here in the Jordanian desert, I recognized that there was a disadvantage to dying slowly of heat exhaustion and dehydration — my life didn't flash in front of my eyes, it ran before them in slow motion. All my mistakes. Everything.

My feet became weights, growing heavier with every step.

Hypnotists and Psychics

I'm trying to go out more, trying to be more social. I picked Mary up at the Lighthouse, and we headed out to see a hypnotist friend perform his act. As we walked to the venue, Mary asked me about more of the files she had from the cabinet.

"Don't you ever get mad?"

"Well, yeah, everyone gets mad," I said. "Didn't you read the beginning of this book? I'm finally admitting just how mad I can get. Seems unfounded for some reason."

Some show anger more than others. But this is some kind of cop-out because I'm mad most of the time. I try not to show it, but you can read it on my face. For years, I just told everyone that that's my face — my thinking face — that happens to pull my features into a frown and furrow my brow.

If I am honest, and there's no reason not to be, I walk around in a ball of anger most days. Usually not at anything specific, just angry. And it sucks because I don't want to be Angry Guy. There's really no reason for it, at least none that I can name right now. I paused at the question Mary posed because although I walk around mad for one reason or another, I have nothing to rail against and therefore I turn it all inside.

It bugs the hell out of me when people toss around their anger — those individuals whom the rest of us tippytoe around, thankful when they're in a good mood. Give me a break, and get some goddamn control over yourself. On the other hand, I'm sitting here on the other side of the spectrum, unable to direct this anger toward where it should go. I know either extreme is not healthy, but there's gotta be a middle ground. It's not good, keeping this all in, pounding the shit out of myself over every little thing. Oh, if you only knew the kind of messed up stuff I tell myself.

All the shit I've been carrying around, all that inside. I never realized how much was internalized, all the crap we hold on to, all the good stuff we let go. I've come to believe that this ball of anger is an actual physical thing that we store in our bodies, something we carry around with us that eats us up from the inside. It manifests itself as illness or bitterness, all kinds of –nesses. We should all let it out, talk some shit, because in the end it doesn't matter.

One of the strangest aspects of anger occurs when I fail to risk something. I chicken-shit out, and then, oh, I lay the internal smackdown of a lifetime. I'm slowly coming to realize that the results of these risks don't matter either. I've gotta take 'em, and a lot of times it doesn't work out, but every once in a while I hit one and it's worth it. The anger goes away, but how come I have to relearn this with every risk? Feel that enormous sense of paralyzing doubt, force myself with threats of being forever alone or forever lost, and only then, with everything on the line, without a net, take the plunge. Even if it doesn't work, I've let go of something, and some minuscule part of that big ball of anger has eroded.

I have two kinds of anger. When I'm in the outside world and I get angry, I completely lose my train of thought, get defensive, and generally want to leave the room. Cowardly, for sure. I have no sense of fight, only flight. When I get angry with myself, it's a totally different situation. I'm all fight and no flight — I guess because there's no getting away from yourself. I can't seem to stay present in a real fit of external anger; it's something I need to work on and figure out. Look, I'm a slow learner, someone not prone to outbursts of emotion. But if you lived in my head, you'd see that in a way, I've been living two lives, lives that I can't seem to connect up. Truth is, I don't like that guy very much, the one who's walking around fake-smiling at people and who is largely invisible. There's a lot going on in here, and I wish I could introduce this person to more people.

Mary and I were sitting in the audience of the hypnotist show when he asked for some volunteers from the crowd. The podcast I produce is making me do things I wouldn't normally do. I figured that since I planned on asking the hypnotist for an interview, I should get the hell up there on stage and submit myself to hypnosis so I could talk to him about the experience.

"Just go up there," Mary said. "Who gives a shit?"

"There's no way," I said. "I'm not that guy who volunteers."

"Come on, coward."

"I can't, I won't."

"Don't be stupid."

"I'm not being stupid, just reasonable."

"Stupid."

I physically forced myself out of the seat with the help of Mary's cane on my backside. Sat down on stage and immediately freaked out over the lights and the shadows of the audience I could only vaguely make out. I assumed they could see me sweating, which made me sweat more. My hands were clammy, and I kept telling myself not to wipe them on my pants because they'd all see and laugh. I was sure I was about to do something I'd regret.

Now, this is a small example — this getting up on stage — of how fear rules my actions because if you're talking about anger, really you're talking about fear. But something happened on that night — dare I say, something important. A lesson. With three other people, the hypnotist started talking and doing his magic. I tried, I really tried. Maybe too hard. There was a struggle going on in my head: one part wanted desperately to listen to the hypnotist, to go under, let go, give in; the other part was so intensely aware of what was happening — the lights, the microphone, the audience — and so self-conscious that I couldn't relax. At one point, when I thought I was starting to go under, the hypnotist played some music and told us to play an instrument along with it. Couldn't do it. Again, heard Mary's voice in my head, *Just do it, just do it, just do it.* But the other part wouldn't allow it. Finally, the hypnotist put his hand on my shoulder and asked me to step off the stage.

I had a drink with the hypnotist at the bar afterward, and he said that people who can focus well easily go under. Also those with high IQs. I can focus well, albeit in a hyper-obsessive kind of way. As for IQ, well, I ignored this comment. We talked about the conscious mind and the subconscious mind, and how easily they can be controlled and manipulated. I must've looked hurt over the IQ remark because he gave me a little test. He asked me to hold out my arm, close my eyes, and think about myself as a child. I thought of visiting my grandmother as a young child and the way she regarded me as more intelligent than I perceived myself to be. I remembered having conversations with her and the way she asked me questions no other adult asked. I remembered her asking me what I thought. I felt some movements along my arm. When he told me to open my eyes, he asked if I'd felt him and Mary pinching me hard along my arm. I had sensed movement but not pain.

Something opened up.

Later on, after a few more gin and tonics, a woman started talking to us as Mary and I were leaving the bar. She mentioned seeing *The Great Gatsby*, and we got into this long discussion about the problems with the movie. As I usually do, I assumed this woman didn't really want to talk to me, that she was figuring out a way to extricate herself from the conversation. At one point, I went over to Mary, who was talking with the bouncer.

"I just made a stupid comment about Leonardo DiCaprio," I told Mary. "She's looking for an opportunity to leave and get out of this awkward situation."

"But she wouldn't be standing here talking if she didn't want to," Mary said.

"She's being polite," I said.

"Why would she bother being polite? Shut up and keep talking."

"She's the one who won't stop talking and create some awkward silence to allow us both out of the situation. Maybe I should act like I have to leave so she can feel better about leaving."

"Stay," Mary said. "Don't be an idiot."

"We should go."

"Shut up, we should stay."

"Fuck."

Let's call her Daisy. I did something stupid with Daisy: I gave her my business card. Jerk. Who gives out a business card? The truth is that I don't even know how to ask for a woman's number without imagining that she's thinking I'm some kind of creep. My reasoning is that if she wants to get in touch with me, I'll leave the ball in her court. This fight and continuation of the argument in my head lasted the rest of the night and the entire next day. The words of the hypnotist came back to me, and I thought about the conscious mind and the subconscious mind. The separation between the perception of my actions and the actions themselves. It's all just fucking fear, man. I mean, who cares, right? What difference would it make if the audience laughed at me when I was onstage? What difference would it make if I asked for Daisy's number and she said, *No, creep.*

Maybe I am truly going mad? My ability to talk myself into any form of risk must surely be a sign of my brain loosening, breaking apart, finally revealing me to be what I always feared: batshit crazy. From here, the arguments can only get louder, and soon they won't just be in my head — it'll become vocal. It'll start with my pacing around my place talking out loud. Then I'll move outdoors, becoming one of those guys walking down the street having a full-blown argument for all to hear and judge, and I won't even hear the people I pass whispering to each other as they pull their kids closer, refuse to make eye contact. My hair will grow long along with a patchy beard, bloodshot eyes. I'll be unable to work, to make decisions, to wash. Let's not go down that road too far.

What this entire book has been about so far is change. Lots of change. Really, it's about fear.

The spring brought some kind of respite from feeling like a complete asshole whom nobody would be interested in. Perhaps there is some truth in the idea that after a breakup, you just need some time to pass. When I was in my last relationship, my body reacted negatively. At the time, when my hair started falling out, I assumed that I was just getting older. Didn't register at first until I kept noticing more hairs left in the shower, more hairs floating around the sink, more around the house. The other thing was I started sweating more, sweating at everything — going out anywhere, having to talk on the phone, going to work. Embarrassed, I always wore jackets and stuck to dark clothes to mask my visible anxiety. I didn't realize until the spring that my hair wasn't falling out anymore, that my pits weren't as sweaty. My body was trying to tell me something but I wasn't listening.

Time to get myself together. Get back in shape. Got some new clothes. Let my hair grow, what's left of it. I'm secure enough in my masculinity to tell you about going for a facial a few weeks ago.

Maybe it was 'cause I was getting older, or maybe 'cause I was single, but all of a sudden, I wanted to do something about the blackheads on my enormous nose. To try and do what I could about this face to make myself more attractive. Vain? Sure, but smiling too much has caused wrinkles around my eyes. Had to start taking care of this before it got too out of hand. Or stop smiling.

So I made the appointment and the place was empty. Naturally, when I returned, it was full of old ladies who all squinted at me, as though I were out of place. A giant snowstorm hit on the day of my appointment, so the woman working there asked me to remove my boots. She provided a pair of small pink Crocs. I hate Crocs, especially pink ones. I shuffled past all the confused old ladies to a private room in the back.

What do you call them? Facialists? She told me to lie down on the bed and proceeded to wrap my neck in towels. She moved over a machine that sprayed steam in my face to loosen up the pores then the facialist left me alone, told me she needed to wait and let my pores open. I felt this time was really for me to be alone with my thoughts, to think about what I was doing.

And I thought, "Is this gay?" Which is a strange thought to have, but I wondered why I associated doing something, yes, maybe a bit feminine, with being gay. Shows how much certain stereotypes enter your psyche and are ready to pop out at any opportunity. I'm not the manliest of men: I'm sensitive and wear my vulnerability too loosely on my sleeve; I'm neat and orderly; and lately, since growing my hair out, I've been using way too much product. I've wondered sometimes, since none of my relationships with women seem to work out, if maybe I were repressing something about myself. It's as though I have certain gay tendencies, except for the being-attracted-to-men part.

The facialist returned and started waving a metal object over my nose. Everything felt nice until she got out a needle and started popping out blackheads. Jesus, what we do to look good. Next she pulled out a small vacuum-like instrument and started vacuuming the outside of my nose. My nose is pretty big, so the vacuuming took a while. After she was done, she removed the cotton balls from my eyes to show me all the puss she had removed from my nose.

Disgusting. She didn't need to show me that. She replaced the cotton balls and started rubbing in different lotions.

The rubbing put me into a relaxed state. And I'm thinking about how this could be gay, but really, who gives a shit if it were. And I start thinking about this one experience I had once, something I've never really told anyone.

In university, I really wanted to get into film school. I missed the cut the first year, but I went to the university anyway with the hope of getting in for second year. During that first year, I kept visiting the chair of the film department, the guy responsible for choosing who got into the program. My reasoning was that I wanted him to put a face to the name, so when it came time for me to reapply, he'd remember me and know just how serious I was about getting in. He was an older guy and always seemed happy to see me. I thought this was a good thing and that I was on my way into the program.

As part of the application, candidates had to take a written test. When I was handing in my test to the chair of the film department, he pulled me aside and asked if I wanted to get a drink that evening. Being naive, I assumed maybe he wanted to hang out with me, as friends, because I was so talented and my radiant youth could shine on him.

That evening, I went downtown — I had never really been downtown on my own before. Found his place, where he immediately offered me wine. He asked me about being a figure skater, something we'd never talked about before but that he must've known from my resume. He suggested we go out for dinner because I was a student and probably hadn't had a decent meal in a while. We went to this really fancy restaurant, and this confused me a bit more. We ate and it was really good food and he paid the bill. Outside he suggested going to a club downtown, and it wasn't until that point that I realized we were out on a date. My realization must've shown on my face because he put his hand on my shoulder and asked, "Wait, you're not gay?" And when I replied that I wasn't, he smiled and said, "That's okay." He offered to take me in a taxi as far as the subway, and before I got out of the car, he said, "Hey, don't tell anyone about this."

I slammed the door shut and was left alone.

Not sure why I felt the need to include that story, but there it is.

A more recent conversation also popped into my head. I was talking to an old friend, telling him about feeling different, about feeling like things are changing, about my daily use of hair products and increased focus on my wardrobe. He happens to be gay, and he compared my experiences to coming out of the closet. A different kind of wardrobe. An interesting statement, it made me wonder if there was a — figuratively speaking — gay man inside me screaming to get out. Maybe this is the answer — a little creativity in relationships? Maybe it's time to move on from the traditional vows of marriage.

So, yeah, the facialist left me alone again, and I wondered why I thought of my one and only date with a man — that wasn't really a date because I didn't know it was a date. And coming out of a different sort of closet. And I just got a facial, which is maybe a little feminine. But it seems to me that we're past the point of determining what's feminine and what's masculine, gay or straight, right or wrong. Everyone's just out there trying to figure their own lives out, trying to get by in whatever capacity they can with a slim hope to find some sense of happiness.

We finished, and I shuffled past the old ladies wearing my pink spa Crocs. At home, I checked myself out in the mirror, trying to see if there was any difference. My face was a bit redder than before, but no one would really notice. This was more my concern, that people would be able to tell that I'd had a facial.

But you know what? They seemed to work, those superficial kinds of self-improvements. The clothes, the hair, the face. I've been walking around like some kind of fool, feeling good, feeling like things are changing and getting better. I'm feeling happy.

And this has me profoundly worried.

After my most recent visit with Mary, we walked through the foyer of the Lighthouse, and she stopped me before I exited.

"The way you ask questions," Mary said. "The way you extrapolate from the answers. Margaret was right, you should be a storyteller."

"Well," I said, "I'm sort of a writer."

She nodded. "You know, there are many ghosts flying around us trying to reach out to us. They want us to tell their stories so they can rest. You're one of those storytellers. Listen to them, they'll guide you."

"Sure," I said and turned to exit out the front doors. Something pulled me back. I turned, and Mary was gone. I took a few steps back inside the foyer — it was large and open, and it led right into the main lobby. She couldn't have moved that fast. I walked through the lobby to the elevators and looked at the numbers — the cars were all at the top floors. Mary is either a very fast and agile old lady, or I am starting to think she's something else...

I headed home, which is not exactly a condo building, more like a townhouse set-up. I'm in the middle: neighbours upstairs and neighbours downstairs. The downstairs neighbours and I had a very Canadian-style, passive-aggressive disagreement. They left me a note in my mailbox explaining all the noise I was making — you know, like footsteps and moving furniture. I don't wear shoes in my place, and the only furniture I was moving would have been my office chair on wheels. Initially I wrote back a strongly worded letter, but started over and ended up saying, "I'll keep the noise down." I got a reply, very apologetic that they even had to bring up this issue but happy things seemed to be resolved quickly.

It wasn't until a few weeks after the incident that I actually met the person downstairs. We don't really talk to each other in the development. I guess it's a city thing. One night I was walking home and I heard this clink-clink-clink behind me. Turned, saw a woman behind me walking with a cane. Clink-clink-clink. Tried not to act like I was noticing her. She caught up to me, smiled, and said, "Hello neighbour!" An attractive woman, Filipina, long black hair. She motioned for us to continue walking. Clink-clink-clink. When we reached our doors, she leaned the cane against her hip and held out her right hand for a shake, a strong shake. With her other hand, she pushed her hair back behind her left ear, revealing a small birthmark on her left temple. I made an excuse and hurried into my place.

Working from home is great. Some days you just don't want to get out of your pyjamas. Other days it can be a bit more difficult and distracting. I decided to try to spend more time downtown, found a collective office space for writers. Members pay a certain amount each month and get access to the space. My idea was to really concentrate on writing and, for the first time in my life, take it seriously.

Often, I'm at my office at night, alone. I don't talk to anyone there. I expect they don't want to talk to me. I don't say this for pity's sake, and I understand it's just a projection, just in my head, but I can't get it out of my head. Thoughts of not being accepted, thoughts of invisibility. I've been working for a while now at rewiring my brain to be more socially presentable to others, with mixed results.

When I was a kid, I staged elaborate wars and created narratives using toys. I enjoyed this and was never bored. These weren't imaginary friends I would talk to, but they did live in my imagination.

I remember hanging out with some friends when they asked me to bike home and get a toy. Acceptance. I rode home as fast as I could, and on my way back I tried to pedal standing up, one handed. Totally wiped out. When I returned to my friend's house, they played with the toy, ignoring my scratches and scars and bloody knee. Even at a young age, you start to understand who your friends are. I remember this as a turning point, one where I turned inward.

As someone who is a creative person, my mind tends to be in constant motion. Sometimes I wish I could turn it off. The trouble with being observant and recording things is that there is a tendency not to be present in the moment. Yes, I keep those thoughts moving, but they can also throw me off balance, disconnect the pathways from the hand to the mind.

I enjoy living in cities, but being alone takes its toll. I don't want to be that guy. I tiptoe around my place so the neighbours won't complain. The doorbell rings, and it's churchy people, and I freeze, not wanting to engage with them in conversations about god. Delivery people can leave packages outside. Unknown phone numbers go unanswered. I clean every week, but for whom? There are moments of extraordinary beauty that happen in my life, and I want the world to correspond with how I'm feeling, but since I've lived an internal life, it is sometimes difficult and disappointing to realize that others don't see things the way I do. The phrase "I'm alone but I'm not lonely" annoys me because I can talk myself into this most of the time, but in moments of honesty, if I go an entire day without talking to anyone, the facade is shattered. Maybe I've lived alone too long, and my ability to establish a stable and healthy relationship breaks down because I'm so set in my ways. Maybe it's too late for me.

Spending a significant amount of time by yourself creates a certain amount of self-awareness. Too much self-awareness. I live in the landscape of my own mind. I question everything around me, and since I have a sincerely modest approach to my own sense of self-worth, well, the perception I have of myself through the eyes of other people can be pretty dim.

It's not been fair to my partners. How can I ask for someone to be with me when I'm not with her? Physically maybe, but not with my head. I've tried, I've done my best, or at least I did my best at that time with what I had. In my last relationship, when we weren't together and I had a night to myself, I felt so disconnected from everything that I would just go on long drives. These times were actually some of the first when being alone just made me feel really depressed. I thought that perhaps I just didn't want to be away from that person. But I think the problem was much deeper; I had lost my way internally. I am in no way laying blame on that person — what was she to do? She stuck around longer than she should've. I do believe she tried, but when I'm lost, I cannot rely on another person to bring me home again. Especially when I don't know where home is.

There have been times when I was in a relationship, and even when I was around that person, I still felt alone. A good kind of alone. Amazing to be with someone but feel like I'm alone? Yes, I'm uncomfortable most of the time, but when I'm alone, I feel comfortable. So if I'm most comfortable alone, but I can get that same feeling when together with someone, that's really something.

I love coming to the office because of the energy in the streets. The energy around here is such that, although I don't talk to anyone, there's life. A pulse. I do admit to wondering what is happening behind closed windows when laughter drifts down onto the street.

The walks are working.

Every day that I go to my office, I take my time getting there. I take my time returning. There's something strange going on, where I'm incredibly connected to everything around me, yet I can still be alone with my thoughts. Like walking through my imagination. It feels like something important has happened, and instead of just keeping my mind moving, I'm getting my feet in on the action.

I am holding on, getting better every day. Every day is a struggle because there is an inherent risk, the risk of not knowing where I'm going. Sure, I can have an idea, I can establish plot points and themes, I can carry with me maps and a compass, but the risk of the unknown can be a scary proposition. But if I don't take or undertake that first step, a truth will remain elusive to me. What if the not-knowing is the truth? What if never arriving anywhere is exactly where I'm supposed to be? One of my scariest moments is asking myself, *what is it that I have to say?* The fear stems from the possible answer: *nothing.* Obviously, I have a lot of work to do before I can get anyone wrapped up in my life or invite a partner in. But also, in that area between the decision to create some type of momentum and the final result, that elusive truth may exist. Perhaps the truth is that not knowing where I'm going could lead me to exactly where I need to be. Or perhaps it will not lead me anywhere. That's the risk.

It was at this moment when I was actually sitting in my office, in the back room, when I heard something. The office is separated into two parts: the front part contains the lounge, kitchen, and boardroom; the back is the "quiet room" that contains a bunch of desks. Alone in the quiet area. When I'm writing, I can be intense, like I'm inside my imagination. I suspect that I look quite funny when I get interrupted, like someone splashed cold water on me while I was sleeping. In the quiet room, there are rows of cubicles. On the wall of the cubicle where I sat, I felt a scratching noise. I said "felt" and not "heard" because that's the only way I can describe it. I felt the noise run down the back of my spine.

Heard another noise in another part of the office. Listened, clink-clink-clink. It was nighttime, and having checked around earlier, I knew there was no one else there. Stepped through the quiet-room door into the hallway that linked to the lounge. The lights were off, but I would have sworn that I'd turned them on when I did my walk-around earlier. Stepped into the room a few steps further. Stopped. All the hairs on my body stood up. Looked around 360 degrees, saw nothing. Felt something. On one side of the lounge, windows went from floor to ceiling. Through the lights from the busy street, my reflection looked back at me. Clink-clink-clink. It was coming from the quiet room.

"Hello?" I said weakly into the darkness.

The printer in the corner started firing off sheets. Scared the shit out of me. Walked over, looked at what was being printed. Nothing. Just symbols and numbers. Clink-clink-clink. Flicked on the lights. Walked back to the quiet room. The lights were off. Okay, someone was playing an elaborate joke on me. Grabbed my stuff, walked back into the lounge, yes, yes, the lights were off again. Kept them off, locked up, left.

On the way home, I couldn't shake the feeling that something had been in that office with me. Walk, the answer is usually to walk. The old woman telling me about ghosts, perhaps an actual ghost in my office, the woman who lives next to me with a birthmark just like ... like...

As I was walking, I found myself looking forward into the future and backward into the past at the same time. I could see what lay ahead, to a certain degree, and I decided to just let it happen. And I kept coming back to someone from the past, Chloe, with the birthmark on her left temple. Chloe, the one I did mushrooms with, and who wrote her story on her walls, on my body. What happened to Chloe?

A simple search through Mary's files on Chloe helped me fill in the gaps. Discovered that she had graduated from university in Vancouver, majoring in journalism. She worked at the *Vancouver Daily News* for three years, covering violent crimes. Seemed about right. I found copies of several of her archived stories. They were balanced and sought sympathy for all parties involved. As I progressed through the stories, her main focus seemed to be on sex workers, the drug problem in Vancouver, and the most destitute of people.

After her stint in Vancouver, she must have moved to New York. Wrote for the *Village Voice* and other weekly newspapers. Her focus was again on sex workers, and her archive included a six-part series where she went undercover to write about how they were treated by police. After this series, she disappeared. No more articles for the *Village Voice*. Her name didn't come up anywhere. She could've changed it, could've been writing under a different name, but you'd think she'd surface somewhere. Checked on the Internet. Nothing. It'd be difficult to disappear in these times of voluntary surveillance.

A small photograph accompanied every article I read. For a few years' worth of articles that I could find, I was able to see Chloe growing up since the last day I saw her. Every photograph was taken to show the left side of her face, hair tucked behind her ear, her birthmark clearly visible. She wanted people to see it.

A friend of mine recently moved to New York and wanted me to visit him. Maybe I'd book a trip to see him and inquire with a few people who might've known Chloe.

I reached home.

Clink-clink-clink.

With my trip to New York booked, I had one more podcast interview to do before leaving. The interview was with a psychic, a friend of my producing partner. We thought it'd be fun to do the interview while the psychic did a reading on me. Never done it, didn't know how to feel about it. I've walked by countless psychics on the street and wondered about going inside, but something always kept me walking. Something made me not want to know about the future.

We pulled up to a nice suburban home. Stella was not the woman I envisioned, very different from my image of a crooked-nosed woman wearing hoop earrings and speaking in a gravelly voice while she caressed a crystal ball. But we went with it. As soon as we walked into her office, she turned to me and said, "Lots of activity around you."

We turned on the recording equipment, started asking her about her gift. Stella told us that she works with guardian angels and that each one of us has our own guardian angels. She claimed that our angels work with her angels and discuss information, kind of like a big office where our angels pull out file folders and share them with her angel.

"There's a woman here who wants you to know she's walking with you," Stella said. "She's been watching you for a long time. She admires your creativity. Feels like a grandmother figure?"

Margaret. I figured something like this might happen. I kept it to myself because I wanted to leave my skepticism intact for a while — I must admit that. I'd been feeling some kind of strange presence. In my office, meeting the neighbour with the cane, with Mary — I couldn't explain it well if I tried, but when I sat alone, really thought about it, really dug down deep, I never really felt alone. Stella told me about a past life when I was a peasant in Europe, crossing large masses of land on foot.

I asked her about women. What the hell else are you going to ask a psychic? Stella instantly asked, with no prompting from me, "Who's Chloe?" And for a moment, I became a believer. How did she know this? She told me that Chloe has been waiting for me, waiting for me to find her. Short of asking for an address, I wanted to know if I would ever see her again. "Yes, you will be guided to her. The grandmother figure walking with you will help steer you in the right direction. You will help each other find home."

Stella went on, asked me if I was going on a trip. Told her I was going to New York. A scared look came over her face: "Don't go on that trip." She didn't want to tell me why. Maybe it was an unexplainable guess; maybe there was something more to it. She went back to the grandmother figure, said that she was restless. She knows that I am restless as well, and maybe, Stella suggested, the two of us could find home together.

Stella likes to say she gives her clients hope, a sense of knowing. I just left confused.

New York

If Cuba was a time to rebuild myself after having been dumped, New York was a bit of purging. A lot of things happened over the past few months and most — I say hesitantly — were good. But Christ, don't I get to the airport to fly to New York and the damn triggers were everywhere. Immediately, I figured out this was the point. You see, the last time I was in New York, it was with my ex-girlfriend. But I love that city. It's my damn city. Many important things happened there. So, I went there to take it back, reclaim it. Make it mine again. I'm not interested in erasing the past — I've been erased from other people's pasts, and it's not really fair. I went there to go even further, but for myself, on my own. I felt I'd smashed through some doors in the last few months, and I was getting there, but I still had a lot further to go.

If you can believe it, a man waiting to board the plane had been on the plane my ex-girlfriend and I took almost two years ago. I knew this because I peripherally knew him from my previous work. I disregarded him, but what a goddamn trigger. Plus, I didn't like him: middle-aged corporate guy, walking around with immense self-importance like he's king shit. I tried to disregard him. In between these two plane rides to New York, I'd seen him one other time. I was in the financial area of the city, walking around in the PATH, an underground system of connecting pedestrian tunnels beneath downtown Toronto. There was Corporate Man having a coffee, and the thought hit me instantly: this was the area where my ex-girlfriend worked — *let's get outta here before an unwanted run-in occurs.* So in that instance, he helped me, but still, it begged the question — why was this guy around to remind me of such things?

The plane was late. When it finally arrived, they had to check it. Please, check away. I didn't want to take off in an unchecked plane. We boarded the plane. No one sat next to me. I always hope no one will be seated next to me. Everyone had settled down, and here came Corporate Man, walking, walking, walking all the way to the back and, yup, he sat down right next to me.

Are you kidding me?

This airline flies to New York several times per day, there are 70 seats in this particular model of plane. And not only was this guy on my flight, but he was sitting next to me? He slumped down, his large frame taking up all of his seat and half of mine. In these situations, I always have a book out on my lap, silently sending the message that I don't want to talk. There's always the hope that the other person won't want to talk either. But I always got the talkers. He obviously didn't recognize me. He pulled out a book: *Outliers* by Malcolm Gladwell. Now, don't take this the wrong way, I've read Gladwell's books and enjoyed them as entertainment. It amuses me that his ability to make sometimes-very-thin connections in order to draw sometimes-very-obvious conclusions has been co-opted by the business elite to generate yet more empty catchphrases. It annoyed me that someone had probably told this corporate guy that he must become a Gladwellian — now that I think about it, sounds like *Orwellian* — and read these books in order to display that he was a multi-dimensional corporate man who craved pseudo-insight and contained pseudo-intellectual curiosity.

Yes, I'm being judgmental, but you should try it before you knock it — it's fun. Besides, I said earlier that I've read Gladwell's books and enjoyed them. So, this also makes me a hypocrite. I'm just admitting that I took a piece of information — what Corporate Man was reading — and spun it in order to not like him, mainly because he represented a connection to my past that I was trying to purge. He read maybe three pages and fell asleep. Woke up with a startle, smiled at me, and said, "I want to read too, but I keep falling asleep." Yeah, sure, this might have been a polite attempt at conversing, but didn't he get the earlier message that I didn't want to talk? I doubled my efforts and brought out earphones. Later on, he was filling out his customs form and asked to borrow my pen. Again, maybe he wanted to talk. I disregarded him. But by then I was getting sort of annoyed that he didn't recognize me. Am I that forgettable, or was the person I had become so different that I'd become unrecognizable? Let's go with the second one.

It was a short flight, and I felt a pang of guilt at pretty much ignoring the person I shared this intimate space with. Maybe he was just lonely. In the airport, we went up the same escalators. Corporate Man leaned over to an attractive woman standing in front of him, "Do I know you from somewhere?" Also obviously not wanting to talk, the woman curtly said no. He kept going, kept trying to hit on her, and I felt that was reason enough to hate him outside of our previous connection: he really was a jerk.

Then I became worried this trip was going to be a series of triggers. Walking out of the baggage claim area, a security guard stood watch. We made eye contact, and when I got halfway down the ramp, he yelled, "Be smooth, baby! Be smooth!"

Instead of ignoring him, I turned and did something I normally wouldn't do. I pointed at him and yelled back, "I AM smooth!"

He pointed back and yelled in return, "You ARE smooth!"

Okay, let me explain something. One of the first drafts of this very book you're holding had a phrase in it. The manuscript was very different from this particular version, but from it, a little mantra developed: whenever I go out somewhere, I just remind myself to be open to new experiences and new people. *Be open.* In the earlier draft, the main character was learning how to speak German and a phrase kept coming back:

As I walked down the street after exiting the hospital, these thoughts swirled through my head. I walked for a long time, I saw this life rolling out in front of me. I walked through the city, out of the city. I walked for a long time, I walked until my feet gave way, I walked until my shoes wore through, I walked until my head was numb. I walked across the earth and over seas, I walked until I wore out my thoughts and those words appeared, the ones that would carry me forth and save me. The words that brought me back: Werde Licht! Werde Licht!

Werde Licht: Be light. So, the saying started off as *be light* and morphed into *be open*. As I walked past that security guard and he said, *be smooth*, all the bad feelings of the trip so far kind of went away. I thought maybe I could actually be smooth. In Cuba, I played with portraying myself as different personas. Before coming to New York, I wondered about not just acting like another person, but becoming another person. True, wherever you go, there you are, but if I were in another city and another country, why couldn't I be another person? A person who is actually smooth, who instead of generally being awkward and insecure, becomes a person who says the right thing at the right time, and who has a natural confidence and charm. Yeah, I've made some progress in the past few months, but there are still many things I'm pushing down and repressing. Get it out already.

Be light. Be open. Be smooth.

I walked to the train that would take me from Newark airport to Penn Station. Sat and looked out the window at largely decaying landscapes of broken down economies. As I got closer to the city, the looming buildings surrounded us and the train was engulfed by a tunnel, shooting the view into pitch-blackness. Closed my eyes until the train came to a complete stop.

Be light.

Grabbed my bag, people everywhere. Joined the crowd to street level, you could feel the energy shooting down the streets, slamming into other energies, the different sources of stuff all mixing up creating some kind of organized chaos. Well, give in, sit down, check out, or join in the chaos and feed off it. My hotel was only a few blocks away, so I walked. Early morning still, the concrete baking in the sun, giving off steam, sweat instantly forming on forehead and under arms. I was carried away by the energy and the blocks zipped by. The hotel was old and not exactly five star, the room only big enough for an uncomfortable bed, sink, and dresser that transformed into a writing table. Perfect. I don't need much. This might even have been too much.

Be open.

Immediately hit the streets. I was staying not too far from Chinatown, so I walked down Broadway. Stepped right into a place called Wonton Noodle Garden, slurped down some soup. In the washroom, there was a metal bar, and on it hung a giant pair of tongs. When I see such things, I know that they are there for a reason, that at one point they were needed, and they might be needed again. Wanted to pay, get out and do more exploring, but had to wait for the old woman at the cash to rearrange her dentures. It took her a while — she took them right out, popped them back into place.

Be smooth.

Rode the subway back to my hotel. On the subway, once the doors closed, three kids yelled out, "Okay, it's showtime!" They put on a stereo full blast and started dancing, doing backflips and handstands. Ran around asking for money, turned off the stereo and exited the train. All in a span of one stop. Anything can happen.

That night, I met up with a friend. We headed out to a high-end restaurant. The servers didn't want us there; our bill wasn't big enough. Headed across a few blocks to the Meatpacking District and entered a beer garden. I tried to fit in, don't know if it worked. Next, we hit up a martini bar where it took ten minutes for the guy to make a drink — it must be good. Down the street we went into a basement. It seems people in that city are either going way up high or down under the ground. We got branded with serpent stamps on the insides of our wrists, our entrance into the secret society. We danced. I don't normally dance. You don't want to see me dance. I danced with a woman. After a while she sat down, and when I offered my hand some time later, she politely refused. I understood. I found my way home, walking through the streets, the chaos: movies being shot, streets shut down, people puking in the alleys, the heat, fights breaking out. A guy with a headset grabbed me, pushed me back, yelled at me to stay off the road. At the moment he grabbed me, a taxi came squealing around the corner, speeding and fishtailing down the street, a door missing in order to fit the camera.

Keep moving.

Hotel.

Sleep.

The next day, I walked down through the financial district. A maze. Came upon the new World Trade Center. Originally it was to be called the Freedom Tower, but I think that would have been a bad idea. I took a photograph and posted it, and a follower called me out on my caption, saying it was a cop-out to say I felt conflicted about this. Conflicted is an easy word to bandy about, a safe word, a sitting-on-the-fence word. Where I was conflicted was about how complicated these issues of war and terrorism have gotten.

Conflicted ain't the right word. Angry, frustrated, helpless, desperate — maybe better. The building represented something that should not be forgotten, but also, there were so many things to take into consideration when discussing these issues. What a vague asshole I'm being. I just didn't really know how to talk about this in a way that did not come off ignorant. So, I just did like the rest of the tourists and took pictures, not really contemplating what this all exactly meant.

Made my way north of Wall Street to the *Village Voice* offices. Entered the main lobby, asked the woman at the front desk if she knew Chloe Qi. She told me she'd just started working there and didn't know people well. I was at a bit of a loss because what was I supposed to do, walk around the office asking people if they knew her? Stepped back to the elevator to head down to street level and come up with a plan. A woman stepped in beside me right before the doors closed. We rode in silence until the ground floor.

"Meet me in the alleyway next to the building," she said without looking at me as she exited.

Walked around the side of the building and there was the woman leaning against the wall smoking a cigarette.

"Why're you looking for Chloe?" she asked.

"I knew her when I was younger," I said. "Just wanted to say hi."

"Thought maybe you were one of those perverts who come looking for her every once in a while."

"Okay, what's going on here?"

"I was a friend of hers," the woman said. "We worked some of the same areas of the city. Even talked about getting an apartment together."

"Where is she now?"

The woman shrugged her shoulders. "She just disappeared. A disagreement between the editor and her. She wrote some pretty racy stuff. Apparently it was all true. She really was — what's the word? — committed."

"The stories about sex workers?"

She nodded her head.

"The series wasn't finished, it just sort of ended," I added.

"Like I said, the editors killed it. Told her she went too far. She walked out of the office that day, never came back. Never called me. I never saw her again. I even went to her apartment. It was already rented by someone else — an Armenian couple."

The woman dropped her cigarette, stepped on it. It was at this moment when I noticed the wall beside her. On the side of the building was a spray-painted image, but not just any image. It exactly represented the birthmark on Chloe's left temple — the same shape, the same purplish and greenish colours. Exactly. Talk about a goddamn trigger.

"I even talked to the Armenian couple and the landlord," the woman said. "Told me she was basically there one day, gone the next. Left half what she owned there. The landlord bitched about having to dump it."

I half-listened, staring at the image on the wall. The woman had to return to work, and I thanked her without looking. Walked for blocks in a haze and ended up, without realizing it, right back at that spray-painted image on the side of the *Village Voice* building.

Our ears popped when we reached the 62nd floor of my friend's building. The view was south. We were looking down on the streets, and yes, the maze analogy came back to me. An organized maze. But once you're in it, can you get out? While I walked home that night, I saw a guy with a scar on his forehead, right where I imagine you'd get a lobotomy. He looked happy. Sometimes I wondered if maybe this would be a good idea for shutting down this racing mind of mine permanently. Not in a suicidal way, just to quiet things down a little, to think about things in a more simplistic way. The problem with a lobotomy was its permanence.

Brooklyn has a different vibe from Manhattan. Hipsters hung out in the park with their dogs. A bit rougher around the edges, but strangely it reminded me of some European cities I'd visited. More relaxed. I could see myself staying there for a bit, fitting in, becoming that guy. Maybe getting a dog.

The subway doors closed, and this time three old men announced they were going to sing for us. The main guy pointed his finger right in the face of a kid, asked the kid if he was ready. The kid, scared, slowly nodded his head. They sang a song called "Come Along Friends."

By the third morning, I felt comfortable, but it was time to leave. Packed up my things and started my walk back to Penn Station to get the train back to the airport. On my way, I saw Ira Glass, with a lunch bag over his shoulder, walking his dog. My ex-girlfriend and I had gone to see a live version of *This American Life* and a live show with just Ira Glass. So my first thought on the street was: *I need to stop Ira here while I go get my girlfriend because she'd love to meet him.* And then I remembered once again that there should be an ex- on the front of girlfriend and that I was alone. I wish I could say that I stopped Mr. Glass and told him my story while he listened attentively. That he was glad that I stopped him and appreciated my sharing my tales of woe with him. That maybe it would make a good episode on his show. But he seemed to be enjoying his walk, and I didn't want to bother him. So I didn't.

On the train back to the airport, my back faced the direction I was going, as though we were all going back in time. Like I was going back to the person I was. But once you had switched over to a different persona, could you switch back fully? Or would you take a bit of that new persona with you? There was no corporate man sitting beside me on the plane, no one sitting beside me on the plane. We shot through the clouds and I wondered—

Wait.

Look, I wrote most of this while sitting at my little makeshift desk in my crappy hotel room, or at a coffee shop, or while sitting on a bench in Washington Square Park. But the trip was finished and I was on the plane reviewing some of what I had written. I'm trying not to do a lot of revising of the stuff I put down here, but goddamn it, this one was bugging me. I felt somewhat depressed, already. I guess it was from coming down from an intense and exciting weekend in a new city, pretending to be a different kind of person. I really tried to be that other guy and at the same time hold on to parts of myself. Largely, it went okay.

But I'm sitting here now rereading this, and I have to stop and really examine what's going on. Why do I feel like crap? Originally, I wanted this New-York part to end with the plane ascending into the sky through the clouds with me sipping a glass of wine and wondering about my identity and my past relationships. And it was all very nice, and it placed a somewhat positive spin on where I am right now as a person and what going on trips like this means to my growth as an individual.

I just couldn't do it. I've talked about letting go and giving up and pushing through and moving forward. Who am I trying to convince with all this? You? Most likely myself. I feel crappy because with every fucking step forward I take, trying to be a better person, trying to reach some kind of potential I might have, I take several steps back. Sure, call this part self-indulgence or navel-gazing — call this entire goddamn book that — but I can't help but return to the idea that at these points, at these low points, with however little esteem I regard myself, and however ridiculous it seems, the insecurities become the reality. Every time I push for something, it doesn't happen. I've talked before about letting go, but I think I need to give up. Give up on any notion of who I think I am, or pretend to be, or want to be. There's an unravelling going on here, still some blockage. The walls are back up and hard to crack through.

Frankly, I'm just a little sick of myself and my need — or desire? — to drudge through all this crap, especially for others to see. I've tried to fit in all over the place, with everything I do, but maybe this is one more thing I need to give up on. Yeah, so it's true: wherever you go, there you are. I'm just so goddamn tired of playing different parts in different places, of thinking and saying things that other people want me to say.

Where, oh, where am I in all this? And if I'm not truly there or really present, if I'm unable to fully understand the deepest goddamn depths of myself, how in the hell do I expect other people to be let in and understand who I am? Or for me to understand who they are? So, you're telling me that after all these months and time and effort, I'm still asking the same goddamn questions. Look, I'm not looking for some instant gratification, some kind of bullshit revelation. I just want to know that I'm getting better in some way, that maybe I am becoming a better person, someone with an opinion and a voice and something to say. But at the same time, I still go deep, deep, deep, look deep down and think I have it finally figured out, but what really happens is that I open my eyes wide and realize I know nothing, or even worse, know less, and have regressed. Be light. Be open. Be smooth. Sounds good. How do I get there? So, yeah, I did sip on a glass of wine, and I thought all these thoughts, and I managed to convince myself that I was okay.

Until.

The pilot came over the speakers: "You've probably noticed that I've turned on the seat-belt sign. Don't worry, we'll probably be okay."

Don't know about you, but I don't want the pilot of the plane I'm riding in to use the word "probably."

He continued: "We've been informed by the Newark airport that there was evidence of rubber on the runway after takeoff. We might have a faulty tire. I've asked that emergency crews meet us when we land in Toronto, and I didn't want you to be alarmed."

For the rest of our time in the air, all I thought about was getting down on the ground safely. I've never really been afraid to fly, but this announcement was testing my usually confident disposition. Nearing Toronto, I looked around at the other passengers, would these be the last people I saw? Would we die together? We flew over the city, approached the lake to the island airport. Yes, you could feel the tension. I'd never believed this kind of thing, but dammit, you could feel it. I sat right over the wing, watched the wheels drop — they seemed okay, but I was no expert. It looked like we were approaching land slowly, but as we got closer, the quick passing of the water, grass, buildings revealed just how fast we were going. We touched down.

Something was not right. Maybe the psychic was right. Maybe I shouldn't have gone to New York.

We slid too far to the right — that must've been the rubber we'd left on the runway. The plane strained, turned slightly, and the wheels, or what was left of them, squeaked. We were all thrown forward into the seats in front of us, the seat belts not doing anything, unneeded oxygen masks dropping. My body twisted, my left leg bent at an unusual angle. All the pain from my polio-inflicted childhood came flooding back. I unfastened my seat belt, got thrust into the aisle as the plane tried to right itself. Finally, we ground to a halt. Since I sat by the emergency exit, it was my responsibility to get us out of there. Tried to stand up, couldn't put weight on my left leg. Limped over, grabbed the emergency bar across the top and turned it, shouldered the window open. Fire trucks and emergency vehicles surrounded the plane. Turned and saw people were frozen in seats. Yelling, screaming. Movement. We all made it out.

Outside, I had my leg checked by paramedics. Not broken, but severely bruised. Told them about polio. Was told that sometimes a trauma inflicted on an old wound could cause phantom pain flashbacks. Took some painkillers, gave my statement, went home.

I arrived home to no one and found no messages. Nothing, like I'd never been gone. Like nobody even noticed. Oh, poor me, I should just get over all this, most importantly, get over myself. Give up. But I needed some sleep first.

Sleep.

Darkness.

Went in and out of consciousness. For days, felt only pain and not much else. Like I said, no broken bones, but my body ached, especially my leg. Maybe my mind, too. On the second night at 3:20 in the morning, a time when angels are out and accessible, my phone beeped, signalling a text message. Or at least I thought my phone beeped. Didn't recognize the number. Fell back to sleep. I think it was the next day, my phone beeped again — a text message: *Hello!* I couldn't reply, couldn't type, fell back asleep. The next day, I reviewed the text messages.

Me: *Hello?*

Her: *I saw your profile on the dating site.*

My first ever message from one of these sites.

Me: *Not a good time.*

Her: *But I liked what you said on your profile.*

Me: *I don't even remember what I put on my profile.*

Her: *Should I remind you?*

Me: *Can't talk now.*

Passed out.

The messages went out of my mind because my phone rang, but this time it was Mary.

"Jesus," she said. "You gotta come down here and visit me. They're driving me nuts."

Felt strong enough to get dressed, look presentable. Went down to the parking garage to my car. When I put the key in the lock to unlock the door, a flood of nausea came over me. My hand wouldn't turn, like it wouldn't allow me to get in the car. Felt this might be a bit of an aftershock from the plane ride.

Went to the bus stop, thought maybe I'd just hitch a ride to see Mary. The bus came along, stopped right in front of me, doors opened. My feet failed me. The bus driver looked at me, all raised eyebrows. I smiled, told him I'd take the next bus. Walked a few blocks to the subway, paid the fare, walked down the steps to the platform. The subway pulled up, and I waited for the doors to open. Another wave of nausea hit me like a goddamn freight train. Ran over to the garbage can and threw up what little sustenance was in my stomach. Went back to street level, started walking.

Reached Mary's place two hours later.

"Amaxophobia," Mary said. "You know what that is?"

"Never heard of it," I said.

"The fear of riding in vehicles," she said. "It's in one of the future files."

Mary walked into the bedroom, opened the closet, pulled out a file. A thick file.

"What do you mean 'future files'?" I asked.

"What is to come," Mary said.

From the folder, she passed some documentation on amaxophobia: *an intense fear of sitting or travelling in any type of moving vehicle. While somewhat rare, phobias of this type are particularly debilitating in today's world. Since the condition impacts the ability to travel by just about any means other than walking, people who suffer with amaxophobia are often confined to their homes, limiting their movements to locations that are within easy walking distance of the home.*

"But how would my grandmother know this?" I asked. "She's dead."

"Don't question it," Mary said. "She knew about me losing my arm before it happened. I didn't listen. Look." She motioned to the empty sleeve.

It had started when Mary developed a pain in her left arm. The pain fluctuated. It was always there, but it was something that could be controlled and diminished down to a dull throb. The throb exploded one day. Mary reached Margaret's place, leaned her forehead against the door, hand on the handle. Closed eyes. Sighed. She didn't want to bother Margaret; after all, she had her own problems. Mary stepped down the steps, missed the bottom two, and crumpled to the ground. Passed out.

Darkness.

The darkness had filled her vision; it was tangible, safe, and she felt it. The next time she woke, she heard the doctor's voice, the word "cancer." In addition to radiation therapy, the doctors performed an experimental treatment involving medical isotopes. The cancer stopped spreading, receded. Mary started eating again, mushy food shovelled into her mouth. She accepted it, didn't — couldn't — fight anymore. The cancer was leaving her body, but the pain in her arm only grew stronger.

Mary's body was, like all people's, a complex algorithm of sophisticated mechanisms that worked together. The cancer was merely an offshoot of a larger problem. The radiation therapy, perhaps the medical isotopes, unleashed a much larger problem, connected two wrongs and created an even bigger one.

One day, a nurse arrived in Mary's room to wash her. The nurse removed Mary's gown and stepped back in horror. Mary's left arm was completely bruised. Mary tried to move it, but the arm wouldn't cooperate. The nurse called the doctor, and the doctor rushed Mary into surgery.

When Mary opened her eyes, Margaret stood before her. The sound came back up. Margaret smiled at her, but then her face turned downward, and she looked at her fidgety hands.

"Mary, I don't know how to say this…" Margaret trailed off.

"So say it." Mary's voice was scratchy from not talking for so long.

"Your arm … amputated…" Margaret couldn't finish the sentence.

Mary looked down to her left arm, or where her left arm used to be. She stared at it for a very long time. Mary worked hard at recovering. She learned how to do everything with one arm. After a few weeks, she was able to leave the hospital for a few hours at a time. She visited the newspaper office. They could offer her only one job, and it probably wasn't one she was interested in: Foreign Correspondent to China. Mary told them she would take the position. What she didn't tell them was how perfectly this fit into her plans. She felt she was being punished, and she wanted to get as far away from her life as possible.

Mary boarded a plane to Beijing. She arrived and settled in this new country, learned the languages, the different dialects. She sent photographs from behind the borders of China. Mary developed many contacts and established herself as an expert on China. She published two quick travel books about travelling through China, forever adopting the name M. Hammer. She did the odd freelance article for the newspaper, decided not to return to her home country ever.

Mary started a new life. Embraced her new culture, actually, new cultures. After moving through the entirety of China, she went through Mongolia and Russia before returning to Europe.

She arrived home to her most recent apartment in Prague one evening to find the door open. She crept in quietly. The lights were on. She poked her head around the corner into the living room, and there, lying on the sofa, was Margaret. Mary put down her bag and knelt down beside the sleeping Margaret. She watched her, moved her hair from her forehead. The movement caused Margaret to shoot up straight. They stared at each other. They didn't know what to say. Mary broke the silence.

"You found me," she said.

"It wasn't easy," Margaret answered.

"But you found me," Mary said.

"Yes, I did," Margaret said.

They embraced, sunk into each other, didn't leave that apartment for three days.

Margaret had found her.

All it cost was her left arm.

Part II

Summer

As the sun set in the east or west or whichever direction it was setting, I walked through the Jordanian desert lost and alone. The burnt skin flaked off my face. My dry hands cracked under the pressure. A slight wind disrupted the sand, shot it into my eyes. I blinked until a limited amount of moisture formed, ran down my cheeks.

In the distance, I saw two large trees and the colour blue. My mind was surely playing tricks on me because as I got closer, the blue turned out to be water. All of a sudden, the fatigue in my feet and in my spirit dissipated, and my steps sped up. I reached the spring, a span of water resembling a kidney-shaped backyard swimming pool out there in the middle of the desert. When I arrived at the trees and the water, I slowly bent down to my knees at the edge. Stopped for a moment, because it's important to appreciate when this happens, when you are lost in the middle of the desert and you find exactly what you're looking for.

Cupped my hands together, reached down into the water, water that was unusually warm and clear. I felt the release of the heat from my rough hands and brought water up to my mouth. Sucked the drops from my palms, spitting it out immediately at the taste of sand on my tongue.

Blinked three times.

The trees disappeared; the kidney-shaped pool disappeared. No water in my hands, only sand. The whole thing a figment of my imagination, the whole thing not true. There was nothing left except rest on my knees and wonder what to do next.

The Long Walk Home

The two-hour walk home from Mary's place was daunting. My head was a bit cloudy, and I took a few wrong turns, started heading south. The Lighthouse Retirement Home was at the northern tip of the city. As the sky darkened, the lights that usually lit the city dimmed and spurted out all at once. The power in the entire city had gone out, creating a darkness we don't normally get in the city. A country darkness. At the same time, fog rolled in.

A moment. One when you're being guided by something else. When you make a decision without thinking, but really couldn't make any other decision.

Checked my watch; it had a compass on its face. The needle shifted around, pulled by the magnetic field of the Earth. It slowly rested on the *N*.

Something told me, guided me, said, *Go, go, go.*

Stepped in the opposite direction. Just like that. Like someone had gently pushed me on the small of the back.

Shopping mall.

The promenade between the Lighthouse and the shopping complex was a new addition. Life-sized iron statues perched on large cement stands. My shadow scanned them as I walked past. The statues represented the evolution of the surrounding neighbourhood, iron people posed in different stages of construction. It reminded me of the stages of the crucifixion that are usually found lining the walls of churches. These people sacrificed the way Jesus sacrificed. The way we all sacrifice.

No one was around. The darkness prevailed, pressed down on the tops of skyscrapers, leaving only outlines of roofs visible. The stars took the sky back, unfazed by their command over the man-made structures, beacons that blinked even as our fires burnt out. The Big Dipper visible. Horologium, Sagittarius, Ursa Major. It didn't matter how far away they were; tonight, the stars were visible with the naked eye.

The moon: full. A spotlight that illuminated the statues, made shadows on the dark, stone ground. The walkway down the centre of the promenade led to the longest street in the city, a straight line on a downward slope directly to the lake, the main artery. I pounded along the sidewalk and realized I could walk down the middle of the street — no one would notice, no one would care. With the North Star at my back, my steps picked up. My spirits raised as the street, my own private walkway, unfolded with each step. There were people about — must've been. Faint candles sparkled in the surrounding condo building windows, resembled still flickering fireflies. Were they scared to come out?

Train tracks crossed over top of the street via a bridge. Connected to the bridge was an old unused station, a water tower shooting toward the sky. A wire fence surrounded the station and extended to a construction zone that blocked the road. I climbed the fence and crossed the abandoned construction area next to the water tower. Water dripped from the tower to the roof and settled along the perimeter of the station. The building cried. I sloshed through its tears, kicked water the way a kid would, climbed the fence on the opposite side. Rejoined the street heading south, always heading south.

A smell hit me: garbage. My senses turned on one at a time; something was happening. I was still me but a different me. Out here, the usually unseen, unwanted throwaways couldn't be thrown far enough away. They just piled up.

A can dropped to the cement, noisily rolled to a stop in the gutter. A greedy raccoon dug into an overturned garbage can. Chucked empty cans over his frustrated shoulders.

I accidentally stepped on a pop can. The raccoon stopped, pulled his head away from his evening snack, watched me. A cat squealed in the distance; I couldn't tell if it was fighting or fornicating. Shadows of bodies bounced off the moon, landed in my peripheral vision, disappeared when I scanned the street. Kept moving, it was only my imagination. The raccoon watched as I walked around him in a large arc.

The soul is only visible in cities. The places people congregate, where energy levels are enhanced. Fires burn brightest in cities, illuminating not the soul of the individual, but the soul of the collective. There are two categories of cities: lucid and grid. Paris is a lucid city: one big sphere of streets that goes around and around and where you can get lost for days. Paris holds the potential for profundity. Grid cities are like this one: streets running north–south and east–west, and it's impossible to lose your way. Boring. But on that evening, something electric was in the air despite the lack of electricity. The grid served me just fine. As Mary once told me: *Die Tränen der Sonne sind nicht sichtbar in den Schatten des Mondes.* The tears of the sun are not visible in the shadow of the moon.

The street dipped into a valley flanked by wooded areas. I heard a noise in the distance, horse hooves on cement. I slipped into the wooded area to the east. The sound grew. I scaled the tree closest to me. The sound approached. A policeman on horseback came over the hill and down the valley. I assumed they were for aesthetic purposes only. He stopped on the road right beside my tree. The horse, a majestic and intimidating animal, defecated on the road, snorted, his nostrils flared as he tried to catch his breath from the run. The policeman scanned the street, shone a flashlight through the wooded area. The beam cut through the dark, unwanted. With his other hand, he unconsciously patted the horse on the neck, stroked him, calmed him. When he was satisfied, the policeman clicked off his flashlight, pulled gently on the reins, and trotted away.

The echo of the hooves dissipated.

My tree sat at the bottom of the valley but rose higher than the hill. Its branches led to the sky, to the stars, and I wanted to reach out and touch them. I climbed higher, right to the top. The trunk thinned, felt less stable. Careful. The city became visible over the hill. Without lights, without electricity, I went back in time. Connect those five stars right there, and they'd form one big star. The Big Dipper. The Little Dipper. Canes Venatici. Camelopardalis. Canis Major. Canis Minor.

Climbing down is always more difficult than climbing up. I hit the ground walking. My vision had completely adapted by then. I noticed rows of planted trees. They didn't randomly grow from the ground. They looked artificial, a human rendering of nature.

The woods led to the cemetery, 10-foot-tall iron gates surrounding the perimeter. The longest road in the city, the tears of the water tower, the raccoon, the horse, the shaft from the flashlight, had all subconsciously pointed this way. One thing connected to another. I had a destination, but it seemed already that something or someone was intent on guiding me. What else could I do but follow? I stood before the gates, another door. Doors within doors. A large chain hung unlocked from a partition halfway up the gate.

Someone forgot to lock it.

The great iron gate creaked, stubborn to open, like it didn't want me to enter. I slipped between gravestones, careful not to step on the plots. People who stepped on plots — I never understood this. You didn't walk into someone's bedroom and step on the bed. The gravestones were pure. Each one a story. Each one a life. Lives had been lived, etched in stone, narrowed down, and encompassed into one phrase.

Gertrude Wilson, 1901 – 1954, loving mother and wife.

Sarah Vabich, 1989 – 1999, too young, too soon.

Corporal John Geddes, 1985 – 2009, died defending his country.

Rows upon rows. The cemetery started small but more land was always needed to bury bodies. Never enough. People died every day. The cemetery was a lucid mini-city within the grid, filled with a deceased population.

John Sims, 1930 – 2002, surrounded by family.

Merriam Glazier, 1980 – 2005, lives on in our memories.

William Geddes, 1895 -1986, yelled out his final bingo.

Walked between plots, checked my compass between strides. The needle bounced with every step. I came upon a giant mausoleum. The moon shone off its domed top, pillars guarded both sides of the door. I rested my hand on the baldheaded marble bust of the mausoleum's deceased resident. The gravestones played tricks on me. Without the hum of the city, without the car horns and the sirens, the people buried here started asking questions. But not questions for me — this was not where my grandmother was buried.

The back exit of the cemetery was about 100 yards away. Someone had been lazy with the front and back iron gates — both unlocked. I reached the border of the cemetery, up the side of the hill, out of the valley, through the opening in the iron gates. Grass turned back into cement. I returned to the longest road in the city and continued on my southbound trajectory.

My steps evened out at the top of the hill, and the road straightened. Red lights bounced off buildings, caused me to squint. An SUV had T-boned a Honda Civic, and the gravity of the police tape, the number of officers, and the three cruisers blocking the road showed that people weren't prepared for the peculiarity of a city plunged into darkness. The paramedics did not rush, a sign of fatalities.

Between where I was standing and the accident scene, a manhole cover popped open with a burst of compressed air. The heavy metal cylinder slid to the side. Gloved hands appeared on the hole's edges, and a figure surfaced wearing a hard hat, goggles, a fluorescent yellow vest with an orange X on the back, and dark blue coveralls. A thin veil of black dirt encased the figure from head to toe. Two other identical looking men crawled out of the manhole behind him.

From behind a parked car, I watched the three men walk over to a van across the street. One talked into a portable radio while the others lit cigarettes, watched the scene. They got into the van and pulled away, headlights cutting through the darkness.

They forgot to put the manhole cover back in place.

A few minutes passed. The police officers' backs were turned as more pressing duties held their attentions elsewhere. I burst across the road, covering the distance to the manhole cover in good time. I shone the penlight on my keychain into the manhole. The light did not touch the bottom; it reached only so far and disappeared. After one last glance at the accident scene, I slipped into the manhole, swallowed like a pill down the throat of the city.

The ladder was slippery, so it was slow moving. Above, the moon was perfectly framed by the sewer opening, a circle within a circle. It provided enough light for me to make my way down. A rumble vibrated through the street, rattled the cement that was now over my head. The van's wheels screeched to a halt, car doors opened–shut, and a radio station played tunes from the 1970s, introduced The Who's "Won't Get Fooled Again." Remembering what they forgot, two of the workers dragged the manhole cover over the opening without looking to see if anyone was down here — why *would* there be anyone down here? As the cover slid back into position, the moon disappeared, and I went from seeing a full moon to a half moon until the heavy metal cylinder slammed into place, leaving me in complete darkness, completely alone.

Only one way to go.

It seemed to take longer to reach the bottom than you would think. The world was different in the dark, even more different in the dark *and* underground. My right foot unexpectedly hit cement, and I felt for the landing with my left foot. Was still for a moment as I got my bearings, whatever they might have been.

Flicked on my small penlight. The ceiling was rounded; slimy block cement stones made up the walls. I stood on a landing and water flowed down the centre of the tunnel. I didn't want to know how deep the water ran. While I surveyed the tunnel, movements caught the corners of the light: rats. A doorless doorway stood on the other side of the trough. I leapt over the water, slipped on the other side, got my balance by grabbing on to a divot that poked out of the wall. Pulled my body toward the curved soggy wall.

The door led into the subway tunnel. Silence. With no electricity, the subways were stopped in their tracks. The tunnel mirrored the sewer with its curved ceiling. I flashed the penlight on my compass watch. The needle went crazy but eventually settled on the *N*. Adjusted the light in the direction of south. The tunnel went on forever. I jumped down onto the tracks. Beware the third rail. If the electricity suddenly came on, that third rail would kill me. I didn't want to see what was actually in the dark. The air was humid, heavy.

Strangely, I felt safe down here, taking toe-steps between the wooden planks that ran down the centre of the tracks.

The subway tunnel veered to the left. A train sat in front of me, trapped between stations. Red emergency lights illuminated the shadowed bodies inside. I approached slowly, stepped on the platform to the right of the train. Peeked through a window. People sat on the floor. Many had eyes closed. One woman rocked back and forth in a cross-legged position on the floor. A man paced.

The woman stopped rocking when she saw me. She got up from her cross-legged position on the floor. Her face appeared larger as she approached the window. She squinted at me, her nose pressed against the pane. She leaned her hand on the glass, fanned her palm so the skin flattened. A thin smile pulled at her cheeks. I placed my hand on my side of the window so it matched hers. I matched her smile with some difficulty as I watched my own reflection in the woman's reflection. It might've been the red emergency lights playing tricks or fooling shadows, but the left side of her face appeared to carry a birthmark covering her temple. Chloe? Okay, what were the chances that I had recently started thinking about her, developed this weird affliction about moving vehicles, started walking, and the lights had gone out, just as Chloe showed up in the city, jumped on a subway, then the subway stopped, I jumped down a manhole, found the exact train she was on and here we were? The woman smiled wider, telling me through her smile that she wanted me to know this was a possibility.

And then she screamed.

Everyone in the subway car sat up, joined in her terror. The scream was excruciating. She backed away from the window, pointed at me. I ducked below the window, crouched and moved quickly along the side of the subway car. Once at the front of the train, I jumped back down between the tracks.

It wasn't Chloe.

Beware the third rail.

The woman's scream pursued me, vibrated off the walls.

I dared not run out of fear of tripping. I speed walked. I wanted out. At the next station, I hopped up onto the platform. The station was empty except for a woman waiting for a train that wasn't coming. She raised her eyebrows, and I shrugged, ran across to the south exit. Music echoed through the station — an old Chinese man sat on a small stool, plucked at strings, bounced music off the walls. He had thick, black glasses on, his head tilted to the sky. Blind, he didn't realize the lights were out. I took the stairs two at a time. The wind had built up, trapped in the subway tunnel, and it spat me out onto the street, to the outside I now needed. Looked behind me while I crossed the street. Returned to my path.

My phone beeped with a text message: *What're you up to? Can you talk now?*

The smooth granite sidewalks from before I entered the sewer had changed, cracked. A different neighbourhood, one not taken care of, where wealth was less visible. Gentrification only goes so far. The street was an obstacle course. Potholes zigzagged, and I hopscotched between them. Shops with barred windows lined one side, broken-down houses the other. An abandoned car, front tires missing, the empty chambers balanced on wooden blocks, rust eating away at the corners of the doors. A group of men hunched in an alleyway, exchanged money. Surrounded by cars with headlights criss-crossed in a lattice of light, they watched me as I passed. The people here weren't afraid of the darkness like those up north. A large man in an ill-fitting sleeveless shirt sat on a white plastic patio chair fingering an unlit cigar. He needed a shave. Beside him, in an identical chair, sat the Virgin Mary. The statue kneeled, hands forming a triangle of prayer. The man had his arm around her like they were on a date, enjoying the stars in the sky. After I passed him, he followed me. Confused cars braked and hit the gas, the blackened stoplights caused chaos. A concerned citizen stood in the middle of the intersection with a whistle, tried to direct traffic. He seemed to be having fun but the cars weren't paying attention, and he seemed to cause more harm than good. At the corner of the intersection stood a different statue: Pope John Paul II. With arms outstretched, he welcomed me to him. There were religious candles lit at his feet. Cigar Man walked right past me, snatched one of the religious candles, held it to the end of his cigar, puffed away until smoke bellowed from his mouth. He returned to Mary. He kept the candle. Was that a sin?

Tires screeched.

The entertainment district.

Bars opened for business, more candles illuminated glassy-eyed faces, acoustic guitars led mass singalongs. A young couple kissed in the closed entrance of the store next door. His hand crept under her shirt. Lots of babies would be made in the dark on this night.

I slipped unnoticed past the bars to where the street opened up and a park ran parallel. A statue of Winston Churchill stood tall. The inscription on the base of the statue read, I HAVE NOTHING TO OFFER BUT BLOOD, TOIL, TEARS, AND SWEAT. Churchill's feet spread like scissor blades, left foot forward and right foot back. His arms rested on the small of his back, coat tucked behind them. He was thinking, frozen, forever trying to figure it out after all these years. Churchill stood watch over the large, impersonal government buildings, a reminder. Over the years, he faded into the background, usurped by the bombastic billboards and advertisements around him.

Catching sight of a public washroom behind Churchill, I instantly had to go. The door latch unlocked. No windows. Saw with my hands, found the urinal.

"Hey, bub," a voice said out of the darkness, almost causing an accident with my pant's zipper. "Don't be scared, bub. If there's one thing I want, I don't want you to be scared."

Focused on relieving myself, I didn't notice the smell. Worse than the sewer. Heat from another body filled the washroom suddenly. My eyes failed to adjust. The body heat came closer.

"There's a toll, bub. For using the washroom. Come on. I got nothing to eat, I've gone blind. Can't see a damn thing. You have anything for me?"

A hand grabbed my arm.

The grip on my forearm tightened in the darkness. The body heat.

The fingers were strong, I pried them from around my arm one by one. Turned, bumped into the wall, rolled along the wall until I found the door. Outside, the smell receded, sealed and contained with the closed door.

My thoughts were still in the washroom; my pants were falling down. Pulled them up, zipped, tripped over three knocked-over garbage cans.

The signs turned from English to Chinese characters. Streets narrowed, and shops were still open here: cheap tourist gifts, clothes for ridiculously low prices, rows and rows of produce, and other things not easily identifiable. Shop owners yelled at each other and at customers, cigarettes dangled from lips. Old women sat on overturned milk crates selling fresh herbs. Men squatted, balanced on the balls of their feet, ignored me as I passed.

The alleyway stretched out to the bottom of the city. Empty. Graffiti enhanced the bare walls. Designs of sad people, skeletons, monsters and aliens lined the cement structures. Graffiti is a language all on its own, a series of messages desperately reaching out to find open eyes. The tags unlock more than the author intends, exist outside our usual realm of communication. They are modern-day cave paintings that wait to be deciphered. I couldn't translate the tags; I wasn't prepared to understand them. But then I saw something in the chaos. I saw the same tag I'd seen in New York, the one on the wall of the building where I talked to Chloe's friend and co-worker. An image that resembled the birthmark on Chloe's left temple. Frozen, I touched the identical image. Electricity shot through my fingers, and I stepped backwards out of the alley to the street.

Tripped and fell to the stiff pavement.

A voice grunted.

A big, burly man was on his back on the ground. His eyes were open, his shirt revealed a sagging belly. A crowd had formed, thought he was drunk, tried to convince him to get out of the road.

A woman blew rings of cigarette smoke around the burly man and shouted, "Come on, man, get up, go home, sleep it off."

A more concerned gawker reasoned, "Shouldn't we roll him onto his side?"

As I stood up, the man grabbed my left ankle. We turned into statues for a long time. His fire was burning out, and he desperately wanted to hold on. Hold on to something, even if it was my ankle. I nodded to him, gently took his wrist in my hand, and he let go. I shifted my weight, lay down beside him on my back. Rolled over until I was beside him. Looked into his eyes.

"I'm not drunk," he said softly.

"I know," I said, and I did know.

"Something else," he said.

I smiled at him and he tried to smile back — there was evidence of effort. We just lay on the road without speaking. His eyes watered; he didn't want anyone to ask questions. Tears succumbed to gravity and slid down his temples, pooled in his unkempt sideburns.

The crowd quieted, slowly dissipated. We lay there, the two of us, holding on. I had to move forward, couldn't move forward. But we weren't alone, this man and I.

As I floated to my feet a second time, the man didn't grab my ankle. He nodded at me, knew I had to keep going. Knew he would find a way to keep going.

Along the street, I came across a line of abandoned streetcars, frozen in their tracks like old men refusing to move. Similar to the subway, the downfall of travel by electricity. The door of one of the streetcars was open. I've always wanted to drive one of these. Looked around, stepped up, and sat down in the driver's seat. Pushed buttons, flipped switches, rang the bell, checked transfers, accepted fares, said hello and goodbye to passengers, and kicked rude ones off. Stamped my foot on the gas pedal and the streetcar lurched forward, a last gasp of electricity must have remained in its bowels. It smacked into the back of the one in front. I exited the streetcar and split down a side street.

The financial district. Signs that usually spelled out the latest rise and fall of stocks had nothing to report. A man in a pinstripe suit paced back and forth before the front doors of the monolithic bank building, his tie undone. There would be no money made tonight. The neighbourhood was eerily quiet, empty except for the pinstriped man yelling at his phone for not working.

I crossed back onto the longest street in the city. It led past the train station, under a bridge. Cars passed, headlights rolling against the brown cement walls. The entrance to the highway cut pedestrians off from the lake. Went up–over the barrier. The water was ahead.

The industrial area that bordered the lake was from another era. The sugar factory was sealed off as though it held government secrets. I scaled the fence. Giant cylinders. Long ramps criss-crossed from one seemingly empty warehouse to another.

Popped out of the factory's promenade onto the docks. The city came to an end. I sat down and looked out over the water. A lonely canoe banged gently against the dock. The ferry had stopped running for the night. The docks were empty.

And I had a grand idea.

And the electricity returned.

And the city lit up: fireworks.

And the fog rolled across the lake.

And I glowed with the city as its lights hit the back of my neck.

And I just kept walking.

Walked through the night. The soles of my shoes grew smooth. Socks chafed the skin of my ankles. Didn't bother me. The land was mostly flat and unchallenging. The challenge came from my will. Still I moved forward. Headed around the lake, just kept to the lake, didn't stray. Wasn't sure exactly where I was going, but felt something guided me as the sun came up.

The trees whistled in the bright sun, swayed with noises of

invisible animals. The animals watched me from their perches, seeing a new sight: a man walking. Cars passed by; drivers honked their horns. And still I kept moving forward. Forward into the future. Brought the future into the present. Made the present my reality. My feet hurt. The blister on my little toe spread, the pain striking across my foot. This neither deterred me nor discouraged me. In a funny way, it pushed me ever forward. My momentum, once accessed, understood the necessary requirements.

The blacktop looked the same everywhere in the world. The night was different but the same. I moved through it, under a clear sky; the stars led the way. The parchedness of my throat spoke of a struggle to reach the end. But what was the end?

The blisters jumped to the other foot. Spread like cancer. Pain shot up my calves — the calves hadn't worked this hard in a long time. The quadriceps tightened and contracted, becoming stronger. Muscles stretched. Spine straightened as I walked. Over the years, my spine had curved, slumped from shoulders that were held too tight to my ears. By holding my shoulders tight, I kept the memories in check and buried them. When they dropped, the pain would send electric currents to my brain, zap me so I felt it in my fingertips. Then my shoulders would jump back up and the whole process would redouble its efforts. Stress endured, made knots that connected, solid masses that could not be altered. These solid masses were cracking, loosening up.

The blisters persisted and a new pain shot up my Achilles tendon. The old pain from the polio and the plane injury returned, caused some limping — the body made adjustments. The pain made me focus on each step, the pain determined to keep me in the present.

Legs tired. The rhythm of forward momentum trumped tiredness.

Out here, there was a force at work. My body buzzed a little more with every step. I imagined that I was coming in contact with the magnetic pull of the earth and this energy provided me with strength. My soles treaded lightly on the ground. The electricity emanating from the earth travelled through my body and created room for other thoughts. This mix of physical pain and potential energy felt useful, something I could bend to my own needs.

The mind starts to think strange things alone on the road. An energy — formed, shaped, unexplainable — mixed up my insides. My steps became more meaningful, each step creating an opportunity. If I could centre this energy, harness this magnetic field and, with my intention, bend this life force and thrust it both internally and externally at the same time, what would the potential be? Each of my steps was an apology, accumulated apologies for years of living inside stasis.

At some point someone will say, "You are forgiven."

At some point I will say, "You are forgiven."

And the blisters will cease to affect me.

Not yet.

I watched the sun rise. A particular stretch of flat blacktop reached to the horizon, touched the sun, propped it up, and encouraged it to travel across the atmosphere. The morning air chilled my bones. Inside and underneath my clothes, a sweaty wetness seeped in and remained. Crept in and wouldn't leave. This moisture wasn't something I could bring out into the warm rays of the sun and wring the wetness out of; it was only cured of coldness and brittleness on its own under my skin.

Bugs buzzed around my head, followed me for a distance. I didn't swat them away, instead thought of them as companions. The carcass of a squirrel lay flattened on the road. The body had tire marks running across its torso, eyes bulged out of its head. It had taken the risk of crossing the street, and sometimes risks don't work out in the end.

With the sun directly overhead, after walking into the day, I saw a sign that read, "Welcome to the County of Batavia, Population 6293." The town sprawled in the distance. I sat down on a rock beside the sign. My feet felt like they were floating, swollen like balloons and ready to take off into the sky.

Don't recall how long I sat there. When I snapped back to the present, the sun was in an entirely different place.

It all started with the boy in the blue cap. I didn't see him at first. I don't know how long he was there watching me. After my recognition, we stared: a standoff. He broke the silence.

"Where you coming from?" the boy asked.

Only a sigh emanated from my body, and I realized I hadn't spoken to anyone since the man lying on the road.

"You walked?" he asked.

"Yeah," I said after clearing my throat. "Yeah, from the city."

"You look tired. You want a drink?" he asked.

"Sure."

The image of a chilled glass of water filled my mind.

"Can you walk a bit more into town?"

"Yeah," I said through parched lips.

The boy whistled and four others appeared from the woods adjacent to the road.

"You must be thirsty. We gotta get a drink for the walking man."

At the edge of town, there was a combination gas station and convenience store. An old-fashioned Coke machine sat beside the wooden steps leading up to the door of the store. The boy in the blue cap kicked the machine, and it whirled and groaned and popped out a bottle of Coke. He cracked it open with the bottle opener attached to the machine, and the boys handed it off from one to another until it reached me.

The bottle was cold in my hand and already sweating in the sun. I walked over to the steps and sat down. Gulped the pop — the fizziness shocked my throat. When I finished, out of breath, I took in the town. The main street a straight line, and you could see the end of it far in the distance. The buildings were all attached — two storeys each — and stores mixed with houses and combined with the institutions found in every small town.

The parade was improvised.

The boys viewed me like I'd dropped from the sky. I wondered what I looked like. Felt my face — the stubble was rough on my chin and cheeks. I must have had that strange in-between look. My bones were still cold from the night, but the boys didn't know this. They also didn't know that I needed something else from them. Or I assumed they didn't know.

We all made the decision at the same time. The decision to keep walking. And so we did, a procession of five with me in the middle, flanked by two boys on each side.

The first house we approached had a porch that was sliding into the ground. A portly old man sat wiping his brow with a handkerchief. The boys ran up the stairs and pulled him to his feet. This was a town where everyone knew each other. They helped him down the sliding stairs and presented him to me like a gift.

"This is the walking man," the boy in the blue cap said.

"I am the old man," the old man said.

We continued our walk down the street. Our steps slowed to accommodate the old man. We didn't mind.

"Why are you walking?" the old man asked.

"I don't know," I replied.

The old man nodded as if he understood, and I think he did.

A few buildings later, an attractive young woman with pointy glasses and grey-as-ash hair stepped out of the library. Her head was down and she bumped right into us, dropping all the books she had clasped in her arms. She excused herself and smiled at me. I smiled back, and she too seemed to understand without my having to explain. This was what I wanted: not to have to explain. The boys picked up her books and carried them for her as she fell in line.

A car pulled up slowly beside us. An old blue sedan with bucket seats. An old woman sat in the driver's seat, barely able to see over the steering wheel.

"Earl, what're you doing?" she called to the old man through the window.

The old man turned to me, saying, "My lovely wife Cheryl." To her, he said, "Out for a walk."

Cheryl allowed us to pass and fell in behind us. She honked her horn, prompting more people to join.

We didn't say much to each other. We didn't have to. There was an understanding between the walkers. A curious lot, we were people who wanted to be on our own but sometimes chose to be with others. We shared an awareness that the second state would not last. Independence always beckoned us. The reasons we started walking in the first place would return. But for now, in that particular moment, the desire to be around each other was stronger than the pull of independence.

Between silences, Earl told me the town was made up of people who worked down under the ground in a mine beyond the outskirts. The mine breathed life into the town. The sun was high in the sky, signalled lunchtime. Earl pointed a crooked finger down the road. There was a group of 15 men walking toward us. Dirty, they wore identical coveralls and had hard hats with spotlights. Some of the lights were still turned on, made them look as if they were having ideas, great ideas. Some of the men were fathers of the walking boys, and they hugged and tussled hair. The boys dragged the men to join us. I thought this was a great idea, especially when I turned to see all the spotlights on. Even though it was daytime, the lights led the way.

Our energy combined, travelled along with us. My intention grew, and my desire to bend this combined energy grew. This energy seemed to hover above us; I conjured it, sent it flying across fields and through cities.

We came upon a hippy-looking fellow. He had long hair, and he sat on his porch with a guitar in his lap. He joined immediately. He played his guitar and added a soundtrack to our thoughts. Urged us on.

And the turkeys.

So far, I had seen owls hooting, squirrels collecting, groundhogs digging, deer running. When we passed the post office, a family of wild turkeys crossed the street. It was the first time we stopped. Earl assured me this was normal; the surrounding lands had been the turkeys' home long before the settlement of the county. And the turkeys had the right of way.

"We don't eat them," Earl said. "We're all vegetarians."

I couldn't help thinking that I should be giving thanks for something. The turkeys were fat but full of life. They marched with their heads held high, chests out. A part of me wanted to follow them to see where they would lead me. The turkeys stopped and regarded us with the same questionable curiosity. They fell in line beside us. Urged us on.

Earl wiped his brow with his handkerchief. The design was the American flag. I put my hand on his forearm, and he shrugged it off. People peeked out windows and flipped signs on their storefronts from OPEN to CLOSED. They fell in line behind us as if this happened every day. We allowed it to happen. It was essential.

We finally reached the end of the town line, and the restaurant on the corner already had the barbecue going full blast, smoke rising from its closed lid. Halfway through our parade, two of the boys ran ahead and alerted the restaurant owner of our approach. Chairs were brought out, and everyone sighed as we sat down. Beers circulated and we cheered to nothing in particular. We ate veggie burgers and veggie dogs, and had more beer, and broke the silence of the walk. We talked about their town, and they told me about the mine, about the generations that have grown up here, about how things have changed.

I sat under the awning of the restaurant. The heat from the barbecue echoed the sun. As the afternoon wore on, the sun lowered in the sky, scared the shade away. The rays kissed my feet. The sun slowly moved up my legs and hit me right in the face.

Earl put his hand on my shoulder, and I looked into his eyes. They were deep. The wrinkles had seen a lot. I opened my mouth to say something, but he cut me off, asked me to stay with him and his wife; they had a bed free in their spare room.

We talked late into the night. I assumed that once the opportunity of sleep presented itself, my body would give in. But we sat at their kitchen table, and I listened to their story, and they listened to mine. Talking felt good. I wondered if it would make me uncomfortable, make me retreat. Earl and Cheryl were old and grew tired after midnight.

I paused, listened to the silence of the house.

Appreciated the shower. The bed was lumpy, but I didn't care. Couldn't care. The room at Earl and Cheryl's house used to be their oldest son's room. They left it the same as when he suffered his tragedy. That's their story to tell. Posters on the wall. Baseball trophies on the mantel. His plaid shirts hung in the closet. History. Dots.

The bed was a single, similar to the one from my childhood. With the lights off, the room was slightly illuminated by the dim glow of the moon, shining through thin red drapes that had a patchwork design. I knew that I desperately needed to sleep, but the position of the bed and the way it faced the window caused the light of the moon to crest a shadow on the ceiling like the birthmark. This room, the innocence of it, the childlike quality brought me backwards in time. I blinked and the posters and trophies disappeared, replaced with crudely written words in black marker, words written with haste and immediacy and emotion.

My phone beeped with a text message: *Why don't you come visit me?*

Me: *Where do you live?*

Her: *The opposite side of the lake.*

Me: *I'm heading in that direction.*

The smell of fresh coffee circulated throughout the house. The aroma found its way under the bedroom door and roused me from sleep. I dressed, made my way down to find a full breakfast with eggs, hash browns, and vegetarian bacon. We didn't talk as much as the previous night; we were hungover from talking.

Easy goodbye. The light conversation and politeness cast melancholy on the scene. I would never see Earl and Cheryl again. Realization came to all three of us at the same time. We smiled in unison.

Renewed perspective. I felt refreshed. Checked my compass watch and followed the lake. The houses became more sporadic. With every block there were more trees. The blisters were sidelined for now. Body ached, but an ache that felt responsible. An ache derived from forward movement.

A collection of dense trees lined the lake, pushing me further from the water, so I walked into the trees. Ten steps in, I discovered this was more forest-like than just a bunch of solitary spruces. Drudging through the moist dirt, avoiding thick, visible roots, the residue and adrenaline of the improvised parade still ran on a treadmill in my head. Walked for hours and came upon a clearing that would be perfect for a fire for the approaching night.

The fire proved difficult. This was something I had never learned — never questioned why I'd never learned it until I found myself in this situation. The closest I ever came to building a fire was the fireplace channel. Some things cannot be learned through the Internet.

Tried slamming two rocks together to make a spark but no sparks appeared — it looked so easy when others did it. I took the rocks and made a firepit, found others to complete a full circle, hoped this would motivate me to actually figure out the fire part. Kindling, that's what was missing — the whole thing needed a base, something to actually catch fire. Kindling, I should have thought about it before. Gathered some small branches, built a solid base but needed more wood since I had turned it all into kindling. Went looking for wood.

That's when the knight leapt out of the woods brandishing a sword.

He was close. He swung the sword on a diagonal, and it came swooshing down and chopped into the ground. The sword was stuck, and as the knight struggled to pull it free, I stepped back and attempted to process the situation. The knight liberated the sword like Excalibur and rushed at me — although "rushed" was not really the right word. He was not used to the movements of the metal and all the weight; he moved as if through water. I easily dodged the sword, twisted his arm until he dropped it.

Brought him to my fireless camp by sword point. He fell to the ground, and I helped him off with his helmet. The image of Luke Skywalker removing Darth Vader's helmet at the end of *Return of the Jedi*, revealing what was left of his feeble father's humanity, popped into my head. I thrust the sword into the ground and it pinged back and forth. The knight was an old man — past 65, at least — with sandpaper skin, chapped lips, and hair shooting straight in the air from the left side of his domed head, hair that he attempted to pat down in an enormous comb-over. Looked like someone's grandfather who had Werthers in his pocket and had forgotten where he parked the car. His eyes interested me: shrunken in their sockets, under joined eyebrows that sprouted from a prolonged forehead. His eyes seemed to be saying something, and that something didn't always match what came out of his mouth. He rooted around under his armour and pulled out, instead of a Werthers, a small flask. He offered it to me.

"I am lost," he said.

"Can you even see through this thing?" I asked, turning over the helmet in my hands.

"It's not as bad as you think," he said. "Sometimes I forget I have it on."

"This helmet—"

"—Bascinet," he corrected.

"Bascinet, sorry. Must weigh like ten pounds."

"Where's the fire?" he said as he thrust his chin toward the pit. He took a swig from his flask.

"First I had to build the firepit," I said, somewhat embarrassed.

"Yeah, and a firepit usually has a fire, or it's just a pit."

"Okay, so, can we back up a bit here?"

"I'm not going anywhere, even if I could get up."

I paused for a thoughtful moment and then said, "I could ask, oh, I don't know … what are you doing out here alone?"

"I could ask you the same question."

"You could, but could you ask me: what are you doing out here alone dressed as a medieval knight?"

It was his turn to look thoughtful. "Maybe," he said. "Depends on the situation."

"Right. Okay. And, well, since we're in this particular situation, I could also ask, what're you doing out here alone dressed as a medieval knight leaping out of the woods attacking people?"

He started laughing. "Let's get a fire going and I'll tell you."

"We need to get some wood first. I turned it all into kindling."

"Help me up. You bring the sword, I'll bring the whiskey."

We made a good team, the knight and I. Although he did a lot of pointing and sitting while I did a lot of chopping. Difficult to chop wood with a sword. Must say, he built the fire quickly and efficiently, using little wood. It kept us for the night.

"Anything to eat?" the knight asked.

"Not really. Some energy bars," I said.

"Will these give me the runs or keep me up all night?"

"Don't think so, but I can't say for sure."

"Good, I can't even drink coffee after 11:00 a.m. or I won't sleep."

Pulled out two bars, handed him one, kept the other for myself. We snacked and watched the fire, listened to it crackle away.

"Not bad," the knight said, his mouth full.

"What's your name?" I asked.

"Tobias. You?"

I told him.

"And what are you doing out here all alone?"

"Just walking. You're not lost, are you?" I was taking a chance here, but so be it.

"AWOL. Damn kids talked me into this, and they get here and take it all serious-like. My son's a captain, and I'm just taking care of the horses. He had me clean out his latrine yesterday. I thought you were one of 'em."

"Don't mean to pry, but what in the hell's going on here?"

Tobias ignored my question and looked down at his armour — apparently I was prying. He fingered the underside of the armour encasing his hip. I thought it was a nervous tic, but I was wrong.

"It's comfortable when you don't move. You almost forget about it. Almost. Help me outta this, will you? I got another fifth of whiskey hidden in here somewhere."

I helped Tobias out of his armour. We stoked the fire higher. We each had a flask now; the second one was large enough for me to wonder where he had kept it.

"My son's a member of the *Medieval Society Re-enactment Assemblage: Keeping the Past Alive for the Future.* He's a captain."

"And you're a...?"

"I take care of the horses. He roped me into it — those damn people don't even know how to ride. And when there's all 500 members on the battlefield, the horses are the last thing they think about. Their era is the reign of King Edward III, around the time of 1365, give or take a decade or two. This out here's their yearly EBUFU — 'Events By Us For Us.' Usually they do banquets, cultural events, or birthdays. I'm supposed to be bonding with my son."

"Not working out the way you thought?"

"They operate under the rules of the time. I work with the horses. He's a damn captain and uses every opportunity to tell me what to do. You should see these people. I know all about it — too much, really. There's three kinds of re-enactors. First, the Farbs, who aren't very concerned with maintaining authenticity with uniforms, accessories, or behaviour. Amateurs. Then there are the Mainstream re-enactors. They make an effort but come out of character without an audience. My son's little troupe is part of the third kind: Progressives, who are so damn crazy, they fully immerse themselves in the lives of the people from the period, in this case 1365. Nothing can be used that was employed after the date of the re-enactment. Nothing — think about that."

We were surrounded, re-enactors were apparently all around us, and I looked, trying to see past the illumination of the fire into the dark trees for foot soldiers. Once I thought about it, it did feel like we were being watched, people out there beyond the woods, regarding my zippers as though they were from the future — which I guess they were, if you looked at things through a Progressive's perspective.

"How'd you know I wasn't lost?" I asked.

"Because you look like you know where you're going," he said.

With help from the whiskey, we both drifted off into a sound sleep.

The next morning I awoke to a sword at my throat. Not again. Surrounded. Tobias snored away until one of the three knights knelt down beside him, shook him awake. Tobias slowly came to, mildly confused until he wiped the cobwebs away and absorbed the situation. His furry eyebrows lowered, and as he rolled his eyes, they seemed to sink farther into his head.

"Tobias, we are off to battle, you must redeem this pathetic display and once again prove your bravery," the captain said.

Tobias turned to me. "My son," he said and turned back to the captain. "Johnny—"

"Captain to you."

Tobias looked over at me, and his eyes said: *See what I mean?*

The captain turned to me. "Who's this? Your stable boy?"

The other two knights laughed, but it was the kind of forced laugh required when a superior cracks a bad joke. Tobias stared at me with those eyes. The captain motioned to the other knights that it was time to leave. I helped Tobias on with his armour, and we kicked the smoking fire out. We marched. I was between the captain and the other two knights; Tobias struggled to keep up, resembled the Tin Man with his metal skin.

Within ten minutes, we arrived at the camp. Rows of tents lined a break in the trees. Knights of all sizes sharpened swords and packed arrow sheaths. Women tended to the children — yes, the children — who were also dressed, I guessed, as children would have dressed in 1365. I wondered if they would even have been present. Things have changed over the last few hundred years, or maybe this was "Bring

Your Child to Medieval Re-enactment Day." There were giant cauldrons filled with root vegetables foraged from the local grocery store. Like in the good old days, there seemed to be a hierarchy at work — the one that Tobias had explained to me and was clearly a victim of. Everyone went quiet when an elaborately dressed woman wandered between the tents. Tobias whispered to me that it was the Queen. I asked where the King was, but Tobias shrugged.

The eve of battle.

Tobias and I were ordered to wash the horses. Punishment. You could have officially referred to me as a stable boy. Tobias and I washed the horses and watched knights sparring and archers aiming at bull's eyes. The clanks of sword on sword filled the air, and the thwacks of bows were interrupted by the cries of archers hurting their thumbs and index fingers, incorrectly releasing arrows.

I should have commended the attempt, but I was more confused than impressed by this full-scale adult make-believe.

Once the Queen had walked by, the hushed tone remained; perhaps she reminded those present what they were here for. Let's put aside the fact that these re-enactments were exactly that: re-enactments. They all knew who was going to win and who was going to lose.

Either way, this was all getting very serious.

I looked into the large eyes of the horse — black-pooled eyes that pointed straight out to the sides. Tobias told me when a horse is born, it can walk within a matter of hours. Since I'd started walking pretty much when I was born, perhaps I had been a horse in another life. These horses belonged to Tobias and were on loan to the Society; that's why he was really here. He wanted to make sure they were taken care of properly. Tobias had a calming influence on the horses. He certainly calmed me down. We didn't speak very much except for his intermittent explanations of this or that horse's name with descriptions of their various personalities. He explained how this horse was from a broken home and had been aggressive until the horse believed Tobias was no threat. He explained how that horse was generational, came from a line of horses that stretched back to when Tobias was a kid.

As we got deeper into the night, ale was brought out for the soldiers, and the camp turned into some kind of bizarre medieval frat house. The ale was strong, and everyone was drunk within an hour. If I had been the enemy and one to completely disregard historical authenticity, I would have pulled a sneak attack. There was an archer face down in the grass, the captain puked behind his tent, the King was hitting on someone who was not the Queen, and the Queen was dancing on a table in a most un-Queen-like fashion. I would have attacked while these sorry re-enactors tried to fire a sword with a bow and have a sword fight with arrows. Was this what happened the night before the big battle in 1365? With a bit of ale, these Progressives transformed into falling-down drunk Farbs.

Tobias and I sat on the grass outside the ring of fire. We were told by two drunken knights to get ready for battle at first light. The enemy had been sighted and confrontation was imminent. We rested for a while longer until it was time. I helped Tobias into his armour; he refilled the flasks and fit them in before we finished putting on the entire suit. We said nothing but everything at the same time.

There was tension in the air — worried looks on the young soldiers putting out the fires, older men sharpening swords, knowing this might be their last chance to see action. This was either the most ridiculous showcase of adult delusion or an extremely earnest display of obsession.

Tobias was ready, and we were summoned.

Johnny — the captain — gave a rousing speech to the troops but had to do it twice because he forgot to turn on his helmet-cam, or Bascinet-cam, I guess you could've called it. I shouldn't talk — me with my zippers and running shoes and all — but a mini-camera inside your helmet for live streaming on the Internet didn't seem very "Progressive" to me. They posted the video for other re-enactors to watch and judge whether it was authentic enough. The speech was not overly inspiring, perhaps due to his hangover —

some people were natural kings or captains, and others pretended to be kings or captains. And then we marched out, all the men. The men seemed to have all the fun while the women and children sat at the camp making candle wax. However, this way, they didn't have to put their lives in pseudo-danger and the men saw firsthand whom they were pseudo-fighting for.

I walked with Tobias stumbling along beside me. Through it all he kept one eye on the horses and the men who straddled them. We trekked for almost an hour through the woods before coming to a clearing where the enemy had already set up. No sneak attacks here — they made appointments to make believe. There was a standoff between the two armies as they attempted to intimidate each other. Even though I knew this was all being re-enacted, there was a sense of apprehension, of holding your breath, of wondering what's going to happen and even wondering if you'd make it out of here alive. One thing was for sure: there were a lot of people who enjoyed spending their time in make-believe places.

Hundreds of people on both sides.

Why would they enter into this? The past was the past and could not be changed — if they were the losers, did they actually go into this believing that the outcome would be different? All this wallowing in what has been.

I was thinking about how pathetic this all was when I looked at myself, looked back years, saw the choices I'd made, and wondered who was worse: these sorry people attempting to recapture a moment in history, or me trying to push history so far back that it ceased to be a part of me and became, instead, a big black hole that I lived in, one where I could safely ignore any and all experiences that had shaped my life. I forgot them intentionally only to have them come back and bite me in the ass. Only I didn't know if it was these memories or experiences because they were gone gone gone never to return, but maybe I needed them, needed to live inside them, needed to feel the feelings of whatever it was that had made me want to forget.

The captains yelled at each other a bit. Each asked for the other to surrender. Neither of them would do it. They both turned toward their own armies and gave the orders to attack. The two armies ran at each other, and there was a series of strange fights where knights swung their swords and sort of hit each other, and pulled back on their bows and kind of let arrows go, and threatened others with lances but didn't actually do anything. They yelled out, "Contact," and the opposing knights fell to the ground and acted dead. It was a flurry of chaos as people yelled at each other, fell down, cheered, died (sort of), and fought. Someone's going to get hurt, but more out of clumsiness than from any form of real battle.

I stuck with Tobias and the horses — the riders had gotten off because the animals were deemed too dangerous to ride into battle. We watched the chaos unfold before us, looked at each other, and realized at the same time that everyone was distracted, busy getting kind-of killed or kind-of killing.

What happened next happened very fast.

I helped Tobias out of his armour. We took everything off except his belt and put the flasks in my bag. He called his four horses, jumped up on one, and yelled at me to jump on the one beside him. I told him I'd never ridden a horse before. He yelled to jump on, that they were the most well-behaved horses he'd ever worked with. I jumped on the horse. Tobias yelled HAY-YA and we were off.

And that's how I found myself riding a horse, an escaped prisoner of war from a faux medieval battle, galloping beside an AWOL old man, naked except for boxers and a Bascinet.

I rode with him back to his truck where we loaded the horses. The riding was something else. Truth be told, horses scared me — those large animals we think we've tamed. I always thought horses had much more intelligence than we gave them credit for. Sure, we put shoes on them and dressed them up, but they could potentially go off at any moment. It was up to them really — if they made the decision that they didn't want people sitting on their backs, what choice would we have?

The riding was fast and I had no time to think about it — probably the only reason I survived and stayed on top of the animal. Kept mentally apologizing to the horse, whose name was Ringo, because if I thought about someone riding on my back, I wouldn't have been happy about it either. The wind was whipping by, and the threat of being thrown to the ground very real and palpable. Doing something with another animal, melding into one, working together as not a horse and its human rider but something more similar to a mythical creature, half horse and half human — a centaur?

We arrived at the truck, and I had to get off this animal that looked taller and further away from the ground than before. Sort of half jumped off–half fell off and when I hit the ground, even Ringo snorted with what I interpreted as a chuckle.

Tobias had already loaded his horse and the other two that were with us: John, Paul, and George. They all looked very happy to be rid of the people on their backs and stepped into the truck without hesitation. I guessed that John, Paul, George, and Ringo were not impressed with the re-enactors either. Ringo dropped his head, rubbed against me in an affectionate gesture. I patted his long nose and helped Tobias guide him into the truck. The door closed and we said our goodbyes. We didn't have much to say — it had certainly been a bizarre two days hanging out with Tobias. He offered me a drive, but I declined and he didn't push it. He wanted to give me something, so he removed the knife hanging from his belt and passed it to me.

"You never know," he said.

Tobias jumped into the cab of his truck, started her up, and held his hand out the window in a fist as dust kicked up in his wake.

I walked for a bit and crossed a farmer's large field, passing between tall stacks of hay that rustled in the light wind. Once through the field, I splashed across a shallow lake. The lake was probably higher at a different time of the year.

After I got away from the rolling sound of the water, I thought I heard something. A voice riding on the wind. Stopped, listened. Nothing. I took a step and heard it again. Stopped again. Nothing again. I waited for a long time — there it was, heard it. Looked around and farther up a slight slope on the beginning of the horizon, an old stone well stood blocking out the sun. The sound seemed to come from all directions, but there was nothing around except that well.

As I approached the well, the sound repeated itself, and it was definitely coming from there. A voice, the distinct words lost in the dry stone echo. I stepped, stopped, listened. A female voice, young. Hearing things? I reached the well and slowly looked over the edge, rooting my feet into the ground and grasping the stones for support in the event that a troll or equally dangerous monster was only pretending to be a young girl to lure me here so he could grab me and pull me into the well to live and die among the bones of his other victims. I crept over slowly, one eye at a time, but I couldn't see anything — complete darkness after about five feet. I pulled out my penlight, flipped it on, and pointed it into the darkness. Two eyes reflected the light and I jumped back, scared completely out of my wits.

The voice talked, and I could understand it now that I was so close.

"Help."

Was this the monster tricking me?

I gathered my courage and grasped my penlight, rooted my feet into the ground once again, and took another look. Flashed my penlight down into the well, but the light didn't travel very far. It reflected in the eyes once again, but I held steady.

I called down, "Hello?"

The voice responded, "Please help me."

"Okay, I'll try to help — stay right there." Brilliant, I hoped she didn't think that was a joke.

I looked around and wondered what I could use as a rope. Wondered also where this girl's parents were, why she was playing out here all alone, and a hundred thousand other things, but I parked most of them. The well looked pretty deep, probably deeper than I thought, and deeper than I could see with my penlight. I looked at the sides of the well and noticed that the rocks it was built with were uneven — good for grappling and potentially climbable. The problem would be getting back up. If we were both down there, who would save me, let alone her?

One thing at a time.

I put the penlight in my mouth, sat on the side of the well, swivelled around so both legs dangled in the darkness. I leaned over and lodged my feet against the side of the well and my back against the opposite wall. Good thing I have long legs. I shimmied down the well slowly, inches at a time. Told the girl to keep talking and wondered when she might turn into a troll, but then I remembered: trolls live under bridges, not in wells.

She kept saying, "Help me."

I asked her to say something else because I *was* helping her. I was coming, sorry if it took a while longer than anticipated. My legs were tiring and my back ached. I tried to point the penlight down to the bottom of the well, but all I saw were rocks. Kept moving and told the girl to let me know when I was close to her.

The girl yelled all of a sudden, and I flinched and fell the last few feet to the bottom. My body twisted around and around, and I landed with a thud on my back, hitting the back of my head on a rock. Luckily, I missed the girl. Dust flew up around me, and dirt caked the inside of my mouth. The fall snapped something inside my head — I was awake, even felt for blood but found none. But there was something else — almost like I crawled into this well and awoke something that was sleeping. Not a monster or anything, but something inside me that had been kept under lock and key. I thought the girl was trying to talk to me, trying to say something, but I couldn't hear her. She might as well not have been there with me at that moment.

The darkness of the well played tricks on my hurt head. Since I was on my back, I faced the mouth of the well. The sphere of light at the top shot down a shaft of sunray that made dust particles visible. It slowly turned from light to dark. My body ceased to feel, dissolved, and my mind went off in a million directions. My ex-girlfriend. She burrowed through the dirt and the earth, shattered the rock wall of the well, and stood before me.

And I felt nothing toward her.

I imagined this was some kind of nightmare because I no longer felt any love or loss toward her. Imagine waking up and not feeling anything toward the people you thought you loved. I should have been horrified, but there was a sense of relief that I no longer had to love her. As long as I stayed here in this deep dark well, I didn't have to love. I didn't have to do anything. With love came pain, with love came loss — it was inevitable. In order to no longer feel the pain of loss, I opted out of love. A sense of calmness filled my existence because nothing reached me anymore. It seemed as though a shift had occurred and someone had gone into my brain, into the very tissue of my being, and performed surgery to remove the pain, but in doing so, the love part had been dislodged as well. My ex-girlfriend tried to say something, but no words come out of her mouth. She was angry, that much was obvious. But there was nothing I could do, not anymore. I was tired but contented at the same time.

A light flashed before my eyes and I wondered if that was it for me. I'm not the most religious person in the world, but I'd heard of this flash of light and that I was supposed to walk toward it.

"Hey, mister," a young, girlish voice said — not exactly what I thought god would sound like.

The rock wall of the well was restored, and the ex-girlfriend was gone. I blinked several times at the light, and the reality of the situation came back into focus. The light was not *The Light*, but my penlight in the hands of the ten-year-old girl who had shone it in my eyes.

"Mister, wake up, please. I need your help," she pleaded.

My body started working again, and I pushed the penlight away from my eyes. I eased into a sitting position, and my head hurt like someone had gone off using it as a nail, hammering it into place. I leaned my back against the well wall and breathed out a mouthful of dust and dirt. Felt the back of my head, and there was dried blood caked in with hair. For a moment I had no idea where I was. Opened my eyes, and there was a young girl sitting across from me, her arms wrapped around her knees, pulling them into her chest. Her face was buried between her knees, but she kept her eyes on me.

"You here to help me?" she asked.

"I don't know. I guess so," I said. "The question is, who is going to help me?"

"I was just playing. I didn't mean to get caught down here," she said.

"How did you get down?" I asked.

"Same way you did, but I didn't fall," she said.

"How old are you?" I asked.

"Ten. How old are you?"

"Older than ten."

"How're we going to get out of here?"

"I don't know. Let me think for a second." I looked to the top of the well — it was farther away from what I remembered, and I had no idea how we were going to get out of here.

I distracted her. "What's your name?"

"Jenna. What's your name?"

I told her.

"Where are your parents?"

"They're off playing with their swords."

I suddenly recognized the clothes she was wearing — a robed outfit, circa 1365.

"I just left them," I said for credibility. "You know someone named Tobias?"

"The horse man."

"Yeah. Good man."

"Yeah. He let me ride one. I wanted to keep riding and use the horse to get away."

"You're not a fan of the re-enactments?"

"Stupid."

"Hmmmm," I said in agreement.

"How're we going to get out of here?"

"I don't know. Let's just sit here for a moment. It is so quiet in here. It's a good place to think."

I rested my head against the well wall and let out a sigh. I thought of my dream and my lack of love and remembered my ex-girlfriend. Did I ever love her? What happens when someone stops loving you? Focus on the future. On the present. Fuck the past.

"I'm looking for a friend of mine," I said.

"What's her name?"

"Chloe."

"That's a nice name. I don't like my name — it's not Jennifer and it's not Jenn. It's stuck somewhere in between. What's she look like?"

"She's unlike anyone."

Chloe could be totally different. I knew nothing about her since we parted. Would I ever find her? Would I even like her anymore, I mean as a person? What if she had turned mean or selfish or unpleasant in some other way?

"I know she has a birthmark on her left temple, but I haven't seen her in a while," I added.

"How come?" This girl didn't mess around with her directness.

"I made a mistake."

"What?"

I didn't know how to answer that, and Jenna understood this. She let me take a pause in the conversation while I mulled it over. Finally, I said, "Because I didn't think I could love her enough. She deserved to be loved."

"Is she with people that love her?"

"I can't answer that either. I don't know."

A silence fell over us.

My phone beeped with a text message. Obviously, I couldn't answer it at the moment.

I wondered if Jenna was silently judging me. I stood up and placed my hands on the rocks that jutted out of the wall. I had an idea and tested it out by myself first. It was not really a new idea, or even an idea that you could call a good one. Pretty much the same way I came down but in reverse. I planned on using the jagged rocks sticking out of the wall for grappling. Tried the method out for a few feet up until Jenna cried out, thinking I was leaving her behind. I jumped back down to the bottom. Showed Jenna what to do: she was going to grab me around the neck, hanging off my back. We looked at each other and she gave me a nod. She jumped on my back, slightly choking me.

Slow moving, one step at a time. This would all be easier if I didn't have the added Jenna-weight. Halfway up I stopped, my muscles ready to give in. They hadn't worked this hard in a long time. Jenna's head was buried in my back as though she didn't want to watch what was going to happen. She looked up as I lost my footing. She screamed and we slipped down a foot or two. I grunted and growled as I tried to stop us — if we fell now, we could both get seriously hurt. We finally slowed to a stop, and my heart pounded and my breathing laboured. Tiny rocks and dust fell to the floor below us. I risked a look down at the bottom but could not see the floor. It looked like a black hole, and I imagined if we fell now, we would just continue to fall forever. In a way, I felt this wouldn't be such a bad thing — Jenna and I seemed to get along. Maybe I could adopt her, and she could be the daughter I was sure I'd never have. As we floated and fell through the earth, through the black hole, into the black hole, out the other side, it wouldn't be such a bad thing. We would have no use for gravity, and we'd learn to accept our new lot in life.

I shook off the thought and Jenna looked at me in the eyes.

"What would you say to Chloe?"

"What?"

"If you were you and she was here, what would you say to her?"

"I would tell her I'm sorry." The aching in my legs and back dissipated immediately.

"She knows you're sorry. Something else."

"I would tell her I have missed her."

"She knows you miss her. Something else."

And I moved slowly upward. My muscles were giving out, but I commanded them to start moving again and they did. It was still slow going, and Jenna buried her head back into my back. And up we went, one foothold at a time. We were almost at the top, but we still didn't see any light — we must have been down there longer than we thought, and it was now nighttime. My head popped over the top of the well, and clean air sucked into my lungs, and the glorious nature of it almost made me slip but I held on. I told Jenna to let go of me and hop over the top of the well. With the extra weight gone, my arms almost gave way. Jenna — bless her — took my arm and tried to help me up but was really only making things more difficult. My body was almost fully over the top of the well, and I grappled for jutting stones. My legs were Jell-O and dangled uselessly under me. I pulled myself up and over the top and fell onto the ground beside the well.

Jenna was at my side whooping and hollering and yelling. "We made it! You did it!"

I shared her joy but needed a second, needed a bit of time to get some feeling back in my legs.

Jenna yelled, "Thank you!" and ran off into the distance.

I raised my head, leaned against the side of the well, and watched her run away. I assumed she was returning to the camp and really, at this point, I was just too tired to fully care. I did care a little bit and had a thin smile on my face, but I couldn't have stood right then if I'd wanted to. As her body got smaller, another little girl ran along with her — almost like a ghost, see-through, and so close to Jenna it looked like a double exposure. The see-through girl stopped, turned, and looked at me. She smiled. The birthmark on her left temple crinkled. I slid onto my side and fell instantly into the deepest of sleeps. I didn't dream of Chloe or my ex-girlfriend or anyone. Dreamt of that black hole and being in it, and someone could have come along and kicked me like a mule, and I wouldn't have felt it.

The climb up the well kicked me in the ass. I checked my compass watch, kept following the lake. Saw no people and few cars — nobody stopped and I was fine with that. The animals watched from behind bushes and hid around trees, scared instead of filled with wonder. They talked to each other but not to me.

The pieces moved together — not the entire puzzle, but images became clearer. The words, the stories were stuck in my brain, and I tried to pull them out. You only go through these things when alone, so alone, no one around, the guilt, the shame, the confusion, the anger — it all comes back.

Okay, first the ex-girlfriend Hannah. Let's get this out of the goddamn way. I thought I loved her, really thought I did, and I can't quite figure out why I can't seem to get by this. The strange thing is that we were probably not so good for each other. We tried, but in the end, there really wasn't anywhere for us to go. I loved her, and herein lies the problem. The problem was love. Goddamn love. And I ain't talking about the traditional love between two people, the kind of love that we're bought and sold through movies, religion, and culture. The kind I just can't seem to get on board with.

I'm talking about being able to accept some form of love. To be able to let it in, and to understand without judgment that it is authentic. Come on, motherfucker, there is no one to blame for the disintegration of all my relationships except myself.

And I went deeper into the past, and I thought of Chloe, remembered things, talked to her. I feel in danger of idealizing the past, of wanting something that no longer exists. But I have to be right about this, have to risk it.

Transported to all those places, all these feelings. The times Chloe and I walked, the times we travelled, when we just stopped and talked and tried different things together. They were just situations, not necessarily special — things that all people experience, but that you believe are special and unique to you and the other person in your life. We were creating love. We were the first, or so we believed.

Remembered when we stayed up all night every night after we first got together. I could have said anything and it would have been all right. We ignored our realities, ignored the people around us. We created our own little world, and it made sense for us to do that. I wanted to believe that you felt the same way, that you could say anything, and I knew you did but that you were holding back on some things. I was okay with that, and it all eventually came out, and I understood why it took you so long. You told me about your family, about what you'd seen, where you came from. I still do not know why you were attracted to me, someone so lost. Maybe that was it: I was your opposite and you were mine. We could experience different lives just by looking into each other's eyes.

I remembered moving you into your first apartment, remembered how we did things that people were supposed to do. Thought about the crazy landlord, with one eye looking east and one looking west, who sold us on that dump. We painted it ourselves, forgot to open the windows, got high off the fumes. We slept on the floor because you had no furniture. But when we got there, things started happening. We did all that we were supposed to. That apartment holds memories for us; many things happened there where we were forced to learn about each other.

And everything was good.

Remembered the insane man in the basement, yelling for someone who wasn't there, barricading his door and knocking at ours at 2:00 a.m., broken. You brought him into our apartment, sat him on the couch, gave him a cup of tea, and listened. You knew he needed someone to ask him questions.

I remembered hiking and walking through dense forests together. Something about the woods turned you on, and these adventurous walks always included more than just walking. On one particular long walk, we trudged through a dense forest. The foliage almost blocked out the sun. You saw a tree and just had to climb it. You picked an adjacent one for me. While I climbed three feet off the ground, hung on, and hugged the tree for dear life, you swung from a branch. And when the branch you were swinging on snapped and you fell to the ground with a thud, you only laughed. It was hot, sticky, and humid. We broke through the trees and came across a beach. The beach went on forever. It was wide with the low tide. You stood on a large rock over a small cliff. Your hand reached out from your brow, looked like a sailor investigating the weather. You could do such things and make them natural. We ran down that beach. Retrospectively, it seemed juvenile or at the very least, out of character. I frolicked. The beach was ours and ours alone. No one for miles. You suggested that we bury me in sand and completely covered me, poked a straw from a water bottle through the sand into my mouth so I could breath. Those were some of the best days, just the two of us, without anyone else around. Believing that we were the last two people alive — I was okay with that and you seemed okay with that too.

Remembered the first time you met my family — a big deal for me as I never brought anyone home. They loved you from the moment they met you. My mother never smiled so much, and she pulled me aside in the kitchen and had tears in her eyes and told me that you were the daughter she never had. I never told you this. Why didn't we tell each other these things? It made me so happy because I'd been so nervous — the most important people in my life were meeting, and what if they didn't like each other? I shouldn't have worried, should have known that they would love you, that you would love them.

Remembered meeting your parents and I was welcomed into their home — your home — and we spent so much time together. You told me I didn't have to go over there so much, that it wasn't necessary, but the truth was, I enjoyed it. I wanted more people in my life.

Remembered how we kept growing, you finished school and were halfway through a first novel. You read me chapters in the night, and I listened like a child at storytime. It was all happening, we were doing what we were supposed to, and it was working. We were happy. You started working at the local newspaper then quickly transferred to a national one. My work was getting noticed. Even though we were busy, we made time for each other, could not *not* make time for each other. Up to this point, we had done everything right.

It was at that moment I was ripped from my memories. Didn't want to remember anymore. Wanted to think of something else. Wanted to stop thinking. Think of a different point in the past that perhaps presented a different future.

A little ways behind me, I saw a man. He was dressed all in black. Black coat, pants, and fedora-type hat. I decided to get moving; something told me this guy was not good for me. I was lost in my memories, the past and the future all falling away, everything except the present. The man in black kept pursuing me. It was probably all in my head, but the thing is, there was no one else out there, no reason for anyone to be there. No reason for me to be out there. I kept looking back, kept seeing the man in black. I took out the knife Tobias gave me — maybe he'd been right, maybe I'd need it.

I realized I had started running a while back. Sprinting, had enough of walking for now. I was a marathon runner; I would keep going, run off those memories. Run like everyone else in this world, run right into my grave without experiencing my experiences, without being fully present, always running into the future instead of understanding the past or living in the present. I ran until I couldn't anymore, collapsed on the tarmac, heard car brakes squeal and swerve. Didn't care. My breath came rapidly, and my back bounced off the road as my heart thudded away at an unnatural pace.

Finally I looked behind me. The man in black was gone.

I needed to rest and recuperate from the previous few days. Bought a case of water and a fistful of energy bars at a convenience store. Looked around for a bit and found a small motel on the edge of town with a sign out front that said VACANCY. I wasn't picky.

Inside the motel office an old man with thin hair, a pointy goatee, and a face covered in moles tried to find the last nine in a Sudoku puzzle on the back of yesterday's newspaper. He looked up at me, squinted when I asked for a room. He already had the puzzle answers in front of him in today's newspaper.

"Busy time of year," said the mole man. "All's I got left is the handicapped room." He said this like it was a problem, but I didn't see one. I signed the register, grabbed the key, and off I went up three flights of stairs to room 3B.

It was the largest motel room I had ever seen, but it was off. Everything in the room — the bed, the desk, the chair, the lamps — was normal in size, but the room was a much larger space. It made the bed, desk, chair, and lamps look like miniature versions of themselves.

Turned the light on in the washroom even though I didn't have to use it: what everyone did after entering a motel room. Again, everything was regular-sized but miniature-looking because of the large space. The only difference was that the bathtub was huge, large enough for at least four people. I turned the light off and sat on the bed. Drank down an entire bottle of water and ate three energy bars. Lay down on the bed and felt someone lay down beside me.

No words.

Sleep.

Wake up.

In the middle of the night, someone tapped me on the shoulder.

I stumbled outside and limped down the hallway, grabbing on to the walls. Followed the ugly motel patterns along the floor. Ice machine. Felt like I was falling apart. All the walking-induced pain flooded into my system. The loud crumbling of the ice falling into the bucket shook my bones. On my way back to my room, I looked up to see the man in black opening a door with a key. Pulled out the knife. He stopped, looked at me, looked at the knife. I couldn't deal with that then. With back against the wall, I moved right past him. He lunged for the knife, and I did something I've never done: I plunged the tip into his torso. The knife was a novelty knife and instead of burrowing into flesh, the blade bent, the point cutting the side of my hand. I dropped the knife and the bucket, the ice scattering on the carpet. The man in black grabbed my wrist, looked deep into my eyes — his eyes were completely black. I scrambled free and ran down the hallway to my room, my joints and my muscles screaming at the pain.

Slammed door.

Locked.

The room had transformed into Chloe's room all those years ago. Saw a black marker on the bedside table. I started in the top corner of the room, started writing. I wasn't alone. This was that night, the time when Chloe, Chloe with the birthmark on her left temple, wrote her story on the walls for me to see. Maybe it could bring us back together again to show her that I remembered.

Late that night, my arms around her and her arms around me. She was asleep, exhausted from writing her story on the walls. From finishing her story on my body. Her hot breath lightly swayed the hairs on my chest. I knew that I desperately needed to sleep, but I turned her story around and around in my head.

In the transformed motel room, I started writing on the walls.

Chloe Jia Qi was born Mayling Qi, in Beijing to a Tibetan father and Chinese mother.

"I remember the night when I was 10, so excited that I could only pretend to sleep, listening to my parents as they whispered in the next room."

The following day, Mayling had been taken to the airport, en route to Toronto, Canada, for an exchange program.

They'd checked her baggage, and Mayling's parents were so upset — something she didn't understand since she'd be back in a month. Mayling and her best friend, Pema, boarded the plane. Mayling stopped on the pathway, looked at her parents. They waved through tears.

That would be the last time she saw them.

Mayling found her seat and pulled out a letter that her father had given her. She was instructed not to open it until after takeoff, but she was too excited. She ripped the corners and pulled out the handwritten note. The note detailed the plans that her father and Pema's father had arranged with the teacher who was supervising them on the trip. Upon their arrival in Vancouver, the teacher was going to take Mayling and Pema to a safe place to stay for a while with some distant relatives of her mother's.

"The passengers all boarded," Chloe continued — Chloe wrote and now I wrote. "The plane pulled away from the gate. I unbuckled my seatbelt and ran down the aisle, pushed past the flight attendants and their emergency procedure demonstrations. I started banging on the door with the palms of my hands."

She grabbed the large handle to open the door and tried to pull it down. Her 10-year-old arms couldn't make it budge. A flight attendant approached her and asked what she could do to help. Mayling hung her head, her shoulders slumped in defeat. She heard a voice and recognized it as her teacher's.

"Sit down now, Mayling," he said. "The plane's about to take off. You're not going to inconvenience the other passengers, are you?"

Mayling turned around. The teacher had a smirk on his face. She relented and returned to her seat. Beside her, Pema asked what was wrong. Mayling thrust the note into her own lap, refusing to look at Pema. The flight lasted longer than Mayling ever imagined. She did not sleep, did not eat. Stared straight ahead at the seat in front of her.

When the plane landed in Vancouver, the class proceeded to the hotel in a pre-arranged bus. The other kids had no idea what was going on in Mayling's head. When everyone was settled, the teacher arrived at Mayling and Pema's door.

A black car waited for them out front. The teacher hustled Mayling and Pema into the back seat. They drove to an industrial area. The teacher led them into an old, abandoned factory, and they were told to sit on two wooden chairs.

Four men came out of the darkness and walked around them in opposing circles. These were not the relatives her father had arranged. The teacher had made other plans for them.

Mayling and Pema were escorted into a different black car with the four men and taken to a house in a suburban neighbourhood. The contrast between the houses and the industrial area was immense. The girls were rushed through the empty house and locked in the basement.

Days passed.

Mayling and Pema measured time with the meals left at the top of the stairs. No one spoke to them, no one told them why they were there or what was to happen to them.

Mayling devised a plan. They worked at dismantling one of the bedposts. Worked for days, freezing whenever footsteps were heard above. They fashioned a crude weapon. Finally, on the 21st day — according to their calculations — they waited at the top of the stairs. When the door opened for the food trays to be placed on the step, Mayling batted the hands with the bedpost weapon, and together they pushed through the door.

Once upstairs, they beat on their captor. They ran outside and were almost blinded by the sunlight. Pema froze mid-step. It was a pause they couldn't afford. Their captors burst through the door and overtook Pema. She screamed from the surprise.

Mayling remembered how Pema's face and body changed. She grew calm and didn't fight her attackers. Her body slackened. She mouthed the word, *RUN*.

Mayling cried as she ran, and she ran until she couldn't anymore. She collapsed in a heap. Forced herself to her feet. Kept going. Some people are hardwired for survival.

She came to a park and sat on a bench. A woman came out of the darkness — much like the men in the abandoned factory. She crouched down and put her hand on Mayling's shoulder. Mayling looked down at the plump woman, who wore thick glasses and had her hair pulled up into a bonnet at the top of her head. She was dressed in a waitress uniform and had a name tag that read, *CHLOE*. The waitress convinced Mayling to come with her to the diner where she worked. She fed Mayling fried chicken and mashed potatoes and refilled her coffee cup several times. Not a single word ever passed between them. The waitress went into the kitchen to pick up an order, and when she returned, Mayling was gone.

"I walked the streets for two days," Chloe said — Chloe wrote and now I wrote. "My parents gave up on me. They left me alone in this world. They did not love me. Nobody wanted me. Not even 10 years old, and I decided to reinvent myself. My mind was a hive of negative thoughts buzzing around, consuming me. The only moments of clarity came when I tasted in my mouth the remnants of the fried chicken and mashed potatoes. My only peace came with the plump waitress named Chloe. I repeated the name like a mantra."

When she arrived in Chinatown looking for work, she introduced herself as Chloe. She knocked on the back door of every restaurant along the strip asking for work or food. Groups of men smoking in back alleys laughed when she told them her name was Chloe.

She finally found a man who would take her in. She worked for food and slept on a cot behind the kitchen. He was an angry man.

Some time later, Chloe was cleaning the table of a regular customer, an affable Chinese man in his early fifties. He would often come for lunch, his office around the corner. He tried to engage Chloe in conversation, but she acted as though she didn't understand him.

"Excuse my daughter," the angry man said while he glared at her.

When he went back to the kitchen, Chloe whispered, "I'm not his daughter."

They went on to have a pleasant conversation. He asked her name and about her background. Chloe made up stories at first, but as the man continued to return and ask more questions, she started telling the truth. The man brought his wife to meet Chloe, and the next day they brought adoption papers.

Her new parents provided as much as they could for Chloe. When the papers were signed, Chloe took her mother's name as her middle name and kept her father's name as her last. Chloe Jia Qi. She wanted to honour her parents in spite of their having given her up. Feelings of anger dissipated over time. She settled into her new life, one of protection and comfort. She was suspicious at first, but her new parents also provided patience.

Chloe often wandered the suburban streets of her new neighbourhood. Hid behind a tree whenever she saw a black car. She could never be sure which house or neighbourhood she and Pema had been locked up in. When she ran from that house, she was running for her life. Guilt over Pema stayed with her. Her parents hadn't wanted her, she reasoned, and with time she could learn to let go of this. But Pema had been right behind her when they escaped. Chloe felt she could have done something. She would never get over it.

"And we met and everything was good. Happy ending, right?" Chloe said that night, long ago. "But after? This wasn't the end. I couldn't forget. I just couldn't get over it."

My mouth hadn't been making any noise, but my mind was reeling. I had so many questions, so many words, and I didn't know how to translate what was in my head and make it real. I needed to rest, so I stopped writing. Something watched me.

I kept writing, wrote about us.

Wrote until I couldn't write anymore.

There was nothing more to write.

It already happened and nothing could be changed.

For the first time I truly understood regret. This person whose adopted parents had lived next door to me, this girl who grew up to be such a strong woman and went through all this, whom I was lucky enough to cross paths with and lucky enough to get to know. I threw it all away because I didn't know how to let someone in as they let me in, didn't know how to let someone love me as much as I wanted to love her.

Alone in the vast space of that motel room, alone with all these words and places that seemed so long ago. The room looked even bigger than before, and I didn't know what to do with all that space.

My phone beeped with a text message. I ignored it.

Walked over to the washroom and looked at myself in the mirror. The pepper in my hair seemed to have fallen out. Sunken eyes. I had lost weight from all the walking. Beard — I always hated beards. I stripped off my clothes and glanced at the skin of my body which looked like a tent stretched too tightly over bones. Ran the water in the oversized tub until it was scalding hot, and turned the shower on. Crawled into the tub and sat on the grimy floor of it. And I just sat there with my knees pulled into my chest, the water slamming into my back and neck. The filth and dirt and experience and wind, fleeting, washed away, off my body. The blood flowed from my hand, and the dried cut from falling down the well opened on my head. I sat in that tub, feeling so alone, so small, not knowing what to do or where to go. Pulled myself ever more into a ball, tried to pull myself into myself.

Tight.

So small.

The beeping phone.

No one knew where I was, no one cared. I didn't know what I was doing anymore. It was gone, all was lost. The water hit me in the back as though trying to make me remember something. But I couldn't remember. It was gone, all was lost. I saw myself from outside myself. Saw a man, small and alone in a tub built for four, shielding his eyes from what he needed to see.

He was alone.

So small, so small.

The desert. Pitch dark. Stars out. Walking. Getting slower. Unsure. Where to go from here? I kept walking and wondering when I would

just die. At that point, it was all I wanted. To be released and forgiven. But would I be forgiven? Forgiven for what? By whom?

I walked up and then down a sand dune. At the bottom of the sand dune, I stepped into what seemed like a hole in the ground. Tried with whatever strength I had left to pull my foot free. The more I struggled to pull my foot out of the hole, the more it sank into it. Up to the knee, the thigh. Lost my balance and my other foot sank into the same sandy area, quickly got sucked in. Up to my waist, my chest. Reached my arms to the sky in an effort not to go completely into the hole. No use, my arms disappeared — only my head still popped up above the surface. Sucked in sand as I panicked. Finally, my head got pulled down into the hole.

Darkness.

Silence.

Trapped, I vaguely remembered thinking I'd like to bury myself in the sand, carry a straw so it could poke through the surface, so I could still breathe. I had no straw in the desert, and really, at that point, I didn't really care or even have the capacity to think to use it.

At first, I struggled, attempted to claw my way out of the sand trap. The more I struggled, the further down into the sand I went. Finally, I stopped struggling, gave in, decided I needed to just finally give up and then perhaps I would be okay. Thought that after that, all these worries and fears and pains and the thirst — goddamn thirst — would go away. Floated in the sand, my body suspended as though gravity didn't exist.

So small, so small.

The stadium darkened. Thirty-five thousand people — mostly men and boys, fathers and sons — hushed. Spotlights darted around the crowd, looking for something. They converged at the wrestler entrance. A steel wall blocked the entrance. A solid-looking wall, the blocks stacked, keeping someone or something inside.

A lonely piano filled the air — Beethoven's Fifth. The chilling sound of glass breaking screeched through the speakers. Hundreds — no, thousands of light bulbs snapped, crackling all at once. A stark contrast to the eerie piano. Someone banged on the wall, and the sound echoed through the silent stadium. The bang turned into a thud; the thud turned into a pounding — someone or something was trying to get through. The pounding became rhythmic, pulsing; the audience started to clap with the noise. The glass breaking screamed over the speakers, building to a climax. The combined noises fell in together, created a soundtrack. Out of the pounding, a steady bass drum kicked in, and then a loud electric guitar amplified a heavy-metal version of Beethoven's masterpiece. It was not so much music as noise. The building shook: the pounding, the breaking glass, the drums, the guitar.

The video screen at the centre of the stadium came to life. Two large men — hulking shadows, really — walked into a mechanic's shop. The shadows were dressed in heavy leather, their faces hidden behind metal masks with glass slits for eyes. They held blowtorches the size of chainsaws. The men, who looked like they were from another planet, walked over to a pile of scrap metal in the corner of the room, sharp edges jutted forever upward. They worked fast, grabbing pieces of metal, soldering them together. The sound of metal on metal added to the noise in the stadium, almost unbearable.

The blowtorches breathed hot fire — the men were making something, but it was unclear what. Various close-ups led the audience through the sequence. Meanwhile, the thumping music and the pounding on the wall continued. Finally, the camera pulled out wide, revealed the otherworldly men as they stood admiring their work: a complex metal sculpture. One of the men lit a fuse and the sculpture ignited. The camera pulled back revealing crude letters that spelled STAINLESS STEELE.

At this moment — and perfectly timed — the steel wall inside the stadium shook from a pressure behind it, and Beethoven's Fifth could not get any louder, exploding into the heavy metal song "Metal on Metal" by the defunct 80s glam band Tortured Soul. The steel wall crumbled from the ground up, destroyed.

Out of the rubble emerged a man, but not just any man: a giant. Stainless Steele, known as "SS." The crowd went wild. Crazy. The floor shook and the audience cheered and screamed with arms stretched toward the sky as if to say *Praise the Lord!* SS strutted down the aisle carrying his chainsaw-sized blowtorch, as seen in the video, shooting flames at the crowd. Some risked the flames for a touch of his skin.

SS was a large man, even for a wrestler, and stood almost seven feet tall. He was cut like nobody's business, with a chest the size of a mid-sized kitchen range. Smooth, shaved head with lightning bolts tattooed on his scalp. Soccer balls for biceps, veins running every which way, taut, tanned skin. His chiselled, square face had kind-looking eyes that turned on you, a small, tight nose, and lots of frown lines that he cultivated to fit in with his character. He wore simple black tights that had STAINLESS STEELE written vertically down the left leg.

SS reached the centre of the stadium, slipped the blowtorch onto the ring floor, grabbed the top rope, and flipped, performing a somersault and landing on his feet in the ring. Agile for such a large man. He picked up the blowtorch, jumped up on the top rope. The stadium went dark once again, and he threw the blowtorch into high mode, shooting a line of fire that almost reached the stadium ceiling. The crowd was beside itself. "Metal on Metal" cut out with an explosion.

The national anthem from the former Union of Soviet Socialist Republics started to play, and the Red Army, another wrestler, known as "RA," came through the curtains and walked toward the ring. He ignored the booing fans. RA was not as muscular as SS — he had more flab — but what was hidden under that pasty flab was anyone's guess. And he looked mad — not mad as in he wanted to hurt you, but mad as in he wanted to annihilate you, eat you up, shit you out, and then perhaps feed you to his Black Russian Terrier. RA carried a bottle of vodka (which was actually real vodka), and when he entered the ring, he chugged the entire bottle and threw it into the crowd, knocking out a wild-eyed fan. The fan fell to the ground and was out cold but quickly came to and jumped up, showing the empty vodka bottle to the stadium like he'd caught the tie-breaking homer at the World Series.

This was a cage match. A twelve-foot iron (not steel!) rod cage was lowered from the ceiling, confining the ring. SS and RA snarled at each other, circling each other in the ring like animals. They were actors building suspense. More than one fan fainted in anticipation. The referee hung the International Federation of Professional Wrestlers' heavyweight belt from a wire hook attached to the ceiling. The first to reach the belt would be the champion. No rules. Inside the ring were assorted props: chairs, tables, broken glass, ladders, tacks, barbed wire, various tools.

Safe to say, there was no love lost between these two. They hated each other for real — even backstage, out of character — and wanted to get right down to it. The referee tried to make them shake hands. They refused. He shrugged his shoulders with great drama and blew his whistle. The bell rang, the match began.

The match went like this:

They beat each other up, used the various weapons at their disposal, bled. SS was going to win — nope. RA set up the ladder, RA got knocked down, they were both unconscious. SS got up, beat on RA, broke one, two, three chairs over RA's back, set up the ladder, almost made it, got knocked down …

The climax of the match came when RA body-slammed SS, leaving him lying on the ring floor. RA set up the ladder, headed toward the belt. SS woke up and slid over to the side of the ring, grabbed his blowtorch. He held it up for the crowd, which went absolutely crazy. Naturally, RA had no idea what was going on below.

SS shot the blowtorch and lit the ladder on fire. The crowd could not believe what it was seeing. RA grabbed on to the wire holding the belt as the flaming ladder fell to the ground. He scrambled, his legs shooting in all directions. He snatched the belt with his hands, but — BUT! — he lost his grip, and both he and the belt fell to the ground. SS caught the belt and held it up to the crowd. RA landed on the ring floor, out cold. SS rolled RA over onto his back and put his foot on his chest. The referee counted one-two-three. "Metal on Metal" blasted over the speakers.

A certain old woman slammed her right hand (her only hand) repeatedly on the table beside her as she watched Stainless Steele claim his victory. She stepped outside on the balcony and lit a cigarette with a mini replica of SS's blowtorch as if she'd just finished a round of very satisfying sex. She could feel the heat of the blowtorch as SS shot flames into the air.

The phone rang, and she picked up the receiver. "Yeah?"

"Mary Hammerstein?" a gruff male voice asked.

She paused. "Yeah, who wants to know? Idiot."

"I'm the manager at a motel near the lake."

"Congratulations," she said.

"Are you related to a ..."

"Yes, I know him."

"He put you down as a contact. The credit card he gave us got rejected, and he's not answering the door. We're going to call the cops soon. People around here don't like the cops."

Mary paused for a second time. Something was wrong. She gave the motel manager a new credit card number and told him to keep the room rented until she got there. She took down the location information and hung up.

The pigeons fornicated. Noisily. Mary's water gun leaned against the wall in the corner of the room. She grabbed it, filled it. Threw open the sliding glass door. Surprise attack. She picked them off quickly, one at a time in a stream of aggressive water. The pigeons didn't know what hit them, and she kept shooting even after they had vacated the balcony. By the time she'd emptied the gun, she had made her decision.

Mary washed the cane, polished the metal — it gleamed, the early morning sun bounced off it. She packed a tiny suitcase, folded and re-folded her garments the way she used to when she travelled — the tricks learned when trying to fit as many items as possible into a limited amount of space. She squeezed in a bottle of gin, a bottle of tonic, and a tumbler. Mary dressed herself, put on her favourite floral-patterned dress. She buttoned it all by herself, slowly, having learned long ago how to do it one-handed. She applied makeup for the first time in years. She realized, looking in the mirror, that she was nervous about leaving the Lighthouse, no matter how much she hated it there. Mary was more than a little concerned over what she would find out in the world, a world she had manoeuvred through and negotiated so easily in the past. She dug through the change bowl and found the keys that had collected dust for many years. She limped her way down the hallway, fumbling with the cane and the suitcase.

Mary heard a rumbling coming from around the corner. A herd of old people shuffled down the hallway, blocking all exits. The Walking Seniors stopped when they saw Mary standing in their way.

A standoff. Cowboy-shootout style.

The air settled and no one breathed.

For years they had woken Mary up unnecessarily. Now they adjusted the grips on their canes and walkers. A beeping sound, then another. The Walking Seniors scrambled to turn off their medication alarms. Mary, using the opportunity, lifted her cane in the air like a sword and headed straight toward the group. She pushed one after another out of the way, knocking more than one of them to the ground.

"My hip!" yelled an old lady.

"My pills!" screamed an old man as his medication spilled onto the floor.

Mary moved through the crowd until a shadow fell over her: Leena, the muscle. A large woman, Leena blocked out the overhead fluorescent lights. Rumour around the Lighthouse was that she had been a wrestler in her native Estonia and had been bumped into the men's league. Leena stood in front of Mary with her enormous hands on her waist. She looked at the wreckage in Mary's wake and slowly shook her head: no further.

Mary slammed her cane down on Leena's foot, and Leena screamed and bent over. Mary used all her weight to push Leena to the side and made her getaway. She pushed the down button for the elevator. Leena regained her senses and headed toward Mary, an angry look on her face. Mary pounded the button a few times, hoping to make the elevator come faster. Leena was slow but almost there. The elevator doors opened and Mary stepped in. A thick, meaty arm stopped the doors from closing, and a giant head appeared in the gap. Mary lifted her cane, placed the four prongs on Leena's face, and with all her strength, thrust the giant woman backwards, pushed the door-close button. The doors closed on Leena's meaty hook. Mary kicked the arm back into the hallway, the doors closed, and the elevator travelled into the bowels of the building.

The doors opened into the Lighthouse parking garage. Mary limped along the rows of cars. The garage was empty and silent except for the ping of her rubber-tipped cane against the concrete. She stopped in front of a car, but not just any car. Her 1981 red Lincoln Mark VI. Mary admired the massive vehicle, the round headlights staring at her, the long hood a receding widow's peak. The Mark VI was traditionally a two-door car, but during the brief period from 1980–1983, the Ford Motor Company introduced a short-lived four-door version. The car had been in hibernation for a long time — many years — and it was time to wake it up.

Mary limped along the side of the car, which had a scotch-tape thin film of dust. She leaned the cane against the car, wiped away some dirt from the driver's side window, looked inside with a cupped hand. The light brown interior was leather, big — SS-type big. Enough legroom for an elephant and a giraffe, and the giraffe could stick its neck through the moonroof.

She slowly slid the key into the lock — even the key was oversized — opened the heavy door, and threw her suitcase in the back seat. Margaret guided the key into the ignition and turned it. The car was stubborn, but so was she. The motor coughed a few times and finally caught, growling to life until it settled into a purr.

Mary let the car warm up, wake up. From her suitcase, she grabbed the tumbler, gin, and tonic. She stepped out of the car and mixed herself a drink using the hood as a table. She placed the tumbler on the hood, mixed her drink through the vibration of the vehicle. She smoked a cigarette while she waited. She had forgotten the lime.

Across the parking garage, the bell from the elevator dinged and the doors opened. An elevator full of Walking Seniors stumbled out — they would have been furious but their medications didn't allow it. Leena led the charge. The seniors spotted Mary, and Leena pointed. Parked beside the elevator was a row of scooters that the elderly used to get around. A row of grey-bearded Harley Davidsons. The Walking Seniors reached their rides, hopped on (as much as they could), and started them up. The parking garage filled with the sound of angry machines. Pulling out of their parking spaces, the seniors made a V-formation, simulating an attacking army but really more similar to a group of docile geese. They followed Leena, who needed no scooter, and they waved their canes like maces.

Mary gathered her bottles and jumped in the car. Placing the tumbler between her thighs, cigarette burning between her lips, she hoped Lincoln was ready. She revved the engine and thrust the stick into first gear. Foot off the clutch … Lincoln rolled forward and stalled. The army of Walking Seniors approached — slowly, but they were getting there. Mary tried to start it up. Lincoln might be angry from being woken up. When the Walking Seniors were only a few car lengths away, the engine roared to life, and Mary threw it into first and peeled out, almost taking a scooter or two with her. She flicked her cigarette butt at Leena as she passed, saw the sparks fly off her massive chest. Mary squealed out of the garage and into the blinding sunlight. She put on her massive sunglasses — the ones that covered half her face — took a sip of her G&T, and lit another cigarette. She patted Lincoln's steering wheel, thanked him for working with her. Before she headed out of town, she got a high-end car wash and stopped at the market for limes.

From there, she stopped only for emergencies.

Once Mary got on the highway, she didn't look back. Lincoln co-operated with her though her lead foot had not gotten any lighter during their years apart. She travelled no less than 140 kilometres per hour. Most times she had the window down while she chain-smoked, and she refilled her tumbler when it was empty. For most people, alcohol and driving shouldn't be mixed. For Mary, it enhanced her awareness. Everything felt more streamlined. She was at one with Lincoln. They were doing this together. She only stopped at liquor stores, for coffee, for the bathroom — she wished she had some kind of catheter to eliminate the need for bathroom stops. She didn't eat, needed no food. Lincoln's hood shook when they went over 140 clicks, so she kept things consistent.

Mary made good time, driving through the rest of the clear day and into the night. Lincoln had no air conditioning, but she didn't mind. Her mind slipped, dipped into the past, recalled her days in India, Egypt, Australia — some of the hottest places on the planet. During the night, apart from the odd tractor-trailer, she was largely alone on the road, left with her thoughts. They drifted, there was no order to them. She remembered the many times she had been in a new country, surrounded by new people speaking languages she could not understand.

Lost and alone.

Mary smiled, knowing that she was never really lost, always found her way. Alone maybe, but she never minded being alone. Preferred it. Thoughts buried deep in her past came right back to the forefront without her even trying to conjure them. She was not lost this time either — she had no map but knew where she was going. Travelled back in time. Lincoln was a time machine, reversed the calendar, allowed her to return to an age when she felt more in control, led her life through instinct. The pulse of her life was close to her heart, right there, and she followed it. After a few hours on the road, she believed her arm had grown back and she could smoke and drink at the same time again. Her wrinkles were gone, her body young, but she retained the lessons from her experiences.

Around the lake she went.

Mary had been on the road a few hours when she saw the sirens. Her hearing wasn't what it used to be, and it was not until she noticed the lights of the police car in the rearview mirror that she realized they were meant for her. She was being asked to stop.

But she couldn't stop. *Damn*, she thought, *I don't have time for this*. She made a choice — probably a choice that the Mary from thirty years ago would have made. Black and white: brake or gas?

The consequence for each decision was obvious. She stepped on the gas. Lincoln balked at the request.

She surpassed 140 kilometres per hour, and the car shook at the effort. Mary peeked at the mirror and saw the officer's surprised look. Mary used the surprise to take a formidable lead. She gunned it, sipped her drink, and lit a cigarette. She moved like a conductor in front of an orchestra; her instruments were a tumbler, a cigarette lighter.

She weaved in and out and around other cars, horn blaring. The sirens behind her grew louder like they had only two settings: "Pull over please" amped up to "We've got a maniac on our hands."

Mary made even better time with a cruiser on her tail. The police car caught up to her, and the officer talked on his radio, motioned for her to pull over. She looked at him and gestured that she couldn't hear.

She floored it.

At the next entrance to the highway, another police car joined them and tried to cut her off. She pretended to slow down a bit, let the officer get out of the car. Then, just as she approached, she stepped on the gas and swerved around the police car. Open road. She looked in the mirror; another police cruiser had joined them, totalling three.

Mary sped around a large hook in the highway to find a waiting blockade. Five police cars blocked the entire highway. Officers were out on the road, directing other travellers through a small opening. They took their guns out and pointed them at her. Just as the initial decision to step on the gas was easy, so too was this one. She stepped on the brakes, and the car swerved to a stop, leaving tire marks on the road in front of the officers. Mary kicked the door open, stepped out of the car with the tumbler, and lit a cigarette.

The police cars that had been chasing her caught up and surrounded her. The officer who had initially asked her to pull over approached. The cops were speechless, didn't even know where to start.

"Was it as good for you as it was for me?" Mary asked.

The police officer grabbed the tumbler, sniffed the glass. Without thinking, he took out his handcuffs and approached Mary to cuff her. She laughed when he stepped back. How to cuff someone with only one arm?

They threw Mary in a jail cell with three other women: one drunk, one huge, one crying. The huge one stood by the bars staring when Mary entered. Mary sat on a steel bench and the huge one joined her, taking a package of cigarettes out of her rolled sleeve, revealing a tattoo of a heart punctured with a silver arrow.

"Who're you, old lady?" the huge one said, as she lit a cigarette.

"I'm pissed off, that's who I am."

"What did you do to get in here? Take too long to cross the street?"

"Actually, I outran a police cruiser in my Lincoln Mark VI and was pursued by several other cops until they blocked the road and arrested me at gunpoint. Now give me one of those cigarettes."

The huge one paused, nodded her head, and offered one from the pack.

"I got to get out of here. Any suggestions? Hey, you—" Mary lit up, pointed at the crying one, "—suck it up, I'm trying to think here."

"Bertha." The huge one offered her hand.

"*Big* Bertha." Mary flicked the smoke into her mouth and shook Bertha's hand.

"Watch it."

"Your wrestling name."

"What?"

"Never mind. I'm Mary. Listen, how do we get out of here?"

"We wait for the right time."

"I don't have time."

"Do you trust me, *One-Armed* Mary?"

They waited three-quarters of an hour. The jail cell was located in a small local police station. It was basically one big room, cut in half with the bars down the middle that separated the cell from a work area. Two desks and chairs filled the other side. There were papers spread everywhere. Very unorganized.

A pudgy officer stepped into the work area and eyed the prisoners. After finding the papers he wanted, he jingled his keys and stepped to the cell door. One-Armed Mary and Big Bertha stood across from each other on either side of the door.

"Time to go, Susan." The pudgy guard opened the door.

The drunk one — Susan — glanced up in confusion. She stood, looked like she was about to pass out, and fell toward the officer. He caught her and the other women attacked. One-Armed Mary stepped on the officer's foot, throwing him off balance with the extra weight of Susan. Bertha clocked him squarely in the jaw, and the two bodies fell to the floor. Mary and Bertha acted fast. Pulled the two bodies in and exited the cell, locked the door, tossed the keys in the wastebasket. It was a bit of a scramble, but Mary found the key to Lincoln — good thing it was so huge — and her cane. They headed for the door.

They stopped. Listened.

They had to pass through another adjoining room with more desks and a waiting area. Two officers sat at desks with their backs to them. Big Bertha and One-Armed Mary stepped silently into the room and toward the door to freedom. Mary could see Lincoln sitting out in the parking lot through the window. They were almost at the door when the wooden floor creaked.

They froze.

One of the officers looked up, paused, scratched himself and went back to work. Beside the door, a key rack held all the keys for the police cruisers. One-Armed Mary quietly grabbed them all. They made it the rest of the way out and crossed the parking lot. One-Armed Mary threw the cruiser keys as far as she could (which wasn't very far, but far enough), jumped in Lincoln, and fired him up. The two officers heard the car start, rushed to the window, and headed to the front door — astonished to find no keys for their cars. They stood still, looking shocked as Lincoln peeled past them. All they could do was cough at the dust kicked up in the car's wake.

The driving was easier the rest of the way. Mary and Bertha took turns. She enjoyed her G&Ts in the passenger seat. Bertha drank only tonic — sober for 10 years. They figured a Lincoln Mark VI could be spotted easily by the cops, so they stuck to back roads. Bertha was a good catch with a built-in tendency to find the best dirt roads, and she seldom got lost. They rarely stopped and risked it only in small towns — really small, one-street small — for coffee and more gin and more tonic and more cigarettes.

They drove all night.

When they reached the motel, they pulled around back, out of sight from the road. Mary and Bertha entered the motel lobby, and the mole man was still doing the same Sudoku puzzle. He'd seen a lot in his days at the motel, but Mary and Bertha were definitely one of the strangest couples he ever saw. Mary asked for my room number and followed him upstairs.

I heard them knock on the door. No answer. Mole man used the master key and slowly pushed the door open. Mary stepped inside first. The room empty. The bed made. The room tidy. Everything seemed in order except for the walls. The walls were covered in black marker. Someone's entire life spilled out in nonsensical sentences. Big letters, small letters, illegible letters. Bertha and the mole man stepped into the room and were shocked into silence.

"Chloe?" A faint voice — mine — came from the bathroom.

Mary stepped inside the washroom.

"Chloe, is that you?"

"It's Mary."

I was still in the bathtub, I didn't know for how long.

"Just hold on."

Mary stepped back out of the bathroom and closed the door.

"You're going to have to pay for the cleaning. I'm calling the cops," the mole man said, switching from shock to anger.

With swift movements that should have been beyond her years, Mary lifted up the cane and pointed it at the mole man, the four prongs pressed to his chest. She pushed him backwards until he was pinned against the wall. "You will do no such thing. From what I hear, people 'round here don't like the cops. If someone comes by to give us so much as a parking ticket, I'll skin your balls and use them to steep my tea. Now scram. Big Bertha here is going to follow you back to your Sudoku puzzle, which no doubt you've been working on for days. She's going to stay with you until we come down."

Bertha crossed her arms for dramatic effect. It worked. My phone beeped with a text message, breaking the standoff. Bertha led the mole man out of the room. Mary closed the door behind them.

Mary walked around the room, reading little bits here and there. She knew right then that it was right for her to have come. She felt the pain in the room. She sighed, stepped into the bathroom, and sat on the closed toilet seat, resting her chin on her cane.

"Where were you going?" she asked.

"To find people I've lost," I said. "Margaret."

"Yeah."

"Chloe."

"Yeah."

"How did you get here?"

"Lincoln. I think I'm a wanted fugitive now."

"We should go then."

"How long have you been walking?"

"Not long. Just took a little detour." I stood up at that point, almost collapsing from exhaustion. The cut on my hand reopened. My left leg would barely support any weight.

"I just wanted to forget some things and remember other things," I said, stepping into the main room, referring to the mess I'd made.

I gathered my things, and we went down to the foyer to meet Bertha. She sat in the waiting room with a very nervous mole man. Mary made introductions, and the three of us, like some demented New-Age rock band — Big Bertha, One-Armed Mary, and me — made our way to Lincoln. When we reached the car, I could go no further.

I turned to Mary and shook my head.

That's when we heard the sirens.

"I'll explain later. We need a plan." Mary felt my eyes on her.

I was a little hazy from the past few days and felt unsure if some of the events had even happened. Now was not the time to ponder.

Bertha spoke up. "I'll take Lincoln. You two go. I'll distract them into following me. Nice to meet you, One-Armed Mary."

Mary was about to argue, but the look in Bertha's eyes told her not to.

"Take care of yourself, Big Bertha," Mary said.

Mary nodded, grabbed her suitcase, and handed over the keys reluctantly, and we headed around to the wooded area behind the motel. We watched as Bertha jumped in Lincoln, started it up, and sped away in the opposite direction to the approaching police cars. The sound of sirens echoed through the streets as they went right past us.

"Now what?" Mary asked.

"We walk," I said.

We took our first steps together.

We walked a fair distance, but it was slow going. We both realized that we were not going to get very far. Mary struggled but tried not to show it. We rested down the road from a combination gas station and convenience store when an old man in one of those old-man scooters drove right past us.

"We need one of those," I said.

"That one looks good to me," Mary said.

"When I said, 'one of those,' I didn't necessarily mean that one."

"Let's do it."

"Haven't you broken enough laws today?"

"I haven't even started."

The old man parked the scooter in front of the store. He slowly got up and entered the store. I stood watch at the door while Mary sat in the driver's seat. The old man had left the key in the ignition, and she started it up.

"Nothing compares to Lincoln, but you'll do," she said.

I stepped inside the store, ready to distract the old man if he headed for the door. Mary put the scooter in reverse, engaging a loud beep that signified the vehicle was backing up.

"What the hell?" Mary yelped.

She looked to me and I looked at the old man, but he seemed not to notice. I saw a hearing aid in his right ear. She quickly floored it — if that's the correct expression for a scooter — and set off down the street. She was not far enough away when the old man headed for the cash register. I walked up to him, tapped him on the shoulder. He turned and regarded me with confusion.

"Excuse me, um, sir," I said quietly. "I was wondering, um, which way is north?"

"What?" he said.

"Which way is north?" I said at the same volume.

"WHAT?" he said louder.

"Never mind."

I hoped Mary was far enough away and got out of there fast. She was already down the street, but I caught up to her and we got back on track.

"I'd love to see his face when he leaves that store." She chuckled.

We walked and rolled right out of that town as quickly as possible. Mary made the scooter her own: ripped off the American flag flying from the back of the machine, and attempted to remove the bumper sticker that read "Ted Kennedy's car killed more people than my gun!!!" But it was stuck on pretty hard and ended up reading "Ted killed people!!!" The three exclamation marks made me want to get out of town faster.

Mary clicked her cane into a slot that tucked it along the side of the scooter, out of sight but accessible in emergencies. This scooter had been modified. In addition to the two normal speeds (slow, slower), the original owner had added "fast." Mary threw the throttle into fast mode, but there seemed to be little to no difference between it and the slow mode. A basket hung from the handlebars. We stopped briefly and fetched her gin and tonic bottles out of the suitcase. The basket was just big enough to hold these supplies.

"Look, no hands!" she said as she mixed a drink while stepping on the gas.

The tumbler settled nicely into the cup holder. Mary was actually enjoying herself. I hinted at the fact that perhaps she should not be drinking and driving, but really, she was going too slowly to cause any damage. Mary christened the scooter Ted.

We walked and rode in silence for a few miles. Maybe it was the open road, maybe it was what I had written all over the walls back at the motel room, maybe it was Mary knowing that something else was at work here.

"Hold on, where're the brakes on this thing? Ah, hell, forget it. Take the wheel. I just gotta—"

Craaaaaaaaaack

"—the ol' kink in the neck is all exaggerated from sitting in the car and in jail too long."

She aligned the bones of her body.

"Don't worry," Mary continued. "That ol' man back there won't need it half as much as we do. Some walking would be good for 'm — did you see the size of his gut? Man's a heart attack waiting to happen. Look at this — slot for my smokes, holder for my tumbler, basket for my bottles, clip for my cane. Man knows how to accessorize. Take the wheel again."

Click, click, puff, puff, cough, cough.

$$\Longrightarrow$$

Hill country. Up and down. The hills were long, drawn out, a constant incline. A break in the road. A valley with a fast-moving stream between two hills. A bridge connected our location to the adjacent peak.

Between the hills, I stopped. Sat down on the side of the bridge, back against the railing. Mary braked, turned Ted's ignition off.

Overwhelmed.

We didn't speak. Enough words for now. Words only go so far.

And that's when we heard the noise. A low hum at first. The hum broke apart, developed into a THUD-THUD-THUD. No vehicles approached from either side. Except for us, the bridge was empty. I looked at Mary, she looked to the sky. A black dot appeared on the horizon. It crossed the sun, blocked the sun, imitated a solar eclipse. The black dot expanded. Headed right for us. The THUD-THUD-THUD intensified — a violent sound cutting through the air. The unnatural bird gradually defined itself as a black helicopter, blades spinning, front drooped forward as it extended, thinning, backwards. The noise overtook the quietness of the surroundings, disrupted it.

The helicopter was stunning and powerful. Floated over the bridge, gently landed in the middle, right in front of Mary and me. Mary stood, unclipped her cane, waited for the next move.

The machine's side hatch opened. Ten men filed out, each wearing black from head to toe. Large belts around waists, thick ropes lassoed around shoulders. Machine guns at the ready. They ran in single file to the edge and lined up along the railing. Pulled ropes over heads, and with lightning speed, looped the ropes into firm knots. Latches appeared from pouches on belts and joined ropes to bodies. All ten, all at once, perfectly choreographed, stepped up on to the railing, faced the bridge, and jumped.

Mary limped over to the railing. I stood, followed. We leaned over, watched the ten men rappel themselves from the top of the bridge to the valley below. Once they had reached the bottom at the same time, the man in the middle gave a signal and they climbed back up. The men climbed up more slowly, each having to lift his entire body with only his arms. Up and over the railing, they untied the knots, removed the lassoed ropes over their heads. When everything was accomplished, they stood at attention, lined up along the railing.

The blades of the helicopter slowed; the noisy machine quieted. A man stepped out of the helicopter. He stood before the ten men, held his arm up in the air. In his hand was a stopwatch.

"You were all faster last week," the man said. He shook his head, returned the stopwatch to a pouch on his utility belt.

The men hadn't noticed us or were ignoring us. Mary limped over.

"Hey," she said. "You think I could try that?"

All ten men and the man with the stopwatch looked over at her, as if seeing us for the first time.

"Sorry, ma'am," the man with the stopwatch said, "but this is an official training exercise."

"Look, just 'cause you have your testosterone-fueled machine and your fancy black garb doesn't mean you can call me ma'am."

The ten men looked to their leader, waited with eyebrows raised for a response.

"Perhaps," he said, "we could do a new exercise. Two volunteers!"

Two of the ten men stepped forward. The man with the stopwatch yelled for Mary and me to approach the men. I put my hands up — this was not something on my to-do list. Everyone ignored me. The men looped rope around my waist and Mary's waist. Tightened it so we were face to face. We shuffled over to the railing, and they tied a tight knot. The men instructed us to sit on the railing and shift around so our feet dangled over the edge. The men followed us, and we pushed, falling off the bridge. The rope slackened. Mary yelped. I hollered all the way down until our feet almost touched the fast-moving stream below.

The howling of the wind as we sliced through the air cut out when we came to an abrupt stop. Slight stillness. We slowly spun around in a circle. I looked over at Mary. She had a huge grin on her face.

"Ha! Now the hard part!" she said to her guide.

These men were strong. They climbed back up the rope only using their arms. One hand at a time, we crawled back up the rope. The way up was not as much fun or as fast as the way down. But it provided the ability to see what was around me. I had been walking for days. You can move over terrain and not see anything but what's in front of you. The trees, the water, the underside of the bridge. Suddenly I had the opportunity to look at something from a perspective I wasn't meant to see.

All this time, my mind had been a building where the lights were being turned off one office at a time. But it was so slight, so efficient, that I hadn't even noticed. You can walk through life without seeing anything. You can turn out all the lights, one by one, and be content with it. Not even notice they've gone off.

The lights were being turned back on.

We reached the top and were helped over the railing, back onto the bridge, by two other soldiers. The man with the stopwatch asked us where we were headed. Mary looked to me. We were going near the great Falls. They offered to give us a ride in the helicopter.

Mary looked from me to them, and said "Thanks, but no thanks."

The blades started turning slowly at first, but the THUD-THUD-THUD became faster and faster. There was a moment where I wondered if we would make it into the air. The helicopter lifted, the lighter back end first, then the heavier front end. It lifted away from us, rose over the trees and over the hills, and sped through the air. In a matter of moments, we were left alone, the THUD-THUD-THUD a distant memory.

Mary sat on the scooter and mixed herself a drink. I consulted my compass watch, pointed the direction. She started the scooter up, and we were off. We made our way through a small town and picked up some lunch. Stayed only long enough to gather some supplies, such as bottled water and tonic. Everywhere we went, there was a fascination with our plight. People weren't suspicious, just curious. Mary enjoyed the curiosity, often spinning wild tales of our destination to those who spoke to us.

Somewhere along a tree-lined area, we came across a natural spring. From the road, we heard a consistent crashing noise, not at all like the sound of a loud tractor-trailer. Mary parked the scooter behind some bushes and unclipped her cane, and we investigated.

We pushed through the bushes that lined the road and cut our own path through some rocky terrain. The rocks led to a small cliff and a path — curiously treaded before — cut along and down to a football field–sized pond below. A slight stream of water curved around the top of the cliff, falling over into the pond, creating a tiny waterfall.

Mary and I made our way slowly down to the pond. Cliffs surrounded us. I took off my shoes and socks, dipped my toes in the water. Surprisingly warm. We stripped off our clothes, down to underwear. I looked over at Mary, her body withered, wrinkled, older, more beaten up than her very active personality would have you believe. The stump where her left arm was amputated had scar tissue around it, evidence of the messy removal.

We entered the water. Mary said she had to go to the washroom. She limped out of the water, grabbed her cane and disappeared into the woods. She was gone a long time.

When I was a child learning to swim, I would often take as much air into my lungs as I could, plow down deep into the water, tuck my knees into my chest, and wrap my arms around my legs. Be still and float. Used to stay down longer than I should have, finally breaking up through the surface, gasping for breath.

The water in the pond was clear but deep, and when I reached a certain level, darkness surrounded me. Stopped moving, curled my knees into my chest, allowed the water to slightly turn me around. Floated. My eyes opened; there was nothing. My lungs started complaining, calling for air. Finally, I went up and up, crashed through the surface, remembered where I was.

When I cleared the water from my eyes, I saw Mary standing on the cliff beside the waterfall. She leaned on her cane, waited for me to surface. She lifted the cane, tossed it off the cliff into the water below. With all the strength of her 93-year-old body, she jumped into the air, floated. Flew. Gravity took over and brought her frail body sailing to the water below. She smashed through the surface, barely a splash. I immediately swam for the area where she landed. Before I reached the waterfall, Mary appeared, a huge grin on her face. I snatched the cane floating nearby, she grabbed the other end, and I pulled her back to shore.

We crawled up onto the rocky surface. Both gasped for breath.

"That was stupid," I said.

"That was fun," she replied. "You should try it."

"No, thanks."

"Why not?"

That's all it took. I scaled the rocks, walked out to the edge, looked down, followed the waterfall with my eyes to where it hit below. From up here, it felt so much higher; everything looked farther down than I'd thought. This idea was stupid. Facing the cliff edge, I backed away to the trees outlining the ledge. Started with a jog, upgraded to a run, calculated where to place my foot, leapt into the air. There was a moment when I felt as though I was flying. Gliding, floating in the air.

Again, the gravity thing.

The transition from slow-motion floating to free falling was immediate. Jarring. My body turned over, my head heading right for the surface. Spun around some more, crashed into the water with my feet. Water gushed into my mouth and nose. Tried to cough, but the pressure of the water pushed it back into my mouth. For a moment, I floated again. My brain took over and reminded me of my self-preserving behaviour — arms flailed, pressed against the water.

My head thrust through the surface. I gulped large mouthfuls of air. Spun around, waved and shouted at Mary. She tipped her tumbler toward me. With the last of my strength, I swam to the shore, crawled up the rocks, and rested on my stomach next to her.

"Now that," Mary said. "That was something."

Rested, refreshed, we rejoined the road. I walked next to Mary until the scooter hit a pointy rock — Mary almost toppled over. The wheel popped, and the scooter rolled to a stop, the weight slanted toward the ground. Mary unclipped her cane, stepped off the scooter, knocked the flat tire with her cane.

"Shit," she said. "Now what?"

I pulled out my map.

"We're almost at the next town," I said. "I'll push, but you'll have to walk for a bit."

The scooter was heavier, more stubborn than I had anticipated. Mary smoked a cigarette while we walked. Luckily, we came upon a gas station with a mechanic's shop, its light glowing in the window like a beacon. We parked the scooter and knocked on the closed garage door.

"Closed!" growled a deep voice.

Mary thumped her cane on the door. Loud. We heard movements, the sound of a large tool being dropped on a cement floor. The door pulled up, and we were face to face with a giant. We both let out a slight gasp.

"I said closed," the giant said through clenched teeth. He turned to walk away. Mary again thumped her cane against the side of the door. The man stopped.

"Listen," she said. "We don't have much time, so get your ass out here, check out our vehicle, and get to work."

He had a large head, bald. He resembled Stainless Steele but looked meaner. His hardness wasn't for show. His eyes narrowed at

Mary. The giant motioned to his garage, pointed at the various motorcycles in different states of repair.

"I only do bikes," he said.

"Ours is sort of a bike," she said. She slammed her cane down on the floor, rested her one arm and her weight on it. Stared right back. He scratched behind his ear, nodded. We led him to the scooter and he shook his head.

"You like wrestling?" Mary asked.

"I used to wrestle," the giant said.

"I knew it. You were Harley Davidson, right?"

The giant's eyes lit up.

"My stage name. Hell, that was years ago," he said.

Mary turned toward me. "This guy was the best. He'd ride in on a Harley. One of the most classic matches against the Razor's Edge. Lasted six hours."

"Still the world record for the longest match," he said.

"Classic," she whispered.

Harley smiled at her. Bent down, looked at the scooter. Poked the flat tire.

"Yeah, I can fix this," he said.

We sat outside Harley's place, and when the scooter was finished, it had four thick motorcycle wheels and a new paint job with flames shooting down the side. Harley had a big smile on his face.

"For a true fan," he said.

Mary started it up — the engine had been replaced with a louder, more powerful one. She threw it into gear, took it for a ride around the gas station parking lot. Harley refused payment for the job.

"You should get back into wrestling," Mary said.

"Maybe," Harley said.

And we were off.

The retrofitted scooter purred, glided along bumpy cement roads. Only blue skies with occasional clouds. We were lucky; rain made everything so much more difficult. Perhaps our unconscious intent had pushed it away for a while. But as the day moved on, dark clouds filled the atmosphere. The pressure in the air thickened; moisture stuck to our clothes. We didn't speak because we knew we still had a while to go before reaching the next town. We were in between towns, too far away from where we had been and too far from our next destination. We held our collective breath, focused on the road ahead — the road that seemed to grow and never end. No cars, no animals.

The rain started.

Mary pulled a thin coat out of her bag, placed it over her head. She lit a cigarette, tried to smoke the wet tobacco, but ended up throwing it away. We moved slowly. The rain beat down on us and beat us down. The roads flooded, our clothes soaked. Still no cars, no animals. No help. I didn't notice because Ted the scooter kept moving forward, but Mary had passed out. She was just too tired, slumped forward. My focus had been elsewhere. I was staring down at my sopping feet, drudging along one step at a time. Feeling sorry for myself. Didn't know why I felt sorry for myself. The scooter veered to the right, right toward me. I got out of the way, and it got stuck beside the road. The new tires spun mud. I looked at Mary — she was lying in the road. After all this time when no cars passed us, headlights appeared on the horizon, closer than they appeared. I ran over to Mary — the car's headlights illuminated us; the horn started blaring. She was out. I dragged her along the road to the shoulder, and the car sped past, didn't even slow down. Mary opened her eyes. Rainwater dropped down, making it hard for her to keep them open. I helped her to her feet. She shrugged me off, walked over to the scooter, turned, and stood beside it, looking at me. The wheels kept spinning, kicking mud into the air.

It hit me out there in the rain, beside the highway, as I looked at Mary and that damn scooter: something was not right. I looked at her and she looked at me, and an understanding came over us, one we both accepted. The rain fell in sheets, straight down, but it didn't matter at that point. She coughed and huddled deeper under her coat. Her body was failing.

I walked over to the scooter, killed the engine. The wheels stopped spinning. I grabbed the front end and push-pulled it back onto the shoulder of the road. The scooter was heavier than it looked. Mary sat down defiantly.

"We continue," she said.

I nodded. "We continue."

We continued: I walked and Mary was aboard Ted. Our clothes could not get any wetter. Up ahead there was a light, a beacon in the night. We hadn't seen a car since that last one almost hit us. We stumbled toward that beacon, hoped it was not a mirage. An unlocked gate opened to a long gravel driveway leading up to a small house. A wrought-iron sign embedded on the top of the gate read: The Elephant's Graveyard. We walked and rolled the length of the driveway, I helped Mary up the steps, and we took refuge on the porch. Rang the doorbell. No answer. Knocked. No answer. We decided to rest for a few minutes and be on our way. Maybe wait out the rain though it provided no indication of slowing.

The door creaked open. An old woman stepped out on the porch, took one look at us, and ushered our two soaking bodies into the house. Mary barely could stand; she leaned on the cane, and it shook under the pressure. The old woman took her by the arm into the living area, sat her down, grabbed a blanket folded on the back of the chair, wrapped it around her. Mary shivered.

"I didn't hear a car," the old woman said. "How did you get here?"

"We walked," I said. "Actually, we have a scooter out in the rain."

The old woman gave me a set of keys that opened the garage beside the house. The patter of the rain was loud compared to the silence in the house. I took the scooter over to the garage, unlocked the doors, pushed them open. What little light came from the house spilled into the musty garage. The layer of dust on the vehicle inside indicated it hadn't been used in a while. Rusted tools hung on pegs above a workstation. On the far side against the back wall, shelves held clear glass jars. I rolled the scooter into the garage, parked it beside the car. Had a closer look at the jars — small animal specimens were encased in formaldehyde.

The door was stubborn and the lock rusted. After shutting everything with more effort than should have been warranted, I ran across the grass and took the stairs two at a time. I was alone in the front foyer. A grandfather clock stood opposite the door. The entire house seemed to be made of dark oak. Pictures of different animals — both paintings and photographs — covered the walls. Giraffes, gorillas, elephants, zebras, monkeys. The clock struck midnight; chimes issued the report. Snapped me from my inspection.

The old woman entered the living room at the same time I did, carrying a giant mug with steam shooting soothingly from the opening. She placed it in front of Mary on a table made from the stump of a tree. The furniture was vintage and didn't match. All different sizes and different colours. Above the red couch, a pair of elephant tusks shot out from the wall, curved so the points aimed at the ceiling. More pictures: bears, camels, birds, fish.

"She has a fever," the old woman said.

Mary shivered, ignored the tea.

"What is this place?" I asked.

"The Elephant's Graveyard," she said. "Bed and Breakfast."

"Lots of animals," I said.

The old woman only smiled at my remark. "My name is Waneta. I assume you need a room?"

I sat down across from Waneta and managed a better look at her. She was old, but there was a glow, almost a radiance coming from her. Her words were measured, weighty, as though she had only a finite number left to her, and she chose them carefully. Her left eye drooped, blinked at different intervals than her right eye. Her age was indecipherable: she could have been 50 or 85. When she took her glasses off, red marks remained on her temples from the glasses being too tight. She squinted. Her dress looked homemade, a patchwork of older garments. Sandals displayed misshapen toes. A big nose was at odds with the smaller features of her face. She had a calming effect. She sat next to Mary and placed her hands on Mary's hands, and almost instantly, Mary stopped shivering.

"Yes, some rooms would be nice," I said.

"Should we call a doctor?" Waneta asked.

"No doctors," Mary said.

We helped Mary upstairs. The steps creaked. The bed was made — it almost seemed like we were expected. Waneta exited as I helped Mary out of her wet clothes and into a robe Waneta had provided. She lay her head down, and as I went to leave, Mary grabbed my arm.

"What time is it?" she asked.

"About midnight."

Mary inhaled, closed her eyes, released her breath. "Tomorrow is the day, then."

"What are you talking about?"

"Tomorrow. Around five o'clock. You'll be on your own."

"Mary—"

"Just promise me no doctors."

"Mary—"

"You won't have to bother with me anymore. You'll make better time."

"But why—"

"Promise!"

"Okay. No doctors."

Mary closed her eyes, released my arm.

Downstairs, I found Waneta in the kitchen. Her back was to me as she prepared some food. She turned with two plates, smiled. Radiant. She motioned for me to sit down, and when I looked at the collard greens, sprouts, kale, potatoes, and green beans, my stomach flipped. We sat and I tore through the food. I wanted to ask more questions, wanted to know more about Waneta, but — perhaps it was the food or the rain — I needed to sleep. Waneta showed me to my own room, the bed welcoming, and I fell into a deep, dark sleep.

I checked on Mary first thing in the morning. She slept. Her fever had come on stronger. The clock read 7:30 a.m. The smell of fresh-brewed coffee filled the house, and I found Waneta in the kitchen making breakfast.

The steps seemed to be at an angle, and I had trouble walking up them. In the hallway, I stood and stared at the door, not really sure what to do. Mary was in bed but with eyes open. I sat on a chair next to the bed, and we didn't speak. She fell back to sleep, her forehead hot.

The grandfather clock chimed: 9:00 a.m.

The rain had subsided, leaving the ground moist, muddy. The air felt good. The sun crept through the parting clouds. I walked from the house to the back property, an open field where wheat used to grow. An old rusted tractor hibernated. A wooded area ran along the perimeter of the field, and a path cut by other walkers led through the trees. The moisture in the air disappeared amid the trees. The humidity held some kind of secret, one I was not going to learn. Beyond the trees, a small dock on the lake, a canoe on the shore. In the distance, a small island floated, still and solid.

I circled back around through a tree-lined area. After a distance, I didn't know how long, my mind was elsewhere. My mind wasn't on my steps. A clearing amid the trees. My mind was pulled away from me, floated like a balloon over my neck. In the clearing was an old cemetery, where crude gravestones jutted out of the ground at odd angles. I stopped, felt the heat and the sweat for the first time since entering the forest.

A rustle in the bushes.

I snapped my head to the right.

A deer.

The deer froze when it saw me. Neither of us expected the other to be here. We thought we were alone. We stared at each other. The deer put a hesitant hoof forward. Determined whether it was safe.

Took another step. Walked right up to me. Sniffed the air around me. The deer stood and stared at me as I stared at it. We stared for an indeterminate amount of time.

I stood up and walked out of the cemetery. At the perimeter of the clearing, I stopped, turned to find the deer still sitting, watching me leave. I retraced my steps back through the trees, through the field, past the tractor, and back into the house.

The grandfather clock chimed after I stepped inside: 11:00 a.m.

Mary woke. Her fever had stabilized but she could not eat anything. I sat on the chair, wondered what to say, wondered what to do. Watched her for a long time. She looked at me.

Silence.

Then.

The door creaked, and Waneta stepped into the room carrying a tray with some broth and two cups of tea. She stopped at the doorway, felt the charged atmosphere.

A smile came over Mary's face.

"Margaret, is that you?" Mary said in a weakened voice, her strength gone.

I looked at Waneta, and she nodded at me slightly. There was an understanding, one last secret to perpetuate.

"Margaret, I'm so happy to see you," Mary said. "I've missed you."

"I am happy to see you," Waneta/Margaret said. "I've missed you."

"Margaret..."

Mary breathed through her mouth. Her eyes drifted, unfocused, the lids closed. The movement of her chest slowed. Her head moved to the side.

The grandfather clock chimed. I checked my compass watch: 5:00 p.m.

"One more walk," Mary said.

I carried Mary down the stairs. Loaded her onto the scooter. We rode around down by the lake. Off-roading. When we reached the dock, the canoe, I pointed out the island.

"We go there," she said.

I guess that's how you get over things like riding in vehicles. At the request of a dying person. A little at a time. Start with a boat with no motor. I'd had little experience with canoes. I picked up Mary, helped her into the canoe.

"Ah, bring the booze."

I pushed the canoe away from the shore, jumped into the other end. The canoe rocked back and forth. I sat still until it settled. Dipped the paddle into the water.

And we were canoeing across the lake.

We didn't speak.

The water was calm and I made good headway. But the farther I got from where I started and the more I looked ahead, the more the distance seemed to grow. It was as though you could only see part of the lake from shore, and once you entered into it, you found yourself in some kind of alternate reality. The water stretched out into its true length. Every few paddles, it looked as if I were going nowhere. At other times, the paddling seemed to thrust us ever more forward at an alarming rate.

Funny thing, repetitive motion. It puts you into a meditative state. A trance.

My left hand grasped the end of the paddle, my right hand grabbed farther down the shaft. I dipped it into the water, pushed-behind-pushed the canoe forward. Switched. Flipped the paddle over my thighs, reversed the hand positions. Repeated the pattern. The water gave me little resistance. Waves were minimal, and I parted the water, crossed the lake one stroke at a time. The little boat was sensitive, rolling to and fro. You had to wrangle it, take control.

The waves were stories. Each one had its own narrative, its own story to share. Some were tall and had lots to tell. Others were small: the quiet ones. They were democratic in their presentations.

I say all this because I failed to notice when Mary lied down. Her eyes were still open; she stared at me. With the waves, it's difficult to say when her eyes closed for good. We reached the island and the waves pushed us up on the shore. I sat there, watching her unmoving body. Made a decision.

I got out of the canoe, pulled her lifeless body onto shore. Walked into the foliage on the island. Found a spot and started digging with my hands. Dug all goddamn night. Retrieved her body, carried it in my tired arms. Laid her in the plot. Covered her body in dirt, stabbed the cane into the dirt at the head of the grave. Got the bag of booze, mixed myself a gin and tonic. Sat down on a fallen tree, lit a cigarette. Smoked that fucking thing down to the filter. Sat for a long time. Sat until the night returned.

Once I was back in the canoe, re-crossing the lake, the weather system coming in from the west snapped me out of my trance. Dark clouds. Lightning. I cocked my head to the left, strained to hear the thunder. My thoughts were too focused on the clouds over there instead of what was happening right here. I got caught paddling in a circle, created a slow-moving whirlpool. Bearings. Spun the canoe around by pressing the paddle into the water on one side. Paddled faster.

Waves inched taller.

Drops of water sprang, landed on me, formed bubbles. I popped them with my palm.

Up and over went the paddle. Waves bounced off the boat.

As morning approached, the sun peeked over the horizon to the east, battling the approaching clouds. The clouds were winning. The sky turned a deep black. I could see the lightning even though it was morning. The wind picked up, and the water got in on the action. The waves were more frequent, taller. They banged against the side of the canoe. The water was angry. Thunder rumbled, turned aggressive with loud violent cracks. The unstable canoe threatened to capsize as I jumped involuntarily in reaction to the thunder.

Within minutes, the waves had grown so large that the canoe went up and over them instead of cutting through. The context of where I was in comparison to the shore was lost to me. I paddled faster, but in paddling faster, I made mistakes and the mistakes slowed me down. Finally, the rain. It came in fat pellets, slammed into me, bordered on hail.

At one point, the boat tipped so much that I was almost parallel to the water. Through the clear water, I saw the fish stop moving, surprised that someone was out here in the torrent. Lightning lit up the sky, thunder snapped. Could I get electrocuted? Were there sharks in the water? I kept heading south. Forced myself to forget the rain, the thunder, lightning. Everything.

It was all too much water for me. It came from above and below.

The waves didn't care. The waves showed no discrimination.

Splashed, sloshed, smacked, slapped. The waves challenged me right to the bone.

I wasn't going to let a little water stop me. Wet. Tired. Cranky. The rain fell with more weight and with machine-gun urgency. It hurt. One raindrop was nothing, but thousands?

The waves had been friendly at first. We had exchanged narratives. But change came quickly. I saw it far out, headed right for me. It grew taller as it approached, yelling, screaming, big enough it could have knocked over a building. The wave punched. Capsized. Cold water gripped me, pulled me vice-like ever lower into the depths.

Stillness.

Everything went quiet. Pure emptiness. Not even any fish around. Bubbles bubbled from my mouth and nose, rose to the surface.

Floated.

I was scared at first then I laughed. The air emptied from my lungs. I hung in the water, my weight suspended. My eyes closed, lids heavy. I remembered reading that drowning was peaceful. Something brushed my hand. A shark?

Summoning all my strength, I opened my eyes. A light glowed deep in the distance. So that thing about seeing the white light was true. My focus was off, shadows played across my face. A figure blocked the glowing light. The light bled into the figure, worked its way around the top of her head. The figure tried to speak, but only bubbles emanated from her mouth. They sparkled in the glow. I tried to talk but got a mouthful of water for the effort. The swallowed water opened my senses, snapped my mind back. I turned away from the figure, saw the outline of the canoe rocking up and down over the waves. I knew I needed to reach it, but my body just would not go. I felt a pressure on my back. The pressure gave me strength. The water was thick, my arms tired, but the pressure guided me toward the canoe.

Broke through the surface, reached the canoe. How do you get into a canoe from in the water? I latched on to the edge, ducked into the water, flung my body up into the air, flew through the air in slow motion, felt the pressure again at my back, flipped my body around, up, over, and landed. The small boat threatened to throw me back out but I steadied it.

I gave in to everything at the same time. Gave in to chance. Gave myself to the elements. Collapsed, sunk to my side. Trusted that something would take me in the right direction.

The rain continued. Soaked me to the bone. The boat drifted, pulled by the magnetic force of the earth.

The rain continued. The sun set. Stars peeked through the clouds.

Shafts of sun stunted across the sky, rousing me. My eyes fluttered, unaccustomed to the light. My hand lifted to block the glow from my eyes. There was still dirt under my fingernails. I squinted.

The paddle rested beside me. I picked it up, paddled. I wrangled that boat until it was under my control again. The brief intermission from the rain was over. The morning passed, and I paddled. And still, the rain continued.

It was still raining when I reached the other side. I jumped to solid ground, pulled the canoe over the rocks, scraped the bottom — like fingernails on a blackboard. Trees. I sheltered under a large pine tree. My bones were wet.

It started in my belly. Moved up my throat. A chuckle at first. Then uncontrollable laughter.

"Chloe," I said.

And the rain drained down the trunk of the pine and pattered down my spine.

From the booze bag, my phone beeped, signalling a text message. And I knew.

And I started walking again.

We're almost there.

The rain continued. I stepped into a truck stop near the Falls. Ate some much needed food. No one noticed me.

The washroom inside the truck stop probably hadn't been cleaned in the last decade. The cracked mirror showed a different person. For the duration of my walk, I had avoided reflections in windows. My cheeks were sunken, sporting a wrung-out wet beard. My hair was stringy, unkempt. My clothes weather-worn. My skin sunburned. I smiled wild teeth at this new person. My physical body had evolved years but emerged strong.

I bought some shaving supplies. Trimmed the beard and cut my own hair. With cold water splashing on my face, I removed my facial hair, stopping every once in a while to look into my own eyes. Flashes of a new person, new but not new. The person I once was appeared in those flashes, the person from before I'd gone into hibernation. These flashes were not of a humdrum human. I would not walk through life unaware. These eyes hungered for understanding. Finished, I washed my face, dried it with a coarse paper towel.

In a department store, I bought some new clothes. Threw away the old worn-out uniform. Emerged as someone ready for the final part of a journey. Someone presentable.

I followed the water to the cemetery. Walking among the plots, I allowed myself to be guided along. I'd been here before but a long time ago. I had an image of the gravestone overlooking a small hill — it was all I had to go on. I walked and walked. It was a damn big cemetery.

The hill. This was it. I walked along a row of gravestones, stopped. Beside two stones, a block of cement was sunk into the ground. The plaque was covered in weeds, barely readable. After I pushed away the weeds and swept away the dirt, I stood.

Frozen.

The name on the grave wasn't Margaret.

The name on the grave was Mary.

All it said was her name and the dates of her birth and death. I looked up, saw a man walking along the graves down the hill. The man was dressed all in black. Okay, it could've been a different man in black, but still. He stopped when he sensed I was looking at him. If you could believe it, he tipped his hat, walked toward the exit. I waved my bandaged hand in his direction. I lowered my gaze, and the sun caught a gravestone up on the next row. I looked at the name.

Jeffrey Paul. 1972–1980. *Little ones to him belong.*

Text message: *Are you almost here?*

On the gravestone was a silhouetted image of a baby, but when you looked at it a certain way, it resembled the birthmark. And I must say that I don't force these things to happen. Sometimes those moments that you wish for, the times in your life where meaning is intensified, where the details of your environment are seen, where you are seen — those moments do happen. The world folds in on itself. Trust me, I didn't want this all to end in such a cliché and well-trodden way. But dammit, without thinking or knowing what I was doing, I actually bent down to my knees on the moist ground. And I saw everything roll out in front of me, understood the past and its way of marking certain moments. Recognized the signposts that had pointed me ever so slightly in the right direction, a direction I had felt many times was wrong. So the past started making sense, but the future — I saw the future in a way where all three — past, present, and future — all seemed to be one thing, one moment.

This was not the way I wanted this all to end, this validation from something external. This was supposed to be an internal walk but, dammit, sometimes you just have to go with things. This need for love outside of myself. Call it random or fate or energy or whatever, it's the only way it could end. It's why I couldn't stop writing and rewriting this damn book. I couldn't let go, couldn't stop, was happy enmeshed inside it instead of allowing myself to step outside, to view things from a different perspective. I couldn't let go because then I'd have had to look at my life.

I stood there on my knees, watching the rollout of what was to come.

A scene played in my mind: I walk into the night, deep into the night, not knowing where I am going, but with something guiding me. Each step builds my strength. Each step builds toward my place in my world.

I come to a house. A modest house. Walk up to the house and knock on the door. Yes, waiting for someone to open the door of a lifetime. I hear the steps on the floor coming toward the door, the turn of the doorknob. The door opens and Chloe is standing there, and we just look at each other with no words. She is older, but still her. I am older, but still me. The birthmark glows a bright purple. She found my profile on the dating site; she is the one who has been texting me.

At first I stay at a brownstone down the street, but we spend so much time together that it makes sense for me to move in. She wants me around. Every night after dinner we walk, hold hands, never stop touching.

Chloe starts writing again, and I make a book she writes into a movie. We find our people, and they find us. We find them together. Everything is done together. We move back to the city, close to friends, close to family. Our house is always filled. We have large meals, surrounded by lots of people. Someone always brings a guitar. I tell the stories of Margaret and Mary over and over again. We all share the stories around us — these stories are important. Essential. The people in those stories live on.

We laugh.

We cry.

We grow older and it is good.

When the time is right, Chloe and I go to the Elephant's Graveyard, but when we find the right place on the map, the house is gone. No signs. We walk around to the lake; the dock remains, the canoe. We push the canoe out into the water, paddle to the island. The cane, now rusted, still stands. Plants and flowers have grown up across the grave.

We are silent.

We end up surrounded by people near the end.

And as I moved from this world, the last moment I remembered, the accumulated moments that drifted in and out and over each other all culminated in six words. On that last moment, the words that were most important, the ones that existed because the ideas permeated my very being, the words that came to define me — those words appeared.

So as I walked down the street away from the cemetery in Niagara Falls, these thoughts swirled through my head. I walked for a long time, saw this life rolling out in front of me. Walked through the city to the outskirts. Walked for a long time, walked until my feet gave way, walked until my shoes wore through, walked until my head was numb. Walked across the earth and over seas, walked until I wore out my thoughts and those words appeared, the ones that would carry me forth and save me. The words brought me back and made me smile — goddammit, made me laugh out loud — and I realized that I didn't have to walk anymore.

Be light! Be smooth! Be open!

Acknowledgements

The road to publishing this book has been long, and my deepest appreciation goes out to everyone I met along the way. I would first like to thank my publisher, Iguana Books, and my editor, Kate Unrau, who caught my (many) mistakes and helped shape the work. Thank you to Lesley Grant for your guidance and first look at the manuscript. Thank you to everyone who participated in the crowdfunding campaign for this book.

Do not underestimate the power of writing groups. A number of years ago, I joined Black Horse Press, a Toronto-based writing collective. It helped me figure out how to present my work. The

Reapers is another group I'm part of, where we share in the art of storytelling; it has not only helped my writing but brought into focus personal experiences. And with both groups came new friends.

I was never very good in school, but my teachers have always been so important. Bruce Powe opened the door of literature for me. Dunja Baus cracked open my creativity. Wayson Choy changed my life. Four years ago, I walked into the Humber School for Writers and met Wayson. Since then, I have been fortunate to be under his writerly guidance and also to have the privilege of calling him my friend. Although I learned so much about writing from him, it's actually way down the list of his lessons. He taught me not only to write with more depth, but also to live life in this way as well.

Before starting the Open Kwong Dore Podcast, Pj Kwong and I had been friends for a while. Since we talked all the time, it made sense to start a podcast. After all this time, my favourite part of the week is finding the time to record with Pj. She's been there for good times and bad.

This book starts in Jordan, and I have a friend there who has been with me through it all. There are many more who have suffered through friendship with me. I can make it difficult sometimes. Someone whose name I won't mention was really the inspiration for this book. I understand now. I think.

Last, I would like to thank my family for giving me everything: Carol, David, Chris, Shannon, Josh, Austin, and Jaxson.

About the Author

Paul Dore has worked in the film and television industry as an editor, director, and producer for almost fifteen years. He is also the co-host and co-producer of the popular Open Kwong Dore Podcast. Embracing the massive changes in the media landscape, Paul has successfully used the innovative crowdfunding approach to help publish this, his first novel. Paul is based in Toronto, but can often be found travelling the world to find inspiration for his writing. For more information please visit pauldore.com.

Iguana Books
iguanabooks.com

If you enjoyed *The Walking Man*...
Look for other books coming soon from Iguana Books! Subscribe to our blog for updates as they happen.

iguanabooks.com/blog/

You can also learn more about Author and his/her upcoming work on his website.

http://pauldore.com/

If you're a writer...
Iguana Books is always looking for great new writers, in every genre. We produce primarily ebooks but, as you can see, we do the occasional print book as well. Visit us at iguanabooks.com to see what Iguana Books has to offer both emerging and established authors.

iguanabooks.com/publishing-with-iguana/

If you're looking for another good book...
All Iguana Books books are available on our website. We pride ourselves on making sure that every Iguana book is a great read.

iguanabooks.com/bookstore/

Visit our bookstore today and support your favourite author.

IGUANA

CPSIA information can be obtained at www.ICGtesting.com
Printed in the USA
LVOW07s0719060115

421611LV00005B/173/P

9 781771 800778